"You want to go out to dinner sometime?"

Mark's words sounded like firecrackers in the quiet night.

"That depends." Adele's gaze didn't move from the fountain.

"On what?"

"Why you're asking."

He wasn't sure. He'd just asked. "We're friends. I'd like a night out and don't know anyone else around here."

Not entirely true, but close enough. He didn't know anyone well enough to want to hang out with them for a whole night.

"So we'd be going as friends."

"Sure, we can keep it at that," he said. *Friends* was what he wanted, too. Except for when he was thinking about making love with her. Which he was trying not to do. And sometimes succeeding.

"Friends is all I can offer you."

He wondered why, but didn't ask. "I'm good with that," he said.

Dear Reader,

Welcome to Shelter Valley! If you've never been here before, you're in for a treat. And if you know and love Shelter Valley, you're going to enjoy being here all over again.

Shelter Valley Stories are about people who look out for each other. This is a town that has a personality of its own, and a people who embody that personality. Bring your hurts, your tragedies, your struggles and shames to Shelter Valley, and the people here will offer you comfort, understanding, strength and a chance to start all over again.

These new Shelter Valley Stories will give you everything you expect from this unique and compelling town, and more. We've got newcomers this time. Three people who've been brought to Shelter Valley on full scholarships to attend Montford University. They didn't ask for the scholarships, didn't apply for them. Didn't even intend to go to college. They don't know each other. They come from different parts of the country. None of them have ever been to Arizona before. All three are well past the age when they'd normally have started college. If you're a longtime Shelter Valley visitor, you'll see the town anew through their eyes.

In this, the first of the three stories, the scholarship recipient is Mark Heber from West Virginia. We also meet Addy. She's a lawyer from Colorado and she moves in next door to him. Addy has a few secrets—including the fact that she was born in Shelter Valley. She doesn't tell Mark or anyone else in town about that. She has her reasons....

Anyway, join us. Settle in. I guarantee that as long as you want to feel love and acceptance, as long as you want to see justice prevail, you'll find a place here. And you'll find ways to deal with a life that doesn't always provide those things.

I love hearing from readers. You can reach me at staff@tarataylorquinn.com. And watch for the next story in this trilogy coming in August 2013 from Harlequin Superromance!

Tara Taylor Quinn

It's Never Too Late

TARA TAYLOR OUINN

DATE DUE		
AG 2 1 '13		
SE 1 8 '13		
OC 2 5 '13		
OC 3 1 '13		
JA 0 9 '14		
FE 0 1 '14		
FE 2 7 '14		
MY 2 7 '15		
JE 2 3 '15		
NO 1 4 '15		
DE 0 8 '15		

Demco, Inc. 38-294

HARLEQU

ISBN-13: 978-0-373-60777-8

IT'S NEVER TOO LATE

Printed in U.S.A.

ABOUT THE AUTHOR

With sixty-one original novels, published in more than twenty languages, Tara Taylor Quinn is a *USA TODAY* bestselling author. She is a winner of the 2008 National Reader's Choice Award, four-time finalist for the RWA Rita® Award, a finalist for the Reviewer's Choice Award, the Bookseller's Best Award, the Holt Medallion and appears regularly on Amazon bestsellers lists. Tara Taylor Quinn is a past president of the Romance Writers of America and served for eight years on its board of directors. She is in demand as a public speaker and has appeared on television and radio shows across the country, including CBS Sunday Morning. Tara is a spokesperson for the National Domestic Violence Hotline, and she and her husband, Tim, sponsor an annual inline skating race in Phoenix to benefit the fight against domestic violence.

When she's not at home in Arizona with Tim and their canine owners, Jerry Lee and Taylor Marie, or fulfilling speaking engagements, Tara spends her time traveling and inline skating.

Books by Tara Taylor Quinn

HARLEQUIN SUPERROMANCE

SINGLE TITLE

MIRA BOOKS

*Shelter Valley Stories
**Chapman Files
‡It Happened in Comfort Cove

Other titles by this author available in ebook format.

For Libby Banks.
Thank you for the emotional shelter...

CHAPTER ONE

"I'M NOT GOING, ELLA."

"Yes, you are."

Sighing, Mark disentangled himself from the girl who'd been his one and only for the past couple of years—ever since his twenty-eighth birthday party, which had taken place at the exact same spot by the lake where he and Ella were right then.

Their lake. Really more of a pond a couple of miles outside of Bierly, West Virginia, where both he and Ella had been born and raised.

Gazing out at the water now, Mark couldn't figure out why everything was falling apart before his eyes.

He'd had it all going for him. The promotion to operations shift manager—making him the youngest manager in the history of the gasification plant that supported their small town—and the small savings account that was going to build until he didn't have to worry about money anymore.

Nonnie was having a good spell.

And Ella...she was nice looking. Content to stay in Bierly her whole life. And faithful to him.

He spun back to her—and found her sexy in her work jeans and T-shirt. "You want to get married?"

ELLA STARED UP AT HIM, her blue eyes and blond hair familiar in the dusky light of the setting sun. They were good together. In so many ways.

"What would Nonnie have to say about that?"

Huh? "I just asked you to marry me and you bring up my grandmother?"

But he knew why. Ella and Nonnie... Things had never been right between them.

A female territorial thing, he'd figured. He'd also hoped the situation would ease as time went by.

"Where would we live?" Feet in front of her on the blanket they'd spread, Ella wrapped her arms around bent knees.

"My house, of course. It's set up for Nonnie's chair." He'd been born there. Figured he'd die there, too.

And Ella lived in a rented apartment in town. A small, one-room place with a hot plate for a stove.

"Nonnie's house, you mean."

With a sick feeling in his gut, Mark sat down, took her hand and stared straight into her eyes. "I think we'll be good together."

"I want to have a family." She pulled her hand out of his and stood with her back to him.

He stared at her behind. He'd just proposed marriage. A once-in-a-lifetime event. It wasn't going well.

"I'll make a great father."

"I know." Her words were muffled by the breeze and the water that lapped at the shore.

Mark's throat tightened. Ella was a decent woman.

The best. He went to her, wrapped his arms around her from behind, pulling her back against him. "I'll do right by you, Ella. I'll be faithful to you until the day I die. I'm a good provider. We have fun together. We can make this work."

She leaned her head against his chest and he relaxed into her. This was home.

The lake beckoned and he thought of the rowboat that he kept stashed in some brush a couple of yards away from where they stood. A couple of yards away from where they'd first made love.

This was the life he'd been born into.

"Do you love me, Mark?"

"Course I do."

"You never say so."

"I'm not much of a talker, you know that."

"You say it to Nonnie."

"She's my grandmother!"

Ella turned to face him, her hands on his chest. "I can't leave this town. It's my home. I love it here."

"I know!" Had he asked her to move? Ever? "I'm not leaving, either."

"I think you will."

He'd have scratched his head if he hadn't been holding her. "Whatever gave you that idea?"

She looked away, off to the trees on their right. And then she took a step back. "Rick Stanfield asked me to a pig roast at his church."

Rick Stanfield was new to town—to the plant.

An operations field tech. Just like Ella. Like Jimmy had been.

"Doesn't he know you're my girl?"

"Yeah, he knows."

"So? What's the problem?"

"I told him I'd go."

"What?" Grabbing her hand, Mark pulled Ella back to him, her hips snug up against his. Reminding her. "You going to invite me, too, Ella? 'Cause we made a vow not to go out single."

"I know. I just think—"

"It's the scholarship, isn't it? You've been acting weird ever since I told you about that letter." A fluke. Incredible. The idea that Montford University, the Harvard of the West, would offer him a four-year full ride without his even asking for it. It was completely ludicrous.

"I barely graduated high school, Mark. I'm no good anywhere but here."

"That's crazy talk."

Her blue gaze was direct as she stared straight at him. "You used to say the same kinds of things. You didn't even graduate high school!" The words weren't unusual; the accusatory tone was.

"I know." He'd never pretended to be something he wasn't. Not even to himself. Especially not to himself. "And I'm not leaving, I keep telling you that."

"You're going to go, Mark. You're going to get some fancy degree, and I won't be good enough for you anymore."

"That's just more crazy talk."

"Is it?" She stared at him.

"Yes!" Rubbing his hips against her, he smiled and then kissed her. A long, wet kiss. "You will always be good enough for me, Ella Holland. Better than me. You're good enough for anyone. But you fit me."

"You said you weren't leaving." Her kiss was fervent as always. Her passion unrestrained. And then she stepped back.

"You *didn't* say you weren't going to get the degree." She was trying to trap him into saying something he didn't mean.

Because he'd been busy saying she'd always be good enough for him.

"I'm going to the pig roast, Mark."

"I don't believe this."

"Bierly's not a huge place. I want a husband and kids and my choices are limited."

"I just asked you to marry me."

"And live with Nonnie."

Yes. Because that one was not negotiable.

"She doesn't like me."

"Of course she does."

"She doesn't think I'm good enough for you."

"Ella." He grabbed her back, held on, as though by doing so he could hold on to the life she was trying to take away from him. "You are my equal in every way."

"You're smarter than I am, Mark. We both know that. You explain things to me all the time."

"At work, yes. That's my job."

"And about finances and world things. You watch the news and documentaries and I like to watch reality shows."

"Difference between girls and guys, is all."

"Nonnie wants you to take that scholarship offer."

"You talked to her?"

"No, but I know."

"I'm not going to Shelter Valley." Because Ella was wrong. He wasn't smart. And he most certainly was not a book learner. "I haven't read a book since before I quit high school."

"But you read stuff on the internet all the time."

A guy had to know about the world around him if he was going to keep his family safe. If he was going to provide.

"Marry me, Ella. Please." He hadn't meant to ask yet. Hadn't really even thought about it. But if marriage was what it took to keep things as they were…

She shook her head. "I can't, Mark. I can't sit here and wait for you while you go off across the country and get even smarter on me. I can't take the chance that you won't be back. Besides, I want a family now. Another two years and I'll be thirty years old, Mark. And you ain't ready. Even without the scholarship. You've said so often enough. You want to save first. And if you go get this degree—that would be another four years at least."

"We've got time, Ella. Heck, people have kids into their forties nowadays."

"I don't want to be an older mother. I want kids now, while I'm still young enough for them to think I'm cool."

That was so Ella, wanting her kids to think she was cool. Ella's mother had been sixteen when she'd had her and the two had been more like friends than mother and daughter.

"Even if I went and got the degree, you'd only be thirty-two when I get back. That's plenty young enough."

Her gaze narrowed and he was pretty sure he saw the beginnings of tears there. But Ella wasn't a crier.

"So you're thinking about going?"

"No! I keep telling you, I'm not going." He'd never make it in college. And had nothing to learn there, either. He was a working man. And he was climbing the ladder just fine. He'd just been talking about the age thing. There was no need to rush kids.

"Even if you came back, you'd be different. I'd bore you in no time."

"You don't bore me, Ella." His boredom was a product of an overactive mind. One that had to be kept busy. He'd never been good at sitting around.

"Maybe I just don't want to live my life with someone who's smarter than me, you ever think of that?"

She had him there. Because he did think of that—about himself being the stupid one. Or he used to. Before Ella. A high school dropout, Mark had dropped out of the dating scene, too. He hadn't liked how he'd felt hanging out with girls who were more educated than he was.

"Do you love me, Ella?"

She lifted her chin, in spite of the tears on her cheeks. "You know I do."

"And you need to know that even if I went, I'd be back for you."

"I'm going to the pig roast, Mark."

IT MIGHT BE SUMMER, but in the mountains of Colorado the evenings were still chilly.

Addy had a cup of tea. Dressed in her favorite jeans, the short ones that she could wear with flip-flops rather than two-inch heels, she hugged the warm rose-embossed china with both hands, legs curled beneath her, and stared at the photo on the living room wall.

The woman in the picture was beautiful. With long dark hair falling softly around high cheekbones and a rounded chin, Ann Keller had always had a kind word for everyone. In most of Addy's memories, Ann was smiling, her brown eyes glistening with love like they were in that picture.

Except for the times when she hadn't been. Those had mostly involved Addy's father. And only toward the end.

Shuddering, she looked away, toward the backyard oasis she'd built behind her small, one-bedroom, one-bath house. The landscaping and yard art, all carefully chosen in greens and blues and yellows, surrounded a pond with a waterfall that ran 24/7, three hundred and sixty-five days a year.

Rock, paper, scissors. She used to play the game with Ely. Paper covered rock, scissors cut paper, rock pounded scissors.

And water killed fire.

No, that wasn't part of the game. Fire had come later.

She listened for the water, a sound that soothed, and glanced back at the photo. Addy was there, too—a pixieish five-year-old with a big gummy grin and missing front teeth. Her straight blond hair was up in a ponytail. She'd loved that red polka-dot sundress. Maybe because of the red patent leather shoes she'd had to go with it—Dorothy's shoes, she'd told her mother the day they'd bought them. Maybe she'd loved them so much because her mother had had a dress and sandals that matched. Or maybe because she could still remember the shopping trip, the day that they'd picked out the attire. It had just been her and Mom that day and they'd played Princess and Queen while they'd tried on lots of different outfits. Addy and her brother, Elijah, were going to be in a publicity photo with their mother, who'd just been signed to her own cooking show. Two years older than she was, Elijah had been gung ho about the photo—but not about tagging along to buy clothes. He'd opted out of the shopping excursion.

But her big brother had been just as excited as Addy had been the morning the three of them had gotten ready—she and Mom in their dresses and Ely in his new suit and red tie—and then piled into the car and taken off for the studio in Phoenix, ready to embark on a great adventure.

After the pictures, Mom had taken them to a nice restaurant and eaten hamburgers and French fries with them—even though she much preferred the fancier foods she'd become known for. And then they'd changed clothes in the lush bathroom just off the dining room, and headed to the zoo.

It had been a great day. Perfect. The best ever.

It had also been the last day Ann and Ely spent on earth.

CHAPTER TWO

"I DIDN'T EVEN graduate high school, Nonnie. College isn't for me."

"You graduated, Mark." Eighty-one-year-old Gloria Heber glanced pointedly at the GED certificate that she'd lovingly framed and hung on their living room wall next to a cheap *Mona Lisa* print that she'd also lovingly framed.

Mark didn't put a lot of stock in a certificate he'd hardly had to work for. But he'd already played his age card. His grandmother didn't think thirty was too old to start college. Not by a long shot. She'd spouted off a list of people, one of whom was in her sixties, that she'd heard of from so-and-so and such-and-such, who'd graduated from college.

"I'm a Bierly boy," he said now, feeling like a twelve-year-old again as he faced down the determined curmudgeon who'd had him quaking in his boots since he wore baby booties. "I've never lived outside this town. Hell, I've never lived outside this house. And you want me to go all the way to Arizona? It's a desert out there! And hot as Hades."

Ella thought he was leaving. She'd gone to the pig roast. And then pretended like she'd had a good time.

She'd also asked if he'd made his decision yet. And he figured, just as soon as he wrote and officially turned down the scholarship, she'd agree to marry him.

"What's wrong with summer all year long?" Nonnie's tone was strong. "I've never known you to have a problem with the heat."

Yeah, well, he didn't like to sweat. At least the kind of sweating she made him do.

"You're good at what you do, Mark, but there's so much more you could be doing. And you ain't goin' to get there from here."

Nonnie quoted a familiar saying in their small West Virginia town.

Technically, wherever he went, Arizona included, he'd get there by way of Bierly. But...

Perching on the edge of the armchair across from Nonnie's wheelchair, he leaned over, elbows on his knees, to face her head-on. "I'm not going to leave you, Nonnie. You can't take care of yourself. They're offering me money for living expenses, but there's no money to hire someone to look after you, and even if there was, I wouldn't do it. You took care of me from the time I was born and now it's my turn. Period. End of story."

He didn't often use that tone of voice with her. Almost never. He didn't use it much at work, either. Didn't need to. But when he did, he got results. Always.

"Fine."

He blinked. "Fine?" He'd been sweating over nothing? She'd never really expected him to accept the scholarship offer that had been delivered by the U.S. postal service the week before?

Nonnie must have written to this scholarship committee on his behalf. He sure hadn't applied. But why would she have done that if she hadn't expected him to go?

"I'm going with you."

"What?"

She handed him a folder. It was half an inch thick, mostly stuffed with pages she'd printed off the internet. Glancing through it, Mark saw housing for rent in Shelter Valley, cost-of-living estimates and driving directions from Bierly, with a map. There were lists of local shopping establishments in the area—privately owned, nonfranchise places with one exception. And a couple of receipts.

"You rented a duplex for us?"

"Two bedrooms are more than we need, but the price was right in line with the scholarship allowance, and I liked the woman who owns the place. Caroline Strickland. She's a Kentucky girl from right around the corner. Moved to Shelter Valley eight years ago and is a little lonely for her own kind."

Nonnie probably knew the woman's birth date and deepest fears, too. She just had that way about her.

"If she's not happy there, how do you expect us to be?"

"She loves Shelter Valley! Says moving there is the

best choice she's ever made. She's just glad to have us joining her."

"You've lived in Bierly for eighty-one years. You were born in this house. And you expect me to believe you want to leave?"

"I want you to have this chance, Markie-boy." She used the nickname she knew better than to utter outside their private communications.

Eyes narrowed, he studied the indomitable woman trapped in a frail body that was all sunken skin and brittle bones—helped along by the multiple sclerosis that had been slowly weakening her over the past fourteen years. "You wrote to the scholarship committee, didn't you? You read about it on the internet and you wrote to them."

"No." Her chin lifted. Mark wasn't going. He adored Nonnie, owed her, but he was a hands-on learner, not a classroom type of guy.

And she'd never survive the trip.

"What about Ella?"

"If she loves you she'll wait for you."

Four years was a long time to wait when you were in your childbearing years. So why hadn't he been in a hurry to start a family before the scholarship offer had turned his life upside down?

"I have no idea what to study," he said. "The scholarship says that I have to complete a four-year degree or pay the money back."

Nonnie's snort would have fit in better at the bar

she used to tend than it did in the clean and pretty home she kept.

"You got ideas springing out your ears, Mark. It's time someone besides me and the dinner table listens to them."

"I just know what could be done better at the plant. And I know better than to shoot my mouth off down there."

"You got life-altering ideas, Markie-boy. I'm old, but I'm not out of touch. Our world's changing fast and the things you talk about, the way things are being redone so fast and the danger in those gases that aren't being tended to, you know how to fix some of that. Look at all the work you've been doing in fire forensics. Hell, even ten years ago they was still using mostly guesswork to determine things about them fires, and you already brung modern science to Bierly with your volunteer fire work. Maybe, if you had the schooling and the position it would give you, you could have saved Jimmy."

An explosion on the line the previous winter had killed his best friend. And now Rick Stanfield was working in Jimmy's place.

"Jimmy didn't follow the handbook, Nonnie."

No one did. The rules in the book didn't coincide with the cost-saving methods upper management expected them to use. But that was his issue to take up with the bosses.

"You're wasting your God-given talents here."

She was his grandmother and, for all intents and

purposes, his sole parent from the day he was born. Her perceptions were a tad bit skewed where he was concerned.

"What will we do with this place?"

"Rent it out, furnished, as soon as someone answers the ad I put out on the internet. Just need enough to pay taxes. Wilbur'll watch it for us in the meantime."

Looking around him, taking in the scarred solid cherry-wood tables he'd learned to dust when he was four, the beige tweed couch that still carried the faded stain of the cherry Popsicle he'd thrown up after he'd had his tonsils out, the threadbare carpet that Nonnie had taught him to dance on because he was refusing to learn with other boys as mock partners in gym class, Mark couldn't come up with any more excuses.

"We aren't going, Nonnie. Twenty years ago, you could have dragged me to the truck by my ear and made me go, but not now. You need me now. And I'm staying here."

It bothered him to play the health card, but leaving Bierly would kill both of them. Nonnie didn't have many years left—not enough to risk four of them in an unfamiliar world across the country while he wasted time learning things he would never use just to have another piece of useless paper hanging on the wall.

Chances were she wouldn't live long enough to frame the damn thing.

He watched as Nonnie's shoulders dropped inward,

her chin falling to her chest as her body leaned forward, and hated that he'd had to cause such abject defeat in the woman who had always championed him. Always fought for him and her right to keep him with her.

And then he saw the folder she'd bent down to retrieve from the thin wire basket he'd designed to fit on the outside wheel base of her chair. A second manila folder. Also half an inch thick.

The mass shook as she reached out bony, blue-veined fingers to hand it to him.

Confused, Mark opened the file. It also contained printed pages from the internet. Housing availability. And receipts. One for a sale. And one for the rental of a room in an assisted living facility.

"I don't understand."

She stared him down silently.

"You just said you were coming with me."

Nonnie was the only person he knew who could deliver a taking-down without saying a word.

"You sold the land?" Ten acres behind the house. Her garden.

He glanced again at the second folder.

She had her own power of attorney. There'd been no reason for her not to have it. She was of sound mind.

But he had her heart. That had to count for something. ...

The folder stared up at him.

"Either we go to Arizona together, or I go there."

Slamming the folder down, Mark crossed his arms and glared at her.

"You are *not* going into a nursing facility, Nonnie. You are staying with me until the end. We're family you and I. We stick together. Take care of each other. That decision was made fourteen years ago. And revisited when you gave me medical power of attorney…"

And then he got it.

That agreement, his promise to her, was what she was counting on.

She had him.

Ella was right. He was moving to Shelter Valley, Arizona.

To become a thirty-year-old college student.

CHAPTER THREE

"HI, WILL, IT'S Adrianna Keller returning your call. I can be reached—"

"Addy?" She recognized his voice as he picked up, interrupting her midsentence. "It's so good to hear from you."

It had been a couple of years. She should have called more often. "How are your folks?"

"Fine. They're trying to arrange a trip to Disneyland with all of the great-grandchildren before school starts."

Will's family—his parents, three brothers and sister—were lovely, not that she actually knew any of them anymore. She hadn't been in touch with his parents, other than exchanging annual Christmas cards, since she was in high school.

"Are they still in the big house?"

"Yes, though Dad finally consented to hiring a full-time landscaper and live-in housekeeper."

The elder Parsonses had bought the desert mansion fifteen miles outside of Shelter Valley when Will was in high school. And ten years later Addy had been a very brief member of their household.

"And how's Bethany?" Addy asked of the baby girl

Will and his wife, Becca, had conceived after twenty years of marriage and numerous miscarriages. Becca had finally given birth at forty-three.

"Twelve going on twenty," Will drawled, but Addy heard the adoration and pride in his voice.

"Getting nervous about the next few years, Papa?" she asked, grinning.

"No more so than I've been for the past twelve. In this town she's not going to get away with much without her mother or me hearing about it."

"Becca's still mayor?"

"Reelected by a landslide."

"And Kaelin?" The Korean boy Becca and Will had adopted four years after Bethany was born.

"Just made first baseman on his Little League team and can't wait for play-offs so that he can spend every waking hour on the field at the park."

A flash memory of summer days spent at the park in town, watching Elijah play ball with his friends, and then going across the street for ice cream, haunted Addy. She sipped her tea.

"How are you doing, Addy?" Will's tone softened.

"Fine. Busy."

"I looked at your website. You're managing on your own without joining a firm, which is impressive. I knew you were doing educational law, but you've got a long list of wins. You've only been out of law school, what, six years?"

Seven. And she only took cases she believed in— something she could do being her own boss. Right was right and wrong was wrong and she of all people couldn't afford to blur the line.

With only herself to support, she could be picky.

"Don't let the list mislead you. I eat dried noodles for dinner more often than most of the folks in my profession," she joked. And spoke the truth, too.

She couldn't even afford a secretary.

"I have a favor to ask, Addy."

Leaning her head back against the couch, she relaxed. "I'll do anything I can for you, Will, you know that. What's up?"

"This is a big one."

Bigger than welcoming a lost little girl into the family and taking time to make her feel as special and welcome as everyone else there? It had been a long time ago. They'd all moved on. Had completely separate lives. Didn't really even keep in touch. But she'd never forgotten.

"I'll do whatever I can."

"How soon could you get away for an extended vacation?"

"I'm waiting on a verdict on a case involving a diabetic kid who was suspended for having needles out during class, and then I'm free. I quit taking new cases as soon as I saw that this was going to trial."

She could only do so much on her own.

"What do you need? Research? Case law?"

It made perfect sense that Will, as president of a prominent university, might need some educational law advice.

"I need it all. We're dealing with possible discrimination charges."

"Does this have to do with Kaelin?" Will's adopted Asian son. "Is someone giving him problems in school?" Hard to imagine in Shelter Valley. Not because the town didn't have bigots, but because of Will's and Becca's standing in the community.

"It's me, Addy." His voice lowered. "I've received a couple of anonymous letters threatening to go public with proof that I'm allowing discriminatory practices at Montford."

She sat up, fully focused.

"What kind of discriminatory practices?"

"It doesn't say."

"Is there more to go on?"

"Unfortunately not. No names, no classes or faculty names, no ethnicities or instances to follow up on. No hint whatsoever."

"And no return address?"

"The letters were slid under my office door."

"Surely you have a friend on the Shelter Valley police force who could find out who's sending them."

"Greg Richards, who's been sheriff here for over a decade, is the only one who knows about the threats besides Becca and myself. I took the letters straight to Greg and he advised that until we know who's behind this, we keep it to ourselves. If for no other reason than if this is just a sick attempt to make me sweat, Greg doesn't want the perpetrator to know he's succeeding. Greg is investigating, but there were no prints on the envelopes. It's common paper. Common ink. And it's not like we have a forensic lab here. Or like this is enough of an issue to warrant involving overworked forensic teams in Phoenix who are trying to convict known perpetrators of horrendous deeds."

It could be enough of an issue if someone was setting up a plan to blackmail Will Parsons who, at fifty-three, was the Parsonses' eldest son and an heir to the family fortune. But she was getting ahead of herself.

"One thing was pretty clear, whoever left the letters has an issue here at Montford that he believes I know about."

"Does he ask for any course of action?"

"No. And no indication of when he'd go public or what I can do to prevent him from doing so."

"Chances are you'll hear from him again. He has to gain something."

"Greg agrees."

Silence hung on the line. And then Will said, "I need your help, Addy. For obvious reasons, we don't want to involve anyone from the area. I trust you implicitly. Your specialty is educational law. And no one here will know you. I need you to look into life at Montford, at my life at Montford, and see if you find any improprieties or wrongdoing that could warrant a civil case against me—or the university."

"Have you knowingly done anything to warrant the accusations?" She wasn't sure she'd believe him if he said he had.

"Absolutely not."

She might not have seen Will in years, but she knew him. With the heart of a child that had once secretly hoped he'd be her new father.

"Then of course I'll help. I'll do whatever I can."

"Even without any truth behind the accusations, if whoever this is goes public with them, the suspicion alone will affect Montford's reputation and could even have bearing on our collegiate rating."

"More likely you'll be given the opportunity to part with a sizable sum to settle out of court and keep the alleged grievance out of the press."

"I don't have a sizable sum readily available." Will sounded beaten. "I need you here. In Shelter Valley. When Becca and I mentioned you to Greg he couldn't jump on plans fast enough. We'd like you to arrive in town posing as a new student, which would give you reason to hang around campus, to turn up in various offices, sit in classes, while doing what you do best."

"Assimilating the facts and smelling the stench." It was a phrase he'd used when she'd first told him why she thought she'd make a good attorney.

"And you can do it without raising suspicion or making it obvious that we're giving the threat any merit at all. Greg is adamant on that one. His theory is that if we appear to be doing nothing, we'll draw this guy out more quickly. We'll drive him to make a mistake. To expose himself."

"I agree with him."

"You'll have access to the secure campus server," Will continued. "And anything else you need."

"Where would I live?" She couldn't think about agreeing to his request. Couldn't think about setting foot in Shelter Valley. She needed to focus on facts.

"That's up to you. We thought an apartment close to school would be most realistic."

"I'd rather be in a single-story dwelling." She could buy a little decorative fountain.

"I'm sure that won't be a problem. Caroline Strickland, the wife of a friend of mine who settled in Shelter Valley seven or eight years ago, owns a few investment properties near the campus. I can put you in touch with her."

The words conjured up memories of Montford's campus. The green quad that had seemed enormous to her as a six-year old.

She quickly refocused, and came up with…math. "I'd have to lease out my place."

She didn't want to do that.

And couldn't afford mortgage plus rent unless she did so.

"I'll lease it."

"You?"

"We have no idea who the source of these threats might be. Greg insists that we go forth as though it could be anyone. So we have to keep as much of your appearance in town as legitimate as we can. You need to rent a place. I can help with tuition, but you'll need money to live and I can't pay you until the job is done."

"I'm making enough on the case I'm just closing to handle living expenses."

"I can't ask you to do that. Becca's going to write a check to your practice, a charitable donation for your current case. Sari just found out her youngest child is diabetic, so the connection works."

Sari was Becca's sister. Addy had a vague memory of being at Becca and Will's house with Will's little sister, Randi, when Sari had come over crying. Will had taken her and Randi home—back to the Parsonses' big house in the desert where Addy had been living since the fire that had killed her parents and her brother.

Sari had a diabetic child. Addy could feel the walls closing in on her.

Will named a sum for the donation.

"That's way too much, Will."

"It should be enough to cover your mortgage, rent and give you something to live off for the next year."

"You expect this to take a year?"

"You're going to need money to tide you over when you get back to your real life."

He'd certainly thought everything through. Her head throbbed. From the back of her neck forward. And she had another thought.

"Your folks know who I am. And Randi will."

"They know you, of course, as is substantiated by the number of invitations they've issued over the years for you to come visit, but they haven't seen you in more than twenty years."

Twenty-five years. Since social services had awarded permanent custody of her to a grandmother she'd never met, rather than to the family she'd known since she was born.

Back in those days the elder Mrs. Parsons wouldn't entertain without Addy's mother catering the event. She'd been known to schedule her social events around Ann Keller's availability. And Addy, who'd been welcome to accompany her mother while she created her masterpieces, had learned to walk standing at a cooking counter in the Parsonses' enormous kitchen.

"Gran wouldn't let me go back," Addy told Will what he already knew. And didn't add that later, after Gran was dead and Addy was the boss of her own life, she still hadn't returned to the town where she'd been born.

She couldn't...

"Greg is arranging an assumed identity for you." Will rescued her mind from the pit she avoided at all costs, getting her back on track.

Becca and Will had already been married when fire left Addy orphaned and Mr. and Mrs. Parsons had taken her in. Seen her through long months of painful treatments for the third-degree burns all the way down her back.

Promised her that they'd love her forever. That she was a part of their family. That she could depend on them because they loved her as one of their own.

They'd meant the words. Addy believed that. Even

as a kid she'd known how hard they fought for custody of her.

But Addy hadn't really wanted to live in that big mansion in the desert. She'd wanted to live with Becca and Will. She had hoped, with childish naïveté, that they'd swoop in and adopt her away from the older folks who were fighting over her.

Becca had lost a couple of babies by then. Which might be why the couple had taken to her as they had.

And she had so hoped…

But no, those roads didn't bear traveling.

"It helps that you never sent pictures in spite of Mom and Dad's repeated requests."

Glancing at the framed photo on her wall, Addy didn't respond. Admitting the truth, that she avoided being photographed whenever she could—as though she could somehow keep her mother and brother closer by not doing so, not getting older, not moving on—would make her sound a bit off.

Gran had never figured out that her yearly bouts with flu had coincided with school picture day.

"You want me there under an assumed name?"

"Greg will help us arrange all of the details. I know it's asking a lot, Addy, but I don't know what else to do. With this second threat, I can't just lie in wait…"

"I haven't been back."

"I know."

He was asking, anyway. Which told Addy he really believed he had no other choice.

And, so, neither did she.

CHAPTER FOUR

THE DUPLEX WASN'T BAD. On her fourth trip in from her car—a small decade-old American-made model that fit her alias just fine—Addy noticed an old woman glancing out the front window from the connecting unit. The frail hand shook on the edge of the curtain. From the woman's height, Addy guessed she was sitting down. She couldn't make out clothes. But the woman's alert and unapologetically curious gaze struck a chord deeply within her.

As much as Addy had prayed as a little girl that the judge would let her stay with the Parsonses and not ship her off to Colorado with a grandmother she'd never known, Gran had been good to her.

Addy missed her.

Shaking herself, Addy looked up once more and the old woman at the window nodded. And dropped the curtain.

She'd met her next-door neighbor.

And she was glad.

PUSHING THROUGH the door, Mark left the air-conditioned hallway of the university and burst out into the blinding daylight. He'd never have believed that the same sun that had been shining above him all of his life could be so completely different here. Brighter. And more active. He didn't just *see* the Arizona sunshine, he felt it clear to his bones.

But it wasn't his bones he was thinking about as he hit the first speed-dial button on the phone he'd pulled from its holster the second he'd left the guidance counselor's office.

Nonnie was alone in a new home in a new town where she knew no one and had no ability to go anywhere on her own.

"I'm fine, Mark," she said, answering after the first ring.

Relief flooded him, and he gave himself a mental shake. He was thirty years old, not ten.

"I'm done with my meeting and on my way home. Do you need anything?" His carefully schooled tone wouldn't fool her.

Nothing did.

"Nope. And you don't have to hurry home on my account. When Caroline told me this place was wheelchair accessible she wasn't kidding. I love that water dispenser on the refrigerator. And do you know, she didn't just put all of the dishes in the lower cupboards, she put one of those As-Seen-on-TV reach things in the pantry, too."

Slowing his pace, he glanced around the campus he'd barely noticed in his determination to get to and through his meeting quickly. He saw lots of green.

Trees. A large patch of perfectly manicured grass in the midst of all the desert rock. Hundred-year-old stone buildings. And some newer ones, too.

Nonnie was telling him about the front-loading laundry machines. They'd missed those when they'd come in the night before.

Truth was, he'd missed pretty much everything except getting his truck parked, unloading the suitcases from the truck and helping his aching grandmother into bed.

Then, after he'd dropped down to the couch in lieu of putting sheets on the bed in the second bedroom, he'd texted Ella to let her know they'd arrived.

She hadn't texted back.

But she would. As soon as she realized that he was not going to desert her.

"I've already washed the clothes we dirtied on the trip. ..."

Great. Something else to worry about. The standard top-loading machines that he was used to gave him one less battle to fight in Nonnie's tendency to overtax herself. She couldn't get clothes in and out of them, which meant she couldn't go about folding them and trying to put them away, either.

Not many people around on this hot August day. Classes didn't start for another week. And the pavement sent up blistering waves of heat.

"So?" His grandmother sounded unusually chipper for a woman who'd recently spent several days in a truck traveling across the country.

And who had to be in incredible pain due to the same.

"So..." His natural reticence holding his tongue in check, Mark kept the phone to his ear and walked toward the truck. And then he smiled. "Okay, Nonnie, you were right. I found it."

"And what is it you decided on?"

"Safety engineering. Fire behavior, hazardous material, physics, technical drawing, regulatory compliance, ergonomics, industrial hygiene..." Head spinning, he reeled himself in. "It's a four-year bachelor degree with a graduate program that adds emergency management," he finished as he reached his truck and unlocked the door. "If I'd had the training already, I probably could have saved Jimmy's life. This is just what the plant needs."

Because he was going home to Bierly. To Ella.

"Good."

A wave of heat engulfed him. He climbed up into the front seat and immediately hopped back down again.

"Good?" He said into the phone, standing there staring at the blistering interior of his truck. "That's all? Just good?" He'd upended his entire existence for "good"?

"It's the beginning, Markie-boy."

Reaching in, he turned on the ignition, set the air

to its coolest setting and prayed the vehicle wouldn't overheat before he could drive it and cool the engine.

"The beginning of what?" He didn't like the sound of this.

"My plan."

"I assume this plan has to do with me?"

"Of course."

"Then don't you think you should let me in on it?"

"In time, Markie-boy. In time."

At least she was counting on having time. He decided to leave it at that.

"'HOLDING TUBE UPRIGHT, lift bowl and slide into place.'"

Addy read. Looked at the piece of half-inch tubing sticking out of the cement base, which was covered in river rock. And then at the river rock and cement bowl that were still in the box on the fold-up handheld dolly that lived in her trunk when she wasn't using it to cart crates of files into court.

Sweat dripped down her back beneath her tank top. She wiped more from her forehead and smeared it on the denim shorts that had been clean at the beginning of this project but now bore various smudges.

The guy at the landscaping store in Phoenix had assured her, as he'd loaded the fountain into her car, that she'd have no problem putting the thing together by herself. It was in pieces, he'd said, and had recommended that she open the box and carry the fountain, piece by piece, to its final destination.

Using a board for a ramp, she'd managed, by climbing into her trunk and getting behind the box, to push it out of her car, down the ramp and onto the two-wheeler.

Then, with her tennis shoes for traction on the hot cement, she'd started the cart rolling to the backyard.

She'd landed the base on the ground by sliding it out of the box.

And now they wanted her to *lift* the bowl? Had the guy at the store even looked at her? She was female. Five foot two. Weighed not much more than that fountain did. There was no way she could lift it.

And no way she was even going to try to live without a fountain. Water sustained her; it was the foundation of her mental and emotional equilibrium.

A girl who'd been burned alive could recover, move on, live a healthy and stable life, as long as she had water close by. And she was better at it when she could hear the water, anytime, all the time, in bed at night, and in the kitchen in the morning.

Right now, with the life of lies she was embarking on, she needed the foundations of her existence firmly in place. Addy, the most black-and-white person in the world, had just taken on a life of duplicity. Her boundaries were already pushed beyond maximum capacity.

Add to that, she was back in Shelter Valley. The desert. Where temperature soared to excruciating highs, drying out everything in its sphere. A fire's breeding ground.

And the land of her personal hell.

She had to have water.

"GO HELP HER."

Standing at the sliding glass door that led out to a small private patio and yard separated by a two-foot-high wall from the small private patio and backyard next door, Mark watched the petite woman sitting on the ground reading instructions. Her hair, pulled back into a ponytail, almost touched the ground.

"You help someone do what they can do for themselves, you make them helpless," he said to the woman who'd just rolled up behind him.

"You let her do for herself, she discovers her own strength," Nonnie corrected behind him. And then, with a snort, added, "Don't be an idiot, Mark. You know the context. And that clearly is not something she should be trying to do herself."

He did know. He also wanted to see what the blonde pixie was going to do next. He'd been home for an hour and on his way out the door to help his new neighbor wrestle the box out of her trunk, when the unwieldy box had slid expertly down the plank she'd set for it.

He'd watched as it landed evenly on a two-wheeler, which she'd then pulled with little effort.

Impressed, he'd walked to the back of the duplex that was larger than the house he'd grown up in back home, expecting to see someone—the husband, maybe—back there waiting to help her.

Instead, she'd opened the box, read the instructions and was now working on putting the thing together on her own.

Fascinating.

In Bierly, the women he knew asked for help first. And got it, too.

No strings attached.

"Go help her, boy. Now!"

And he'd been afraid the cross-country trip would be more than Nonnie's frail, disease-ridden body could handle.

"Do you mind if I lend a hand?"

For a second Addy wondered if the heat was getting to her when she glanced up to see the dark-haired, exquisitely proportioned man climbing over her wall from the unit that adjoined her temporary new home.

The navy muscle shirt and navy-and-white running shorts he wore framed his assets perfectly.

Wow.

"You aren't the older woman who lives there," she said inanely, certain now that the heat had done a number on her.

"No, I'm her grandson."

Made sense. The woman probably had family all over town stopping in to check on her—help her out.

Shelter Valley was like that.

She might have been a little kid when she'd been shipped off to Colorado, but even at that young age, she'd been aware of the camaraderie and neighborliness of the folks in the town where she'd been born. A whole group of them had gathered downtown to wave goodbye as she'd ridden off in her grandmother's car.

"Lucky woman," she said under her breath, and then winced. That had come out louder than she'd intended. What in the hell was the matter with her? She was around good-looking men all the time. And didn't care one way or the other.

His grin unsteadied her nerves. "What was that?"

"I said it's my lucky day." Addy straightened up to her full height and passed him the sheet of instructions. "If you could just lift that basin, I'll guide the tube and then I can get the rest."

She'd just lied. She'd said "lucky woman," not some tripe about "her lucky day." Adrianna Keller, straight-and-narrow line walker, had knowingly and deliberately told an untruth for no other reason than to protect herself from further embarrassment.

"I beg your pardon, ma'am, but I don't think that's what you said." His grin had grown into a full-blown smile. But there was something kind about the glint in his eye.

"That's quite the accent you have there, cowboy." She figured two could play this game.

"I'm a West Virginian through and through." Looking from the instructions to the box, Grandson dropped the sheet she'd handed him, bent down and lifted the basin. "Ready?" he asked, as though holding two tons was no effort at all.

Moving more quickly than she'd have figured possible in the heat, Addy did her part. She held the tube and guided it into the basin.

And in seconds, her fountain was in place. Not working yet. The most important ingredient—water—came next. And she had to plug in the power source....

"I'm Mark, by the way." Gorgeous Grandson held out a hand.

Wiping her sweaty palm on the seat of her shorts, Addy placed her hand in his. And melted a little more.

"I'm Ad...Adele," she stammered. Not Addy. Or even Adrianna. Not Keller, either. "Adele Kennedy."

The sheriff of Shelter Valley had advised that they choose a name not unlike her own in case she had slipups. And here she was, slipping up on her very first try.

"I hope we weren't too loud when we arrived last night. I'd planned to make it in earlier but Nonnie had a spot of trouble in the hotel yesterday morning so we got a late start."

"I wouldn't know," Addy said. "I just got in this morning."

"You were out of town?"

"I'm just moving to town," she said, wondering how often he visited his grandmother if he didn't even know that her neighbor had left.

"No kidding." His warm, friendly gaze continued to mesmerize her. "We're just moving in, as well."

"We? You live with your grandmother?"

His grin faded. "Yes." His sudden change of stance, arms folded at his chest, told her that he was ready for her if she wanted to make something of the fact that he was a grown man living with his Nonnie.

"I'm sorry." Bowing her head, Addy took a second and then glanced over at Mark. "I didn't mean that to sound as though I was shocked."

"But you were."

"Maybe." She shrugged. "But probably not for the reason you'd assume. I think it's great. Just coincidental. I lived with my grandmother, too. Was raised by her, actually. She died a couple of years ago and I still miss her so much." Squinting up into the sun, she offered more of herself than she should have, considering her new persona —more than she usually did upon first meeting, even when she was living her own life.

His grin was back. "Then you'll understand if I sometimes seem a little forward. I learned a long time ago that it's easier to give in to the hand at my back than it is worth fighting it."

"The older they get, the more strong-willed they become," she said.

"And more outspoken, too," Mark added, nodding.

"And the more willing you are to do everything they ask because you know your time with them is limited."

His head tilted at her words and he studied her silently before saying, "I have a feeling it's going to be good living next to you, Adele Kennedy."

Addy smiled, nodded, mumbled something appropriate and wished, just for a second, that she really was Adele Kennedy.

CHAPTER FIVE

HE'D FLIRTED WITH the woman. It had been less than a week since he'd left Bierly, since he'd sent Ella a goodbye text promising her that he'd be back, whether she waited for him or not.

A text she hadn't answered.

Balancing the pot holder and small casserole dish in one hand, he raised his other to knock on the door six feet from his own, an apology for the intrusion already on his lips. He'd deliver. And go.

Shelter Valley's online want ads awaited.

A dead bolt clicked. "What did she make you bring me?"

Adele's smile reminded him of the Arizona sunshine. Or maybe the sun had blinded his vision.

"It's a party casserole. My favorite when I was growing up and what she makes for every single special occasion for which she's well enough to cook."

He could make it now, too. Just as well. But he didn't share that tidbit. He held out the dish. "If you've already eaten, don't worry. It's even better reheated. Gives the flavors a chance to comingle."

"Your grandmother's not well?" She took the casserole and set it down on something in the darkness behind her.

"She's got multiple sclerosis. It's nothing new. Just more severe as she gets older. The trip across country has caused a bit of a flare-up."

"Is her condition life-threatening?"

"No." Nonnie might not be with him forever, but he wasn't losing her yet.

"Tell her thank you for me, for the casserole."

He nodded. Stepped back.

"So are you going to Montford?"

She leaned casually against the edge of the door as she spoke. And, standing as she was on the raised ledge leading into her home, her breasts were in a direct line with his eyes. Straight ahead. Right there. Firm and shapely and…

Want ads. Waiting.

"I only ask because I was told that while this is off-campus housing, it's reserved for students. And if your grandmother's not well, I figure she wouldn't be enrolled as a senior student, which was what I initially thought—"

"Yes, I'm enrolled at the university," he got out—naturally, he hoped—as he dug his brain out of his pants. And then asked, "Do you live here alone?" and when he heard how personal the question sounded he quickly added, "Nonnie said that she saw you unloading your stuff by yourself. She sent the food over, insisting that you were alone and shouldn't be left to fend for yourself on your first night in town."

Adele's brow creased, sending another ripple of desire to his nether regions. "How'd she know it was my first night in town?"

Because we were sitting over there, on the other side of the wall, talking about you. "I told her."

Afraid she'd make too much of that—or exactly enough—he quickly added, "After she asked." And to solidify his idiocy, he continued rambling. "I hope you'll forgive her nosiness but she's spent her entire life in a town the size of a pea pod and believes that knowing everything about everyone makes her a good neighbor."

Where in the hell was his reticence? Or any vestige of the intelligence he'd been born with?

"Nonnie? Is that her given name?"

"No. It's my name for her. My version of *Grandma* when I was kid. Or so I'm told. But that's all anyone at home has called her for as long as I can remember."

"I like it." She stepped back, taking the door with her. "And yes, I live here alone."

He glanced again at the empty ring finger he'd noticed earlier that day. Because noticing was free.

Hard to believe a woman as gorgeous as she was wasn't married.

"And you're a student at the university?"

"Yes."

"Since you're just new to town I take it you're a freshman? Or are you transferring?"

Was there a chance his new neighbor would be in any of his classes?

"I'm a freshman." And she was over eighteen. How much older he wasn't sure. And he wasn't asking, either.

"I had to work to earn enough money to attend college," she continued, looking away. "I was a receptionist in a law firm."

She seemed uncomfortable, embarrassed by her circumstances.

"My grandmother didn't believe in accruing debt. If you couldn't pay for it with cash, then you didn't need it. I heard it so much growing up, I just couldn't make myself take out school loans. I figured that if I wanted to go to college badly enough, I could save the money. And if, by the time I had tuition money saved, I no longer wanted to go, then Gran was right, I didn't really need the education."

"That's how you can pay for the duplex and attend class? Because you saved enough money to do so?"

"Yes."

"So why Montford?"

"Horticulture…I'm studying horticulture," she stuttered. Was he making her nervous?

The sensation wasn't completely unpleasant.

"Desert plants are full of medicinal properties," she added more easily. "And Montford has one of the best programs."

He would have stayed to chat, but he heard the whir of Nonnie's chair as the old woman moved closer to the door.

Eavesdropping.

Wishing his beautiful neighbor a good-night, Mark went back to his own place to talk to his grandmother about meddling. And manners.

IF SHE HAD TO COME back to Shelter Valley, at least she was there incognito. As a new student in town, Addy could keep to herself. There was no one to answer to. No flood of decades-old invitations that she'd feel duty bound to accept. Because there was no doubt in her mind that many of the folks who'd seen that scarred little girl off all those years ago were still in Shelter Valley, living and loving in the unique Western town nestled into the desert that surrounded it.

But no one knew Adele Kennedy. No one who would notice that the short route between the university and home, a route with a grocery store on it, was the only route she ventured upon. Will might have reached out to her if he could have done it without jeopardizing her cover. Becca certainly would have.

Thankfully, they couldn't. Which left her alone to peruse the hundreds of electronic files he'd opened up to her during the week before classes started. She was enrolled full-time for the fall semester. With a horticulture major. Maybe she'd learn something about raising beautiful plants during her stay here.

And maybe... She stopped, looked away from the laptop set up on her kitchen table and listened. There. It came again. A tapping sound. On the shared wall between her and the gorgeous man with the Southern drawl who drove the older but well-cared-for black truck that would fit right in back home in Colorado. *Tap*. And then again. And again. Over and over. Sometimes with more force than others.

What was he doing over there? Not hammering, there wasn't enough force. What else did one do that required tapping on a wall?

Except send Morse code to a prisoner on the other side?

Whatever, it wasn't any of her business. He wasn't any of her business. As she'd been telling herself repeatedly for the past four days.

She went back to student handbook changes and complaint files. She'd already been through all student discipline actions taken in the past five years, and would search further back if need be. So far every complaint had been handled with no untoward legal implications.

Tap. Tap. Tap, tap, tap.

Addy stopped. So the information on her screen was tedious. She was used to tedious. Actually liked losing herself in tedious. Researching tedious information to expose the smallest of inconsistencies was a large part of her job. One inconsistency could be the basis of winning—or losing—a case.

Tap.

The sound was in the exact same spot on the wall. Over and over.

What if Mark wasn't home? School hadn't started yet, but he'd certainly come and gone a lot more than she had during the four days they'd both lived in town. What if Nonnie was over there alone?

She'd yet to meet the older woman. Or to speak with Mark again since she'd returned the empty and cleaned casserole bowl.

But she heard them on occasion. Heard the timbre of voices when she left her window open so she could hear the fountain. Heard doors open and close. Heard pipes groan as water ran through them.

She thought of them, next door. Took an odd sort of comfort in their presence.

Not that she needed comfort. Addy had been living on her own for a long time. She liked the solitude.

Tap. Tap. Tap.

The sound came from the back of the duplex, in the kitchen area. She couldn't just ignore it. Not if Mark wasn't there. Nonnie was elderly. Sick. And in a wheelchair.

Slipping out the sliding glass door off her kitchen, she knocked on the one next to it. And then, with her hands to the glass, she peered in.

She saw the wheelchair first. An electronically powered one coming straight toward the door. And then she caught a glimpse of the tiniest elderly woman she'd ever seen, sitting upright in the chair that engulfed her, her gnarled knuckles covering what must be the chair's control.

Upon reaching the door, the woman reached up, hooked her hand around the latch, and with a couple of clicks the door slid open.

"I'm sorry to bother you, but are you okay?" Addy asked, taking in her neighbor's sharp-eyed gaze with a sharp breath. If she blinked, and focused only on that expression, she could almost be looking at Gran—the only family she'd known from the time she was six.

"Fine, and frustrated and how do you do?" Nonnie said all in one breath, her voice soft, but clearly discernible. "My grandson tells me your name is Adele and I would have been over to greet you myself, but the trip out here zapped me for bit. I'm better today."

Addy smiled. She couldn't help herself. How a woman as frail and shrunken as this could, at the same time, be such a bundle of strength and energy she didn't know. "The casserole was wonderful," she said now. "I hope Mark conveyed my thanks."

"He did. Which gave me the chance to tell him, 'I told you so.'" The bony chin jutted upward.

Laughing, Addy remembered why she'd knocked on the older woman's door. "I heard a tapping sound. . . ."

"This darn thing," Nonnie held up a metal rod with a plastic handle on one end and a claw-looking thing on the other. "I'm trying to get a package of beans off the top shelf over there and I cannot get this thing to close around it. Reminds me of a game they brought into the bar. You pushed buttons to drop a claw and it was supposed to grab a stuffed toy. Of course it never did."

The bar? This woman hung out in a bar?

"Can I get the beans for you?"

"I'd rather you show me how to work this thing," Nonnie said instead. "I've used it to reach for things at counter level, but up high, I'm not doing something right."

Following the chair until it stopped beneath the highest pantry shelf, Addy took the grabber, played with it a minute and saw the problem. The older woman was clutching it just fine. She just didn't have the claw around the beans.

Obviously the woman's eyesight wasn't all that good, either.

Helping the claw connect to its prey, Addy watched as Nonnie brought the beans down and dropped them in her lap.

"I'm making soup," the woman proclaimed, and wheeled herself over to the stove where she bent, opened the bottom drawer and pulled out a Crock-Pot that she also put in the chair with her.

"I can get that." Addy reached for the pot. And had her hand lightly swatted for her effort.

"I know you can get it," the woman said. "But the important thing here is that so can I. And I intend to get this soup on before that stubborn and pigheaded grandson of mine gets home. He thinks he's helping when he does things for me, but I swear, that boy's going to have me in an early grave if he doesn't let me do things with my day. I can't just stare at the computer screen all day long."

The whole time she was talking, Nonnie was using

a combination of claw, hands and chair to turn on the faucet, measure water into a pitcher, pour it in the Crock-Pot, add beans and a Baggie of freshly chopped onions and plug it into a waist-high outlet by the stove. She pulled out a drawer—one that held dish towels in Addy's half of the duplex—grabbed some spices and sprinkled them atop her mix.

Entranced, and afraid of offending the dynamo a second time, Addy stood frozen and watched.

"Sometimes Mark forgets that his old granny is a tough woman," Nonnie was saying. "Couldn't have tended bar all those years to pay for his keep if I'd been a swooner."

Nonnie was a bartender? Eyeing the tiny woman in the flowered cotton dress, Addy couldn't make the two images meld into one woman.

"I'm guessing he just loves you and wants what's best for you," she said when it appeared that it was her turn to speak. She should go. If she studied reports from then until Monday when classes started, she still wasn't going to be halfway through this first batch of information. Once classes started, not only would her research double, she'd also have homework assignments to complete if she wanted to maintain her cover. And a campus to investigate for any possible civil suit infractions.

Just how she was going to do that, beyond attending class and keeping her ear to the ground, she wasn't yet sure. But she knew the answers would come to her. They always did. She'd see or hear something that raised a question and off she'd be, following some lead or another.

Most of them would lead her straight to dead ends, too.

In this case, she hoped all of them did.

"Be nice if he had a clue what was best for me," the older woman was grousing, mostly to herself, as she worked. Then she added, "Mark's a good boy. And he's on the right track now. That's all that matters."

With the lid on the Crock-Pot, Nonnie wheeled herself backward and around and headed toward the living room where the television was on, the volume down low.

"I hope you can't hear that thing over at your place," she said, as though expecting that Addy would have followed her in.

"Not at all," she said, and wanted to ask if there was anything she could do for the older woman before she left.

"My grandson says that you're over there alone."

"That's right."

"You don't have a ring on."

"I'm single."

"Have you always been?" The voice was fading, but the hawkish look in Nonnie's eyes was not.

"Yes, ma'am."

"How come?"

I beg your pardon? The words were there. For some reason, Addy didn't say them. What she did say was, "I'm a bit of a loner."

"Pssshh. No one's really a loner," Nonnie said. "Who was he?"

Was dementia a problem here, as well? Mark hadn't intimated as much. But sometimes the family was the last to admit. "Who was who?"

"The man who hurt you so much you'd rather live alone?"

"There was no man." Anyone else she'd have told to jump in the lake. In polite terms, of course. "I date. I've just never met anyone worth giving up my solitude for."

Arms crossed, Addy stood there, taking on the bird of a woman.

"You ain't gay, then."

"No." She laughed.

"Didn't think so, but these days, you can never be sure. There's lipsticks and dykes and—"

"Mrs. …!" Addy broke off when she realized she didn't know Mark's last name. Or even if his and his grandmother's last names were the same.

But she was fairly certain the woman was being purposely outrageous.

"Call me Nonnie," the woman filled in without pause. "Everyone does. And don't mind me, dear. I said what I thought when I was young enough to know better. No hope of stopping me now."

"I don't mind," Addy said, perplexed as she realized that she spoke the truth. She should mind.

"Mark minds. But he worries too much, that boy of mine. My fault, not his. I was so certain I could handle raising him all by myself, but my body had other plans for me. Been the other way around longer than it should've been."

"I've only met him a couple of times, but he doesn't seem to mind having you around." What did she know? Really.

"Nah, Mark don't mind 'bout that. Like I said, he's a good boy. Always taking care of everybody. That's why I had to get him out of Bierly. That town was going to eat up my boy's whole life and he'd never have known any different. Folks're nice there, but they used my Mark. Always asking him to do the jobs no one else wanted to do 'cause they knew he would. And he was too nice to call 'em on it."

Not sure what that meant, but completely sure she had no business having this conversation, Addy heard herself ask, "What did he do there?"

"Worked his ass off," Nonnie said, and then, with a grin said, "Sorry, dear, I meant 'butt.'"

"Doing what?" *It's no business of yours, woman. You're here under false pretenses for one semester— fingers crossed—and then it's back to Colorado and private practice for you.*

"Anything anyone needed, during his time off. On the clock he was in management at the gasification plant. Pretty much everyone in Bierly either works at the plant or has someone in the house that does."

"Is that one of those places that turns coal into natural gas?" There was one in North Dakota that thought itself one of America's best-kept secrets.

Addy knew of it only because the Colorado-based daughter of one of their line workers missed too much school the year her father was killed and had been facing twenty-four hours in juvenile detention for truancy.

"Yep. Takes the coal straight from the mines and cleans it up."

"I've heard the work's dangerous."

"Hell, yes, it's dangerous. Mark's best buddy was killed in an explosion on his line last year. Mark took it hard. Real hard. Not that he'd say so."

Shuddering, Addy stepped back. "Was he there at the time?"

"Yep. He's the one who pulled Jimmy out of the fire, but he was too late."

"Is that why he left?"

Made perfect sense now why a man obviously past the usual age to enter college was starting out fresh.

Sometimes a fresh start was the only way... Turned out Gran's idea to get her out of Shelter Valley after the fire had been the best thing for her....

"Hell, no," Nonnie said. "I mean, heck, no. Trying to clean up my act a bit now that I'm getting closer to meeting my Maker."

"Why'd he leave, then?"

"'Cording to him, he hasn't left. He's just here because I blackmailed him into coming. I was hoping he'd get interested in something completely different, new. Safer. But no, not my Mark. He's got himself enrolled to study safety engineering so he can go back to Bierly and implement newfangled 'protocols' for keeping folks as safe as possible under the circumstances." Nonnie's opinion of Mark's plan was obvious from the sarcastic way she pronounced the word *protocols*.

"You don't think he should go back?"

"You ever been in a gasification plant?"

"No."

"They're filled with chemicals. Dangerous chemicals. Can't tell you how many times Mark's come home burning with frustration because one or another of his crew ended up in the bathhouse."

"Bathhouse?"

"The shower they put them under when they've been exposed to contaminated substances."

Addy had sporadic memories of the aftermath of the fire. Mostly pain-filled ones.

"I've got to get back to wor—what I was doing." Addy made her excuses and turned to go out the way she'd come, adding, "I'm home almost all the time, and will be, except when I'm in class. If you ever need anything, let me know. I'll leave my number here on the counter. And you can always just knock on the wall. I won't take so long to respond next time."

"You got a second before you go?" The woman sounded tired. Dangerously tired.

"Of course."

"Could you help me into that chair?" Nonnie nodded toward the blue flowered recliner that exactly matched the one in her own living room.

Addy was at her side in an instant, and where she would have steadied the woman, Nonnie just had her hold on to her arm while she slid herself from one chair to the other.

"I can handle my own weight." The woman's words were more sigh than sentence. Addy had a feeling she could have handled the woman's weight, too. By herself. Nonnie couldn't weigh more than eighty pounds.

Eyes closed, the woman's features relaxed, providing her with a glimpse of the beauty she must have been in her younger years.

Remembering Gran during her last year, when the emphysema had taken most of her air away, Addy figured Nonnie was already asleep, and crept back softly toward the door.

"Mark's on a job interview."

She turned. "What?"

"Darn fool's set on working in spite of the living expenses he's getting. Didn't want you to think he just up and leaves me."

"The thought never entered my mind." Surprisingly, in spite of Addy's natural distrust of mankind, it hadn't. Something to ponder later. Maybe. Nonnie's eyes were still closed. Addy reached the door. Pulled the latch.

"Thank you."

The barely discernible words followed her home.

CHAPTER SIX

HE GOT THE JOB. Both of them, actually. One was a work-from-home thing—doing small-unit repairs for the local hardware/electronics store. The second was just outside of town at the cactus jelly plant, working as a part-time floating shift supervisor. The position was perfect as it allowed him to work various shifts throughout the week, based on his school schedule. Cooking cactus plants was vastly different from cooking coal, but production theories and processes—and the machines used to run assembly lines—were surprisingly similar.

Still, his job was not to oversee cactus, or jelly, but to oversee people—the line workers who actually ran the machinery and created the product. He would oversee scheduling and deal with performance issues.

He'd pump gas or clean toilets if he had to—both jobs he'd done before—as long as he had work.

Both jobs, and the close proximity of his temporary home to campus, allowed enough flexibility that he could tend to Nonnie if an occasion arose. Enough flexibility that he could check in on her throughout the day. There wasn't anyone else to keep an eye on her for him. They weren't in Bierly anymore.

And when he'd tentatively suggested hiring some-one to come in, he'd received another nursing home threat. If she was going to be treated like an invalid, she might as well live like one, she'd said. Or some-thing to that effect.

The threat hadn't gotten to him as much as the tears, though. He'd seen her eyes well up before she'd blinked them away. His insistence on babying her upset her. When would he get that?

And he remembered what Bertie—one of the few people Nonnie considered a true friend—had said to him not all that long ago. Quality of life was better than quantity. If he wanted Nonnie around forever, he could try to baby her. Try to prevent anything bad from happening to her. But if he wanted her happy for the time she had left on earth, he had to let her fend for herself for as long as she possibly could.

And if he lost her during one of her attempts to care for them?

Turning the truck toward town—the center of town where Montford University stood as the town's foun-dation—Mark sang along under his breath to the country music station on the radio. Out of a pristine blue sky the sun was shining down on the mountains that housed Shelter Valley, and his voice rose with the swell of the music in an attempt to drown out the thoughts in his head.

Someday the trick might actually work.

On Sunday, the night before the start of the fall se-mester, and only a week after he'd arrived in Shelter

Valley, Mark sat alone in the kitchen of the duplex, country music playing softly in the background as he bent over the DVD player, in pieces, spread out over the table. According to Hank Harmon, the owner of Harmon Hardware and Electronics, the DVD player's owner couldn't get the thing to play and was ready to replace it. Hank wanted Mark to see if he could find what was broken and fix it for less than the replacement cost. Because Hank didn't just spout customer service—he insisted on providing it.

As it turned out, all the player needed was a good cleaning. Something had gummed up the gears.

From what Mark had gleaned in the couple of days he'd been working for Hank, the older man had been in the hardware business his whole life. And his father before him, too. They'd just branched out into electronics in the past couple of years.

With technology changing so rapidly, Mark figured that as far as business decisions went, the choice was a sound one. Only problem was, Hank knew hammers and nails. Not technology.

Mark, on the other hand, was fascinated by every new toy that came out on the market, and had been the guy in Bierly that everyone called when they ran into a technological glitch. He didn't have an iPad yet, but he wanted one. He just couldn't justify the expense for what, for his purposes, would only be a toy.

With precision care, he gingerly picked up and, with a special cloth and solution, gently cleaned the metal pieces spread before him. Over the years he'd amassed an impressive collection of tools, from eyeglass-size screwdrivers to an air compressor that pretty much every citizen in Bierly had borrowed at one time or another.

He'd packed his collection of manly necessities in the bed of the truck. As long as he had his tools, he'd be able to provide.

With pressure from the tip of his finger, he picked up a screw from the table, set it to the tip of the miniature screwdriver and proceeded to attach part of the tangential deflector assembly, freezing midturn as he heard something.

Background on the Linda Davis tune playing from his MP3 player?

The sound was human.

And, he was pretty sure, female.

He didn't move, listening for a repeat—hopefully in rhythm with the sound track.

It came again. Louder. More hoarse. Dropping the fragile component and screwdriver in a pile on the table, Mark ran down the hall to his grandmother's room. Throwing open the door, he was at her bedside before he'd taken a full breath.

Nonnie lay still. Silent.

And while he watched, she took several long, even breaths. Normal breaths.

Relieved, he backed quietly out of the room, revisiting his sound track theory for explanation of whatever he'd thought he'd heard, until the sound came again.

Louder still. Human? Or animal? Maybe coming from the living room?

"Ahhhh. *Ahhhh!*"

Animalistic. Growing in intensity. An expression of severe pain. Looking out the front window he peered into the darkness. Had a cat been run over by a car? Or been attacked by an owl?

From what he'd heard at the plant during his first shift of work the day before, wildlife in Shelter Valley was nothing like the nonhuman inhabitants he'd grown up with in West Virginia. Cats and dogs weren't safe roaming the streets in the desert. The food chain was far too active. Lizards ate crickets. Rattlesnakes ate lizards. Roadrunners ate rattlesnakes. Coyotes ate roadrunners. And rabbits and dogs and cats, too.

They also had a distinct howl. That happened mostly at night. A desert mating call he'd been told. Was that what he was hearing?

"Help!"

One word. Completely legible. Mark flew out the front door.

THE SCREAMING WOULDN'T stop. Her throat was on fire. Burning. Hurting so badly she couldn't suck in air. And still she screamed. But sound wasn't coming out loudly enough.

Others were screaming, too. As long as they all kept screaming they would be okay. They'd be together. They just all had to keep screaming. She was crying, too. Tears clogged her throat. Choked her. But she couldn't stop screaming. She had to let them know she was still there.

So they could find her.

She wasn't sure where she was. She just had to let them know.

One of the other screams stopped. Or maybe she just couldn't hear it because she was making too much noise. But she wasn't making enough. They had to know she was here. Still screaming.

But she couldn't breathe. Couldn't keep breathing. And screaming. She had to.

Another scream stopped.

Was she the only one?

But there was hollering. Really loud. Male hollering. Was that good? Or bad? Should she be quiet now?

Let her throat just hurt until she couldn't feel it anymore? That's all "here" had become. Her burning throat. And hollering.

And...

Addy bolted upright. The T-shirt and running shorts she'd put on when she got out of the shower clung to her. Sweat dripped down her neck and the sides of her face.

Head pounding, she jumped to her feet.

Someone was hollering. It wouldn't stop. Spinning around, she whimpered. A frightened sound. Weak. One she recognized. And didn't.

The pounding didn't stop. The urgency in the

male voice echoing her dream. She moved toward the sound.

Stood on cold tile. Her house had wood floors. Hotels had carpet. And...

"Adele! Adele, open the door! Let me know you're okay. I'm calling the police."

Adele. Realization slammed home with brutal force and she fell against the front door of her rented duplex.

"Don't! Don't call the police. I'm okay," she said, praying that she sounded normal. And she absolutely did not want Greg Richards called to her home. Everyone in town would know. The sheriff's calls went out on radio. And enough people in Shelter Valley listened in—to offer aid in case of emergency—to ensure that those that didn't would know by morning if a woman new to town had an emergency.

She had to stay under the radar if she was going to make this work.

"Open the door. Let me see that you're all right."

She peered through the peephole. Mark stood there, cell phone to his ear.

And the inanity of her first thought—that he didn't have a smartphone—brought her more completely back to reality.

She pulled open the door.

"What happened?"

She had to get rid of him.

"Nothing."

"You look like hell." He stood firmly in the doorway, staring at her, and then past her.

"I wasn't expecting company. I just got out of the shower."

"I don't mean your... Your looks are fine," he said, glancing her up and down quickly and then focusing on her eyes as though he was avoiding the rest of her. "You're flushed. Your bangs are sticking to your forehead. And...you're shaking."

Men weren't usually so observant. Leave it up to her to move next door to one who was. "Are you here alone?"

He motioned for her to nod or shake her head in lieu of a spoken answer.

She nodded. And then added, "Yeah, I'm here alone."

"Then you won't mind if I come in and check, will you? Either that or I call someone else to do so."

He wasn't giving up. And while a small little something deep inside of her was comforted, Addy didn't want anyone in her house. She didn't want anyone near her at all.

She especially didn't want the sheriff of Shelter Valley at her door.

"I'm fine," she said aloud. To Mark. And to the rest of Shelter Valley, too. But she stood back and held open her door.

Better Mark than anyone else.

He made quick work of checking out her living

quarters—helped, she suspected, by the fact that his unit was identical to hers.

She waited in the living room. Stood by the couch with her arms crossed against her chest and held on until she was alone again.

"There's no TV on."

"I don't watch a lot of TV."

"No radio, either."

Did he have a problem sitting quietly with his own thoughts? Or think it odd that someone else chose to do so?

Not that she entertained personal thoughts all that much. Most of her quiet time was spent pondering other people's problems. And more particularly, figuring out solutions to their problems.

Or holding internal debates with opposing counsel in an attempt to prepare herself for anything with which she might be presented.

"I heard you."

"Excuse me?" Did he want her to believe he was a mind reader?

"You were in pain. Crying out. I heard you."

The nightmare.

The screams. They'd been real?

She hadn't had an episode like that in years. Not since she was a kid.

"I fell asleep on the couch," she said. "I must have been dreaming."

"That was more than a dream. Care to talk about it?"

Dare she hope he'd believe that she didn't remember? Did she really want to step so far into her alternate persona that lying became habit?

One of the reasons Addy spent so much time alone was because if she was in a situation where she couldn't hold her tongue, she'd tell the truth even when it hurt. Her, or someone else. She didn't like causing pain. But she disliked lying even more.

It made her a horrible lawyer. And a great one, too. She hadn't lost a case. But she had turned down a number of them.

Mark touched her hair, ran his fingers down it to her shoulder and then stood back. "You're still shaking."

Staring at him, she nodded. He was so gentle. So... there.

"You should sit."

What was it about this man that sparked her interest and felt safe at the same time? And what was wrong with her that she was open to either?

She sat.

So did he. And she didn't tell him to leave.

"Maybe it would help if you talked about it."

She shook her head. It wouldn't. "I closed the window," she said as the thought occurred to her.

She'd been on the phone with Will and needed to make certain she had complete privacy. Classes started the next day. It would be the last time she spoke directly with him until she turned in her report.

For all intents and purposes she was alone in Shelter Valley. She'd hung up the phone and remained sitting on the couch after the call. Preparing herself. Warding off the memories…

She'd fallen asleep.

"You want me to open the window?" Mark asked from outside her private hell. "Are you hot?"

"No. I mean, yes. I'd like the window open. But I can get it." She stood. So did he. And she sat back down.

So unusual for her.

"The kitchen window, if you don't mind," she said.

"Of course, it opens to the backyard."

It opened to the fountain.

She waited. Listening. And felt a lessening of the constriction in her chest when she heard the familiar tinkling. Water was right there. As always. She was in her own life. Her adult life. She was perfectly fine.

She didn't have to listen for anyone. Didn't need anyone to save her. Didn't need anyone, period.

Mark sat down.

Nonnie had told her he'd pulled a man from an explosion.

She shuddered.

"Tell me about it."

She looked him over—six feet of muscled, gorgeous male, acting as if he had all the time in the world. For her.

A man who cared for his grandmother when a more logical choice would have been to put her in an assisted-living facility.

"I don't know your last name."

"It's Heber."

"How old are you?"

"Thirty."

"I'm thirty-one."

He shrugged and watched her as though waiting for more.

"Do have them often?"

"What?"

"The nightmares."

"No," she assured him quickly, in case he was worried that hearing her "crying out" as he'd put it, would be a regular occurrence. "Not since I was a kid."

"A young kid or a teenage kid?"

The question was innocuous. His presence oddly calming. "Teenage."

"Something happened?"

"Yeah."

She didn't offer more. He didn't ask.

He'd pulled a man out of an explosion. He knew about the heat...

"I was in a fire."

His expression intensified, as if she'd hit a nerve. As if he knew...

"I was five," she said, because it was the easiest part to tell.

"Were you burned?" He glanced from her face to her bare legs and arms.

"Some." The final skin grafts she'd received when she was in high school had taken care of the worst of the scarring, smoothed all the edges. What was left, no one saw—not even her. "The worst damage was internal. Smoke inhalation."

And psychological, if she wanted to believe the things the counselors had told her. Gran had insisted she talk to them, but she'd never felt the need.

Still didn't.

She was like her mother. Strong. Determined. Positive.

Gran had hated Ann Keller- -because she wasn't of the faith she'd raised her son to be, and her son had left the church to marry Ann.

Gran had refused to attend the wedding and disowned them both. They'd died before she had the chance to make things right.

It was Gran's biggest regret. And the reason she'd spent every second of the remainder of her days dedicated to Addy's life and happiness.

"Was anyone else hurt?"

The constriction was back in her chest. And her throat. She stared at Mark wide-eyed, as though, if she tried hard enough—filled her vision with enough of him—she could block out the memories choking her.

"Who was hurt?"

She shook her head.

"Where were you?"

Here. In Shelter Valley. "Home."

"Your house caught on fire?"

She nodded.

"Were you in bed?"

Another nod.

"Being five, you wouldn't have been left home alone."

She didn't say anything.

And then his entire being softened. It was as though he reached out, wrapped his arms around her and cushioned her from life's blows.

As if anyone could do that.

"Were there any other survivors?"

Addy shook her head.

CHAPTER SEVEN

IT WAS LATE. He had to be out of bed at six the next morning so he could prepare breakfast and pretend he wasn't paying attention to Nonnie's morning routine as she got herself up and around. Afterward, he'd get ready to leave for class.

But right now, Mark wasn't about to leave Adele Kennedy. Even though her blank expression told him she didn't want to talk about what happened on the night of the fire anymore.

He had more questions for her, but they'd have to wait.

"Do you have a DVD player?"

"Yeah."

"Do you have any movies?"

"I have Netflix."

He had an account for Nonnie, too. She watched it through the secondhand PlayStation he'd picked up from a guy at the plant the previous Christmas.

"You ever watch *Andy Griffith?*"

Her smile was mostly dead, but it was there. "Who doesn't?"

"The town I grew up in is a lot like Mayberry, even

now. We have one sheriff and he's got a couple of deputies and they pretty much keep everyone in line."

"I have a feeling this town is pretty much the same way."

"Maybe. How about you? Where'd you grow up?"

"Colorado."

"What part?"

"A suburb of Denver."

"That's where your grandmother lived?" She'd told him, the first time they'd met, that she, like him, had lived with her grandmother.

Now he knew why.

She nodded.

"You want to watch an episode of *The Andy Griffith Show?*"

She blinked and looked at him as though he'd suggested they eat chocolate for breakfast. And then she smiled a real smile. "Yeah. That sounds good."

Opening the drawer next to her, she pulled out a couple of remote controls and within minutes they were engrossed in a world where good always won out over evil, kids were safe and you just knew that everything was going to be okay.

MARK HEBER WASN'T the only person who knew about the fire. He was just the only person in her adult life whom she'd told.

It didn't really mean anything. He understood fire. And he only knew that a house had gone up in flames. Not where the house had been.

He had no knowledge of the circumstances....

She wasn't even sure Will Parsons knew the whole story. Sheriff Richards could find out the official version—if he had a mind to. Maybe he already had.

But from what little Gran had told her, and the things she'd overheard, she knew the official version had been adjusted.

Okay, fudged. Mostly for her sake.

If a man committed murder and then suicide, insurance wouldn't pay. If he simply died in a fire with the rest of his family, it would.

And if the man was a firefighter, one of their own, if he'd risked his life over and over for the good of the town, if he'd only made one mistake in his life, then the powers that be—which in this case meant the firefighter's best friend, who also happened to be the fire marshal—could fudge a report.... Which meant, in turn, that the man could get away with murder.

Her father's best friend had stopped in to visit Gran several years later...to ease his conscience and make sure his lies had done good—not harm. He'd come to check on Addy.

And she'd overheard more than she should have.

She'd been twelve at the time.

Gran had been right to cut her off from Shelter Valley so completely. She'd been back for a week and she was already falling apart.

Or she would be if she allowed herself to dwell on the past. If she gave in to the self-pity that Gran had taught her to avoid. As a child she'd had every reason to feel sorry for herself.

But if she'd done so, she would never have found the focus to finish law school. Never have been able to contribute to society as she did, making her life worth living.

As it was, Addy left for classes Monday morning, determined to take life head-on and win. She had a job to do. A job she wanted to do. If someone was out to frame Will Parsons, Addy was going to do everything she could to help Greg Richards find the evidence he needed to arrest the creep.

She wasn't in Shelter Valley on vacation. She wouldn't visit any of the places she'd been with her parents, wouldn't drive by the school she'd attended with her brother, or see the park where they used to play. She'd attend her classes. Stick her nose in every nook and cranny on campus—she'd never spent time there as a child. Most of the research could be done from her duplex. And when she needed groceries or anything else, she'd shop in Phoenix—or at the new big-box store outside of town.

She wouldn't develop relationships with anyone. Not even the casual kind. She wasn't here to stay. And had no intention of ever coming back.

Couldn't have anything calling her back.

Her mind firmly set, Addy sat through an introductory botany class and a first-year biology class, watching students, analyzing teacher response, and then headed to the campus bookstore with a wad of cash to purchase textbooks she'd sell back just as soon as she could.

The place was a zoo—long lineups of students with not as many books in hand as she'd expected. Montford provided students the opportunity to purchase most of their classroom materials in ebook form and, by the look of things, a good many of them were doing so. Not sure about the buy-back policy on ebooks, she was opting for print copies.

In spite of the amount of traffic, there were no exceptionally long waits. Standing in the cash line with her satchel over her shoulder and her arms filled with heavy tomes, Addy marveled at the efficiency of the store. The three lines immediately to her left were reserved for credit card users. And to the far right was a line designated for scholarship recipients.

Probably students on a full ride whose books were included as part of their monetary award. Scholarship recipients were on her list of people to investigate. Lawsuits had been filed—and won—based on education being denied to some while it was offered freely to others of equal merit. And a degree from Montford came with external economic value.

As Addy was mulling over that thought, her heart suddenly tripped. Mark Heber, looking sexy in jeans and a white polo shirt, had just joined the back of the scholarship line.

God, he looked good.

He couldn't see her. She couldn't let him. Not yet. Not so soon after last night. At least not until she had her emotions firmly in check. Turning her back, Addy stepped up to the counter, her sob story in place for the cashier as she attempted to get a pass on paying for her books. When she was told in no uncertain terms that she had to pay, she asked to see a manager, asked to speak with the manager's boss, asked if students in the scholarship line got their books for free and what she'd have to do to reap the same benefit.

She'd be doing spot checks like these all over campus to ensure that employees at every level knew university policy and applied it across the board. A lapse, regardless of how minor it was, could point to a bigger personnel problem—or aggrieved student. If employees didn't follow policies—like those related to hiring, conflict of interest and so on—rigorously, they could put the university at risk of a lawsuit.

So Addy did her best to get someone to make a mistake....

She did it all without raising her voice, or causing a stink. And when she left she was happy to know that Montford's bookstore employees, at least those who were working that day, could not be persuaded to budge from university policies.

Stepping outside, she wished she could call Will— and almost walked straight into Mark.

"What was going on in there?" he asked, falling into step beside her as though they met on campus every day and hadn't just met for the first time the week before.

As though he hadn't been sharing her living room couch, smiling at Barney Fife's antics, mere hours before.

"Nothing, why?" she asked, conscious of guarding Adrianna Keller's secrets—and Will Parsons's.

"You seemed to be having trouble. I heard you ask to see the manager. So I waited."

Maybe she was still vulnerable from the night before, or maybe Mark Heber was just a genuinely good guy, but Addy was touched by his concern.

And bothered, too. She was there to work while living a lie. She couldn't encourage friendship.

But she also had to try to fit in—and a new student in town would be eager to make friends....

"One of the books I need is in ebook format only." She couldn't believe the ease with which the lie escaped her lips. "I prefer print and was checking to see if there was a print-on-demand option."

"Is there?" He stepped closer to her to avoid colliding with a group of young guys going in the opposite direction. Addy felt the brush of his arm as acutely as if he'd just kissed her.

Books. He asked about books. "Yes." A pair of girls were coming toward them. One had tattoos all the way down her arm. Addy focused on the tattoos. "It'll take a few days, though."

He reached for her bag of books. "Are you headed to your car?" he asked. "I can get these for you."

She could carry her own books, but she gave up her bag. "Yeah. How about you?"

"I've got a break, two afternoon classes and then I've got to go to work."

He had a backpack slung over one shoulder. No bookstore bag. But she'd seen him in the scholarship line. It didn't surprise her that he'd won a scholarship.

Only that he'd applied for one, if what Nonnie had said was true and he was in Shelter Valley only because she'd blackmailed him.

The man was occupying far too many of her thoughts. She needed to focus them elsewhere so she could free Will and get out of town. But Mark smelled musky and masculine and...

"You don't have any books." She didn't know what else to say.

"I prefer ebooks." He shrugged, grinned and then said, "And I just found out this morning that my scholarship provides for a tablet to read them, too. You're talking to the owner of a brand-new seven-inch e-reader. Not quite an iPad, but it's still pretty cool."

He sounded like a deep-voiced kid at Christmas. He was smiling broadly as they walked across the campus, the sun shining warmly down on them. Addy wondered if he liked Christmas, if he and Nonnie celebrated in a big way. She wanted to tease him about his obvious affection for electronic devices. But she was there to work.

Period.

"Your grandmother said something about blackmailing you to go to college," she said, even though she knew that she should be taking back her bag of books and getting the heck away from him. "Was that just B.S.?"

"Nope." His smile faded a little. "She did."

"But you seem happy to be here."

"Yeah, well, that's the hard truth about Nonnie. She mouths off, but she's generally right."

Oh, God. She was liking this man more and more. Getting herself all twisted up when she absolutely shouldn't.

And still she smiled again. "So, what, you applied for scholarships hoping you wouldn't win any so you could be off the hook?" Or he'd applied because he actually wanted to attend college to begin with— which Nonnie had probably known and that knowledge had been the basis for her blackmail scheme.

Addy had it all worked out. Like she knew the two of them that well. And had any business at all speculating about them.

Or caring about them in any way.

"I didn't apply," Mark said.

"Then who did?"

"My guess is Nonnie," Mark said, stepping down off the curb as they reached the lot where she'd parked her car. "She insists that she didn't, but there's no other explanation. It was crazy. I came home from work one day and there's this letter in the box addressed to me. Nonnie acted like she knew nothing about it. I opened it and it's this packet of papers telling me that I'm a scholarship recipient, giving me details of the award in terms of financials and including forms I had to fill out to accept the offer."

"No explanation of where the money's coming from or on what basis you earned the scholarship?"

"No."

They'd reached her car. "And Nonnie won't admit she applied, even now that you're here?" She unlocked the door and swung it open.

"She's too stubborn to admit she lied." With a hand on her door frame, Mark handed her the bag of books, waiting while she slung them over to the passenger seat.

And then the two of them were standing there, eye to eye, trapped between the opened door and the car.

Time to get in. Get home.

"Thank you for carrying my books." She stood there, as if she was waiting for something.

"You're welcome." He grinned again. A different kind of expression. One that sent shards of pleasure shooting clear to her toes.

And when the moment turned embarrassing, she ducked into her car, pulled the door closed and waved goodbye.

MARK HAD BEEN looking for his new neighbor in every class that first morning of college. They were both freshmen. It stood to reason that they'd be in a freshman-level mandatory class together. He'd been disappointed that she hadn't been in any of them.

And then he'd seen her in the bookstore. Telling

himself that he'd watched for her because she was the only person he knew, he allowed that it wouldn't be disloyal to Ella if he waited for her outside the bookstore.

He told himself he waited because he knew she'd had a rough time the night before. Because he wanted to make sure she was okay. It was the neighborly thing to do.

But then he'd failed to ask her if she was okay, to mention the night before at all. Hell, he'd almost kissed her.

Almost being the operative word. He hadn't.

Ella had predicted that he'd move to Shelter Valley and move on from her, too. That she wouldn't be good enough for him once he met college women. She'd broken up with him because she was afraid of losing him, but he knew she loved him. And he cared about her, too.

He'd given her his word that he would come back to her.

With his resolve firmly in place, Mark texted Ella. But she didn't respond.

CHAPTER EIGHT

ADDY PULLED OUT of the parking lot and headed straight home, forcing herself to focus all of her mental energy on the task at hand—on a question raised by some numbers she'd come across before falling asleep on her couch the evening before.

A question that preceded the nightmare and all that had come after.

She'd been looking through professor rating statistics—a series of measurements collated from performance reviews and anonymous student ratings. Near the top of a chart showing the rankings of all the professors to have taught a full semester at Montford over the past fifteen years was a woman named Christine Evans. The woman had taught English. Her performance reviews were excellent. Student ratings placed her at the top of the chart. And she had only taught for one semester.

Why? Had Will Parsons found something untoward about the woman? Fired her? And was there a paper trail, documentation, to support his decision?

Proof of wrongdoing in case the woman was somehow involved in the threat against Will?

Or had the woman quit? And if so, why?

It might be nothing. Probably was nothing. But her job over the next four months was to pursue every single lead that raised any question at all in her mind, from a legal standpoint.

The fact that Mark's scholarship had shown up without any effort from him at all was also odd. Nonnie had to have applied. She'd know all of Mark's pertinent information, including his social security number, but still, the circumstances were curious.

She was going to have to look him up—find out where the scholarship came from. She had to look at scholarships, anyway, albeit just a sampling. But she couldn't ignore this. Not if she was going to do right by Will.

If she was still in contact with Will, she'd have called him to ask about the scholarship—and the professor. But not only was she staying away to avoid risking her cover, she and the sheriff had also determined that Addy's work would be more valid, less likely to be influenced, if she worked separate and apart from Will. She didn't want her research tainted by bias.

"Psst."

Climbing the couple of steps to her front door, Addy stopped at the sound and glanced around.

"It's me." Nonnie Heber's voice sailed loud and clear through the screen door next to her. "You got a minute?"

"Sure." She stepped up to the door and peered into a room barely discernible from her vantage point, standing as she was in the bright sunshine. Nonnie was in her wheelchair, but Addy couldn't make out the expression on the older woman's face. "Can I get you something?"

"No, got all I need. 'Cept someone to chat with."

Addy had work to do. She wrestled with silent thoughts, searching for words to excuse herself without hurting the older woman's feelings.

"Door's open. Come in."

Addy pulled on the handle.

Fifteen minutes later, she was pouring iced tea for herself and her elderly neighbor.

"I told Mark he didn't have to stop off at home between school and work at the plant," Nonnie said as Addy carried the cold glass into the living room. "I'm fine here. But he insists. At home in Bierly, folks were always stopping by to see me, and Doris, next door, I've known her since she was born. She came in every morning whether I wanted her to or not." Nonnie's diatribe stopped long enough for her to sip.

"I did something this morning," she continued shortly. "I don't want Mark to know." She lowered her voice, leaning toward Addy. "Not yet. But I have to tell someone."

"What did you do?" The older woman appeared to be fine. The kitchen looked normal.

"I sold my house."

"Your house?"

"Was my grandparents' place to begin with. Grandpa built it on a piece of land his daddy gave him when he married Grandma. My daddy was born there. And so was I."

"And you sold it?" Was Nonnie getting senile? She didn't seem to be, but it wasn't like Addy had had multiple conversations with the woman.

"Yep. This morning." She named a price that sounded decent to Addy, but not knowing the area, or the size of the home or land, she couldn't be sure.

This wasn't her business.

"You said Mark doesn't know?"

"Nope."

"Don't you think you should tell him?"

"Nope."

"I really think you should."

"Can't."

"Why not?"

"He'd have a fit."

"Maybe he has reason to."

"No, he don't."

"The house has been in your family for generations."

"Yep. And now it isn't."

Alarmed at Nonnie's pragmatic manner, at the possible mistake being made, she asked, "But you haven't closed on it yet, right?"

"Wrong. It was a cash deal. Closed this morning."

Oh, God.

"Medicare doesn't cover my most expensive meds."

"Do you have supplemental insurance?"

Nonnie shook her head. "Canceled me a few years back."

"Canceled you? Did you miss a premium?"

"Nope."

"Did you omit key medical information on your application?" She was a lawyer. The question just slipped out.

"No. They said I did, though."

"What was the basis for their claim?"

"I disclosed the multiple sclerosis. I said I wasn't in a chair." She motioned toward her chair. "Because I wasn't at the time. Then I fell again and was sentenced to the damn thing. I put in a claim for it and they denied the claim and then canceled the insurance."

Addy didn't know a lot about insurance law, but she knew enough to know that insurance companies had done some unethical things regarding policy cancellations.

"Did you talk to an attorney?"

"Found one on the internet. But he wasn't sure I'd win and I couldn't afford to pay all the money it would cost me to go to court on a chance I'd lose."

"What did Mark say about all of this?"

"Nothing. I didn't tell him about it."

"Don't you think you should have?"

"Sometimes. But mostly, no. That boy has sacrificed too much of his life because of me. He was already working two jobs and getting nowhere. I got by using my Social Security." Nonnie's words were raspy and growing more so, as though she was out of breath. Hands shaking, she picked up her glass of tea and took a sip, sloshing the liquid over her top lip and onto the lap of her cotton short-sleeved dress.

Got by. Past tense?

Addy had to get back to her work. The Hebers' problems were not hers. Nothing in Shelter Valley belonged to her. With the exception of Will's problem. That she'd agreed to take on.

Still, Nonnie Heber was new to town. By her own admission the woman was used to having people stop in and see her every day. People who likely heard the same stories Addy was hearing. Or renditions thereof.

The woman was lonely. Addy thought of Gran, those last years after she'd left for college. And of the neighborhood women who'd kept her grandmother company.

"I take more meds now." Nonnie's voice was fading. "Didn't expect to live so long."

Addy understood. "Social Security isn't enough to cover the difference."

The response earned her a self-deprecating smile. "Who knew I'd outlast Doc's predictions?"

"You have to tell Mark. He'll help you."

"No!" Nonnie sat upright and winced. "My grandson has this scholarship. This chance. The house was just a building. A piece of property. In a town that won't give him nothing more than he's already had."

"He mentioned going back there."

"Probably would, too, if the house was there."

Shrewd eyes appealed her to understand.

"You don't want him to go back."

"He has so much more to offer than that place can give him."

"Shouldn't that be his choice?"

"Should be, but it ain't. He's saddled with me."

"He loves you." She didn't need to know him well to know that.

"And I love him. So I sold the house." She paused to breathe. "The money'll pay for my medicine. And my burial, too, when the time comes."

"I still think you should tell him."

"Not yet. But I had to tell someone. Thank you, young woman, for having compassion on an old woman. Now, if you don't mind, I need to rest."

With that, she closed her eyes. Addy rinsed their tea glasses and let herself out.

She should have asked Nonnie about Mark's scholarship.

ON HIS BREAK, Mark texted Ella again. He sat in the student union and set up his new tablet, playing with the features. He signed on to Wi-Fi to register for a class bulletin board.

And tested internet speeds because…that's the kind of thing he did. A guy had to know his specs.

As a test case, he typed in fires in the Denver, Colorado, area twenty-five years before. Just on a whim. Addy's house fire was none of his business. Unless she chose to tell him about it.

He was only looking because he was studying fire safety and engineering. Because he was curious about the details of the fire in a purely scientific sense. And because he'd lost a friend to an explosion and could relate—if only minutely—to his new neighbor's suffering.

He didn't find anything.

PROFESSOR CHRISTINE EVANS was deceased.

Standing at her kitchen table, Addy stared at the woman's file on the secure Montford server accessible only by Will and one or two other people. No one could legitimately accuse Will, or Montford, of poor record keeping. A scan of Christine's death certificate was in the woman's file.

Cause of death was a fatal blow due to a car accident.

But the shocking part was that she'd died before she taught that semester at Montford.

Scrolling back to the first page of the file, Addy read again, checked dates. And then brought up the chart depicting a historical account of professorial ratings at Montford. She double-checked the dates of Christine's student ratings and her performance reviews.

She was right.

The woman had been dead before she taught a course at the college.

Which meant that someone had tampered with the records.

Addy was onto something. And the something wouldn't be good if it meant that someone Will trusted enough to have access to the secured database was altering records.

With her finger on the page down key, she quickly flipped through the pages she'd read and then slowed when she came to the parts of Christine's employment file that she hadn't seen.

A newspaper article written by a local reporter, dated January 2001. Just a few weeks after Christine's one semester at Montford had ended.

Dead Sister Saves Lives

Addy read every word of the story. Two sisters, traveling together. An accident. One dies, the other lives…and the attending physician mixes up their identities.

She read it again. And then, hands on the keyboard, typed quickly. Furiously searching for more. With her memberships to online sources, she accessed local public records. Legal and criminal records from the county courthouse. Montford databases.

She looked at marriage licenses. And found adoption papers, too.

And wondered if Greg Richards knew what she'd

just learned. If that was why he had her looking into Will Parsons's activities. Was it possible the sheriff was using her to find out what a prosecutor might uncover if Will Parsons was brought up on the charges that were alleged in the anonymous letter he'd received?

Were they both using her? Because they knew there was something to find?

Feeling sick to her stomach, she stumbled outside, fell into the cheap lounge chair on the tiny patio and sat listening to the tinkling of water in her fountain.

Just listening. Focusing on the water. Searching for peace.

Will Parsons was a good man.

He would not lie to her.

CHAPTER NINE

NONNIE WAS IN BED asleep, her chair parked beside the lowered double mattress in her room that allowed her to slide easily from bed to chair without assistance, when Mark got home shortly after eight that evening.

It felt good to put in a full day of work again. Good to be providing. And he felt guilty as hell that Nonnie was spending so much time alone. She'd put him in an impossible position with this move of hers. He couldn't not work. His scholarship-allotted living expenses would not cover Nonnie's disposable undergarments. Or the heat therapy bands that eased her pain. They wouldn't pay for her vitamin supplement drinks or, God forbid, any emergency that might arise.

Closing her bedroom door—because she insisted on maintaining her individual privacy as a condition of continuing to live with him—Mark showered, pulled on a fresh pair of jeans and a sleeveless undershirt and helped himself to a beer from the refrigerator. As he sat at the kitchen table, nursing his beer, he looked through the small window over the sink into the equally small backyard, and wondered how the boys back home were doing. Pretty much every member of his crew had texted him at least once in the week and a half he'd been gone.

He missed them.

Missed knowing everyone in town and everyone in town knowing him. He missed the acre of land that greeted him when he looked out his back window at home.

There was movement out there. Slight, but there, just the same. Giving his eyes a chance to adjust to the darkness outside, Mark watched the far corner of his neighbor's patio.

And was rewarded by the sight of her. Sitting in the dark all alone.

Was she reliving the horror from the night before? What had happened to trigger her nightmare? Especially after so many years?

Figuring he should probably just leave her be, he turned away from the window.

She was new to town, too. Didn't know anyone, either. Was she over there missing the town she'd come from? The people? The familiar?

Was she dreading the homework that awaited her, too?

He opened the refrigerator. Grabbed a second beer.

And headed outside.

"WANT A BEER?"

Addy stared up at the tall figure standing next to her in the darkness, knowing that she shouldn't be glad he was there. He was wearing a white undershirt—like the macho, working-class hunks de-picted in the old beer and cigarette commercials. "No, thanks," she said. If he'd offered her a glass of wine she might not have been able to refuse.

She'd heard him come in. Had been imagining him with Nonnie, asking about her day. Thinking about the things that his grandmother wasn't telling him.

He had a right to know.

And telling him wasn't Addy's place.

Nonnie was allowed to have her secrets.

"How was your day?" He took a sip from his beer, still holding the other in his hand.

"Good." *Mention the nightmare,* she implored him. *I'll assure you that it was an aberration. I'll be calm. Unaffected. I'll make it seem like a nonentity and we will never have need to speak of it again.*

"Nonnie said she'd called out to you. Invited you in."

"I visited with her a bit."

"How was she?"

"Tired, but she seemed fine."

"I dropped by for a late lunch," he said. She already knew that. She'd heard him come home. "She seemed tired to me, too. Hopefully she's still just recovering from the trip out here."

His expression, or what she could make of it in the shadows, appeared pinched. Worried.

"Is her disease progressive?"

"Not so much as it comes and goes. At times it

completely incapacitates her and then she goes into a form of remission and can get along fairly well."

"Can she walk at all?"

"Not anymore. Her bones are too brittle and the arthritis in her knees makes walking too dangerous."

Mark hopped the low wall that separated their patios and returned with a chair that matched hers. He set it down a foot away from her and opened his second beer.

She focused on the fountain. Searching for equilibrium in an unrecognizable world. "She told me that people dropped in on her all the time back home."

His gaze swung sharply toward her. "She's homesick?"

"She didn't say that."

"Oh." He turned back toward the fountain and was silent.

"Other than when I'm in class, I'm here, Mark. Pretty well all day and all night, too. I'd be happy to sit with her, look in on her. Anything you need."

It was the right thing to do. For the Grans of the world. The women who took on other people's children and loved them as their own.

And for the children of the world who were the sole caretakers of their elderly loved ones.

"I appreciate the offer," he said. Addy had thought about the older woman on and off all afternoon. Nonnie was an example of the type of woman Addy longed to be. Independent. Strong. Capable. No matter what life threw at her.

And Nonnie posed no threat to her, unlike her grandson. She had to go in.

Still, the night, the darkness, held her trapped in its shadows.

With a man she was drawn to as much as she needed to get away from.

Staring at her fountain, she watched the jeweled droplets of water chase one another over the rocks.

"It's like they're playing hide-and-seek."

"The fountain's important to you." There was a personal note in his voice.

"I like fountains." She watched the water, needing to be transported to a place she felt safe.

"I know."

His tone was far too personal.

"People give away things about themselves by the priorities they choose. Before you moved into the house, you set up your new fountain."

He was trespassing....

"You're perceptive."

He was quiet, and she waited, on edge.

"Why fountains?"

He wasn't going to ask about the nightmare. And she couldn't stay.

"Hmm?" She sat forward in her chair, picked up her glass and sought a suitable way to say good-night that wouldn't offend him.

"What is it about fountains that speaks to you?"

"The water." Maybe it was all the lies she was being forced to tell that compelled her to speak the truth.

Or maybe the water was too sacred to lie about.

"The water?"

"I find it peaceful." She didn't want him to think she was crazy. Coping devices were enlightened. Not crazy.

"A lot of people find fountains peaceful," he said, watching her now. "But it's not their first priority when they move into a new home. Sheets on a bed, food in the fridge, those kinds of things usually come first."

She was going to tell him.

As she sat there, her heart beating a mile a minute, Addy realized she wanted to tell him. Because he was a stranger passing in the night? Because he knew her as Adele, not Adrianna?

Because he'd rescued his best friend from a fire?

Not because she felt connected to him on any personal level. Please, not that.

She was outside herself. Analyzing, as always. Watching from afar. And there was something different. She was *feeling*...

"After the fire...I had panic attacks." Counseling hadn't helped. Sleeping in the same bed as Gran hadn't helped. "The only thing that made them go away was knowing there was water nearby."

There, she'd referred to the night before. Gotten it out in the open. They could move on.

And if Adrianna Keller was crazy, if she had some mental or emotional shortcoming, her secret was still safe. This man only knew Adele Kennedy.

"Were both of your parents home that night?"

"Yes." *Yes.* That one word held so much hurt.

"You were screaming last night. Over and over. Were you reliving the fire? Or had you been asleep until they rescued you?"

"I screamed."

"What about the others? Were they asleep?" The words were delivered with a warm, soft tone, sliding over her with nonthreatening concern.

She was okay. She was Adele. She could give him this. One stranger to another.

"Mom and Ely were screaming, too."

"Ely?"

"Elijah. My brother. His screams stopped first."

"How old was he?"

"Seven." It sounded so young. He'd been her big brother, not a little kid.

"I thought if we all kept screaming, we'd be safe. I had to do my part. And then Ely stopped."

"Who else was screaming?"

"Mom. She was screaming for Ely and me." Over and over. Just their names. *Ellllyyyy! Aaaadddyy!* Over and over. She could hear her so clearly, even now. "I kept answering." Ely had, too. Until he hadn't.

"Then she stopped."

"But you didn't."

"No." She had felt compelled to keep calling out, to keep playing the strange game even though the air was so hot and hurt so badly.

"What about your father?"

"He didn't scream."

"But he was there."

She looked away from the fountain into the darkness of the walled-in yard. "Yes."

Everything went black inside of her mind. Not blank. Just black. She couldn't picture her father. She could just see the blackness.

Charred black. Burned black.

"Adele?"

Turning her head, Addy focused and saw Mark. Even in shadows, his face was gorgeous—his features strong and chiseled in all the right places, his gray-blue eyes filled with emotion.

He'd called her Adele.

She was safe.

Adele knew things that Addy had never told anyone. Adele could talk for Addy, and then roll up her imaginary life and disappear as Addy moved back home to the life she'd built for herself in Colorado.

Mark would understand. He'd pulled his friend out of the fire. He was studying fire safety and engineering.

"Mom and Dad were high school sweethearts," she told him. "Dad had always wanted to be a firefighter and started training while he was still in high school. He became an EMT, too. They got married and Mom stayed home to raise us kids."

Such a happy story. A happy family in a happy home. That's how she remembered it.

Mostly.

Mark's silence, his lack of judgment or commentary, left her back in time.

"She was a great cook. It seemed like she was always in the kitchen, whipping up new things for us to taste." She'd been five. How could her memories be so vivid?

She'd prayed for them to fade. And prayed that they never would.

"At first she just cooked for us and then, when people started asking, she cooked for parties and events around town. Eventually she entered some competitions and sent in her recipes to places and somehow was offered a cookbook deal in conjunction with a television show." She remembered it from the perspective of a five-year-old. Her mother's beautiful smile. The way they'd run together at the zoo that last day, Mom laughing and telling her and Ely about all the fun they were going to have.

A warm hand covered hers on the arm of the chair. She turned her hand over and he wove his fingers together with hers.

"My father couldn't take her sudden fame. He felt threatened by it." She'd never been told as much, but she'd figured it out. As an adult, she understood. "I remember him yelling at Mom, telling her that if she took the deal, she'd be ruining the perfect life they'd built together." She hadn't understood at the time, but she did now.

It wasn't her mother who'd ruined things.

"He was jealous," she said. That last day, picture

day, she'd gone to her parents' room, excited to have her mother see how she'd done her hair all by herself, and had overheard urgent whispering between her parents. Fearful, she'd stayed hidden outside the door so she could hear if she or Ely were in trouble. Her father had been telling her mother that if she picked fame and fortune over him, that was her choice, but he wouldn't let her take his children, too. She hadn't understood what that meant then.

"He wanted the stay-at-home wife he'd married. A normal, ordinary family to come home to." Some of that she'd heard. Some she'd later surmised. That photo shoot that had been one of the highlights of her short life had been her father's undoing.

"It's what he knew." Mark's comment jarred her.

"He set the fire." Her words shattered the night air. Like that, Addy's secret was out.

"Oh…God…I'm sorry."

"He knew fire," she said. "He knew how to make it happen quickly and all at once."

"A man who knows fire does not subject his family to that kind of hell."

Intellectually she had it all figured out. "A rational man doesn't subject his family to hell at all."

She looked at Mark and wanted to curl up into him and lose herself within the strength and compassion he offered. "We were supposed to go instantaneously. All at once. It was his way to keep us together forever."

At least that's what she made herself believe. It was the only thing that made sense.

Nothing was forever. Not childhood. Not one's safety. Not even life. The thoughts rolled over one another, gaining momentum until more than just her silence had been shattered. There was no great rumbling in her ears as the walls, weakened from the night before, tumbled down. No warning.

No big switch from Adele to Adrianna.

Just blistering rawness. Around her. On her. Inside her…

She was five again. Back in Shelter Valley. Shaking. Cold and hot and wet and scared. Tears running down her cheeks. Choking. Huddling in the thunder and the eerie silence. Thirsty. Waiting for someone to come get her.

Mark gave a gentle tug and she leaned into him, letting him lift her over to his lap where she settled in his arms. "I'm so sorry." He said the words over and over as Addy finally admitted, full on, the horror of knowing that her father had killed her mother and brother.

And had tried to kill her, too.

CHAPTER TEN

MARK KNEW THE second his neighbor resurfaced from the hell she'd sunk into. She stiffened in his arms and he let her go immediately, acting as if nothing unusual had happened as she crossed back over to her own chair.

"I'm sorry."

"For what?"

"That." She motioned toward him, but she was looking at her fountain. "I hardly know you and that was inappropriate. I'm not a crier. I assure you."

The night was dark. Quiet. Warm.

"Don't, Adele. Please." Unlike him, who had Nonnie, she was alone. Completely alone. "I know we haven't known each other long, but I consider you a friend. And you needed a friend. I'm not sorry. I'm glad I was here. Any time you need to talk, or need anything, I'm here."

In Bierly he'd never have had to say that. Folks just knew.

He could barely make out her nod in the darkness. And so he sat with her. It was just the silence, the night, the glistening water fountain and him. There with her.

Ten minutes passed in silence, and then she shook her head.

"You okay now?"

"Yeah." She glanced at him, a half smile on her lips. "I don't know what came over me. It was all so long ago. And I'm fine, really. I don't make a habit of falling apart. Ever. I hardly even think about that time in my life."

He wondered if maybe she should.

"Something's obviously bringing the old memories to the surface," he said. "Maybe it's just that you're away from home, out of your element. Starting a new life…"

He was going through similar adjustments. Reflecting on the life he'd had, the perceptions he'd held, all the things he'd thought he had known.

"Mark?"

"Yeah?"

"Back home, people call me Addy. Would you mind doing so?"

Did he mind? Hell, no. "Is that what your folks called you?"

"My mom, yeah."

She sat straight up, apparently back in control of her emotions. It was as if she hadn't just been sobbing in his arms minutes before. Her strength was impressive.

Her compassion—Nonnie couldn't say enough about her—was noteworthy. And she was sexy as hell.

No wonder he couldn't go an hour without thinking of her.

She seemed to need silence and he was happy to sit with her for as long as she wanted. Sleep was irrelevant.

"No one knows about my father."

"That he set the fire, you mean?"

She nodded. "The fire marshal…he was a friend of my father's. And back then, fire investigation was based almost solely on the opinion and theories of the fire marshal."

"They didn't have fire forensics like they do now." She was in Mark's territory now.

She nodded, and said, "If he'd ruled that my father started the fire, I'd not only have been emotionally scarred, but I'd have lost his benefits. There'd have been no money for the funerals, or for my care. So he didn't. I'm sure the fact that my father was a firefighter and friend had something to do with it, too. They protect their own."

"So what makes you think your dad set the fire deliberately?"

"I know he did. Several years later, my dad's friend came to see my grandmother. I think he was checking up on me, actually. Anyway, they were in the kitchen talking and I could hear them through the register in the bathroom."

"Did you say anything?"

"No. Not to anyone. Ever."

So why him? Why now? And why wasn't he feeling the least bit cramped by this…thing…between them? He wasn't receiving replies to his texts to Ella, but things were still somewhat unresolved in his mind regarding the woman he'd expected to marry someday. The woman he'd mentally committed to.

He'd promised Ella he'd be back. It was a matter of his word, not whether or not she believed him.

Or maybe the situation was resolving itself. Maybe his heart knew what his mind was not yet processing—that Ella was not his one and only. That leaving her wasn't reprehensible. Or wrong.

"You want to go out to dinner sometime?" His words sounded like firecrackers in the night.

"Depends." Her gaze didn't move from the fountain.

"On what?"

"Why you're asking."

He wasn't sure. He'd just asked. Kind of like asking Ella to marry him. "You're patient with my grandmother. We're friends. I'd like a night out and don't know anyone around here." Not entirely true, but close enough. He didn't know anyone well enough to want to hang out with them for a whole evening.

"So we'd be going as friends."

"Sure, we can keep it at that," he said. That was what he wanted, too. Except for when he was thinking about making love with her. Which he was trying not to do, semi-successfully.

"'Friends' is all I can offer you."

He wondered why, but didn't ask. "I'm good with that."

When she didn't say anything else he asked, "When do you want to go?"

"I'm assuming you're talking about going to Phoenix, right? Other than diners there's not much here."

He hadn't thought that far ahead.

"Phoenix, it is. When?" He could hear himself pushing her. And didn't stop.

"Your schedule is a lot more complicated than mine," she said. "I'm good with just about any evening."

He was pleased to hear it. "I'm working the rest of this week and through the weekend," he said. "As soon as next week's schedule is posted, I'll let you know." He was a fill-in supervisor, good for any shift that he wasn't in class. He'd told them he'd work seven days a week.

So far, they were holding him true to his word.

"Sounds good."

He held back a grin, already looking forward to their non-date to nowhere in particular, and feeling guilty as sin, too.

ADDY DIDN'T HAVE class Tuesday morning, but she was up bright and early, eager to get her homework done so she could get back to her purpose for being in Shelter Valley—the investigation. With yesterday's find still chafing at her, she was afraid that she would un-cover more—that Will was in more danger than she'd initially suspected. More danger than he'd feared.

She was planning to go through all of the personnel files on record, looking for any other inconsistencies in hiring, firing, commendations, raises, nepotism or relationships—all fodder for lawsuits.

She was eager to immerse herself in the job, and forget about the past. Forget, too, about Adele Kennedy—and her relationships.

Her cell phone rang five minutes after she was out of the shower. Recognizing Nonnie's number, she picked up immediately.

"Can you do hair?"

She'd done Gran's toward the end when her grand-mother couldn't get enough air in her lungs to make it across the room, even with her oxygen tank, let alone make it to the hairdresser's.

"Yes."

"Can you get it done before my grandson stops in after class? He thinks he's going to do it for me before he goes to work, and as good as that boy is at some things, I don't ever want him touching my curls again. I look like a damned boy when he gets done with me."

"I'm sure someone at the shop in town would come out and do it for you," Addy offered, because she was Adrianna Keller and had work to do. And because she wouldn't always be next door to Nonnie Heber.

"I don't want Mark to have to spend the money on it. If you can't do it, I'll be fine looking like a boy. ..."

She heard the ploy even as she gave in to it. "Do you want it cut and curled or just washed and cut?"

"I want whatever much you can do."

"You got hair scissors and rollers?"

"Brung 'em with me."

A full do would take her about an hour. Looking at the clock, Addy said, "I'll be there in five."

THREE DIFFERENT GIRLS made it privately obvious that they were vying to be Mark's lab partner in his entry-level fire and combustion class. Three of the four girls in his class. He asked Jon Swartz, a guy he'd seen walking with a kid into shop downtown, to partner up with him.

He was the oldest guy in class. Jon was easily the second oldest. He didn't need coed complications.

He wasn't there to interact with students. He was there to learn about things he used to think he already knew.

"You want to light it or should I?" Jon asked, referring to the small mound they'd built in the stainless-steel utility sink—their rendition of combustible composition, solid fuel. They'd used a piece of construction paper, rolled and standing upright. They'd doused the paper in chlorine, which was an oxidizing agent. The dousing was their chain reaction. All that was missing was the heat.

"You light to flash point," Mark said with a grin. "I'll do fire point."

Jon smirked. "Sure, man, you take the easy one!"

He had. And next time, Jon probably wasn't going to give him the choice.

Half an hour later, they were walking out of class, both of them heading to the parking lot. "Good call, standing the paper vertically," Jon said as they separated from the rest of the students in their lab.

The quicker burn, as opposed to the horizontal, slower burning position all of the other students had used, had won them bonus points on top of their A.

"Can't say that I came up with that on my own," Mark told his lab partner. "Cylinders at the gasification plant where I work are manipulated on a vertical axis when a quicker burn is needed." He was only one week into his classes and just beginning to comprehend all that he had yet to learn, but at least some of what he'd learned back home was relevant.

"Where is there a gasification plant around here?" Jon kept pace with him.

"Sorry, where I used to work, back home. I work out at the cactus jelly plant now."

"No kidding. I tried to get a job there. I really need the benefits. They work around your school hours?"

"Yeah. They've been great, so far."

"You on the line?"

"Supervising." It sounded egotistical so he added, "I've been doing full-time plant work since I was sixteen. My experience is what got me the position."

"You're supervising?" The dark-haired guy sent him a sideways glance. "You think you could get me in there?"

He had no idea but said what came naturally, "I'll see what I can do, buddy. You working now?"

"At the gas station. But the hours suck. I can't make enough to pay bills and I got my kid to look after."

"You have a kid?"

"A son, yeah."

"Where's his mother?"

"In New York, last I heard. I thought we were in love but she was just having fun. When we turned up pregnant, she wanted an abortion. She agreed to have the baby instead as long as I took full custody. And here I am."

They were almost at the student parking lot outside the building that housed most of the chemistry labs. Mark shook his head. "How old is your son?"

"Two."

"Are you in touch with his mother?"

The younger man shrugged. "Nope, but Abe and me, we don't need her, either."

They'd reached their cars. "I'm on my way to work now," Mark said, unlocking the door of his truck. "I'll ask around and see what I can find for you."

"That'd be great, man." Jon's vehicle was a an older truck, too, but unlike Mark's his had a car seat in the back. "I'll sweep floors. Anything they need."

Mark believed him.

WASHING NONNIE'S HAIR wasn't hard at all. After rolling the old woman's chair up to the bathroom sink, she'd draped her bony shoulders with a towel and then helped Nonnie slide down in the chair until her head hung in the sink.

Addy took extra time massaging Nonnie's head while she lathered and conditioned and rinsed.

"I think Mark likes school," the old woman murmured while Addy's fingers worked gingerly on her frail scalp.

"I know he does."

"He told you?"

"Yes."

"Good."

"He told me you applied for the scholarship for him," Addy said. She was in Shelter Valley to do a job. And had to find out everything she could about anything having to do with Montford University.

"I told him I didn't."

"He thinks you lied."

"What would be the point? He's already here. Besides, I'm not afraid of my grandson."

With the help of a cup, Addy rinsed Mark's grandmother's hair. Letting the warm water wash over Nonnie's head as the woman scoffed.

"So you didn't do it," Addy asked, just to be clear.

"Nope."

"Who did?" One of Nonnie's friends? Someone else the old woman had wrapped around her finger?

"I've been wondering that," Nonnie said. "I didn't know a thing about it till it showed up in the mailbox. Just like Mark."

Frowning, Addy wrapped a towel around Nonnie's

head, used a second to drape her neck and helped her to sit up. "No one's come forward?" she asked. "Even after he accepted?"

"Nope. I got my ways of findin' out things and, hard as I tried, I couldn't find a damn thing."

The situation was definitely odd. She'd get to the bottom of it. Now that she had personnel concerns, scholarships were further down on her list of avenues to investigate, but she would look into it.

CHAPTER ELEVEN

MARK WAS WAITING for Addy when she got out of her last class Wednesday morning. They'd compared their class schedules and locations the night he'd stayed with her after she'd had her nightmare. It was hard to believe that had been just three nights ago.

She saw him leaning against the side of the building as she exited the doors with the rest of the crowd leaving the lecture hall. In his usual uniform of jeans, a polo shirt and leather shoes he should have looked ordinary to her.

But he didn't.

"I wanted to thank you for yesterday," he said, taking her books from her as he walked beside her toward the parking lot as easily as if they made the trek every day. Which they had, considering this was only her second day of class.

"No need to thank me," she said. "Being with Nonnie is a treat. She reminds me of Gran."

"For some reason I thought your grandmother was conservative. Proper."

"She was."

"Nonnie's outrageous."

"She's smart. Savvy. Perceptive. And most of all, she adores you more than anything in the world."

His head dropped and she added, "My gran was the same way with me. It's nice. Everyone should have someone so firmly in their corner."

"Tell me she didn't tell you about me spitting out my peas in my dresser drawer."

Addy laughed. "You spit your peas in your dresser drawer?"

"I'd seen it on TV or something. A way kids could get out of eating vegetables they didn't like."

He didn't like peas. Good to know. For what purpose, she had no idea.

It was time to change the subject. To stop being friends.

Because she wasn't who he thought she was.

They weren't even halfway across campus yet.

She had to focus on the job she was there to do.

"I read the most incredible story." She heard herself say the words before she'd fully decided to utter them. "I was looking up professorial ratings, checking out my botany professor." She altered the circumstances by which she'd found the information on Sunday to fit her current situation. But she needed to run this by someone—to get another reaction. "And that made me curious about the woman at the top of the ratings charts, so I looked her up." She was skating a fine line. Melding reality with fiction. Adrianna with Adele.

If she wasn't careful, people would get hurt.

"They have professorial ratings?"

"Yes. I'm not sure all universities do, but I know that Montford prides itself on maintaining the highest levels of academic excellence. I did a lot of research before choosing a college," she ad-libbed as she floated close to dangerous waters.

And scooted closer to him to avoid a pedestrian crash. The main sidewalk through campus was crowded, with lanes of students hurrying in all directions. It felt like she and Mark were a bubble in the throng, part of the rest, but separate, too.

"So who was the professor with top marks?" he asked. She couldn't talk to Will. Or anyone. Her job at Montford completely isolated her. Had Will screwed up beyond her ability to help him? Could she be friends with Mark without letting things go too far? "A woman named Christine Evans. She taught English."

"As in past tense? She's not here anymore?"

They turned a corner, embarking on another, less-traveled pathway, and Addy shook her head. "She had a sister, Tory, who drove out here with her when Christine was hired to start her new job as an English professor at Montford. Tory was divorced from a rich, influential, abusive older man. He was after her, which was why she was coming out here to live with Christine in Shelter Valley. Christine, the older sister, thought Tory would be safe here. They were still in New Mexico when the ex-husband's henchmen found them. There was a car accident and, according to the coroner, Tory was killed.

"But it wasn't Tory who died in the crash. It was Christine. Afraid for her life, and for the lives of anyone around her were it to be known that she was still alive, Tory allowed the mistaken identity to stand and came to Shelter Valley and assumed her dead sister's life."

So much about the story bothered Addy. And not all of it was professional. Or to do with the job. Lines were blurring. Which was why she was talking about the case at all. She, like Tory, was living an assumed life.

Doing something wrong—but for good reason.

But she wasn't taking on power that didn't belong to her, wasn't in a certified position, living a life of duplicity in a way that could directly affect other lives. Was she?

"She taught classes?" Mark asked, his tone suggesting that he found the story engrossing.

He didn't seem to find it odd that she'd allowed her curiosity to drive her to follow the trail, either.

"Yes, she taught Christine's full load."

"She had a doctorate degree, then, too?"

"No. A high school education was as far as she got."

Mark looked at her as they walked. "Wait a minute. This is the teacher that was at the top of the professorial ratings you were talking about? The ones that prove Montford's high standard of excellence?"

"Yeah."

"And she was a fraud?"

"Yes."

"You said you found an article about it, so I'm assuming she was caught?"

That's where things got really sticky for Addy.

And for Will.

"In a manner of speaking," she said. "The abusive ex-husband apparently had a lot of money and he hired detectives to watch Christine, just to verify that they hadn't pulled a fast one and pretended that Tory was dead. When he heard that Christine was doing so well as a professor, he became convinced of her death and, leaving a note to the effect that if he couldn't be with her in life, he'd be with her in eternity, he shot himself. Someone who worked for him, but was loyal to Tory, got word to her that he was dead and she immediately came clean."

They were nearing the parking lot.

"Before the end of the semester?"

"No. Word came during semester break."

"What happened to all of those students who took her class? A class she didn't have credentials to teach?"

"They received full credit for the courses they took from her."

"Can you do that?"

Legally, if the institution determined that they'd met class qualifications of learning, they could. It would be the same as though they'd all tested out of the classes. But ethically?

"They did it."

"Students could have sued, couldn't they?"

"Yes. But because they all turned in work to exhibit their mastery of the subject matter, their damages would probably have been negligible."

Addy froze inside for a second. A college freshman who'd only read an article wouldn't know that. Would she?

"Did anyone try?"

He didn't miss a beat—either on the sidewalk, or in their conversation. She started to breathe easier again.

"The article didn't say."

And she couldn't ask Will.

"What about Montford? The university pressed charges, didn't it?"

"No." Not that she'd been able to find. There'd been nothing filed, that much she knew. And he'd just hit on the other problem she had where Will was concerned.

Not only did Tory Evans get away with her deceit, she was still right there in town. Married to a Ben Sanders, according to the records Addy had pulled up the previous afternoon. She'd adopted Ben's daughter and the couple had had a child of their own, too, Phyllis Christine, born in 2001. The child would be twelve now.

More damning, though, was that Ben Sanders was

a descendant of the Montford family—town founders and Montford University patriarchs.

And based on what she'd found in the local paper, the Phyllis Tory had stayed with when she'd first come to town was one of Becca Parsons's best friends. Becca Parsons, as in Will's wife.

"I'd say they're lucky no one pressed charges."

Not the words she'd wanted to hear. But exactly the same conclusion she'd drawn.

It appeared to Addy, with sickening dread, that Will Parsons had played favorites. That if his anonymous threats had anything at all to do with Tory Evans, he could have a tough road ahead of him. She figured he had a fair chance of winning—but the battle wouldn't be easy. And he could lose his job.

Addy was really beginning to regret coming back to Shelter Valley.

For more reasons than one.

On Thursday, Nonnie volunteered Mark to change Addy's oil. The truck was due. He'd mentioned taking care of it before work. And before he knew what was happening, his grandmother had called Addy and told her Mark would be changing the oil on her car, too, while he was at it.

He could only hear one half of the conversation, but figured Addy was trying to refuse when he heard the old biddy say, "I can't let you do for me if you won't let us do favors back," in a pleading voice that didn't come naturally to her at all. She'd never have gotten away with it if she'd been talking to him.

"No, really, he'll have the oil pan out there, anyway. Won't matter if he lets a little extra drip in."

Sitting at the table, finishing the tuna sandwich she'd had waiting for him when he'd come in from class, Mark shook his head. He was going to have a serious talk with his grandmother.

Words at the ready, he waited for her to get off the phone. Seeing him, she wheeled down the hall toward her bathroom, assuring Addy that he'd know what kind of oil to get and she could settle up with him later.

By the time she hung up, she was in the bathroom with the door firmly locked behind her.

The ploy might have worked if he hadn't just helped her change her padded undergarment half an hour before.

"Nonnie." Standing outside the door, he used his most serious tone on her.

"I'm busy."

"No, you aren't. Come out here."

"Nope."

"What you do in my life is our business," he said through the door. "You can't interfere in someone else's life."

"Who's interfering? I'm being neighborly, is all."

The toilet flushed. She could be going. It wasn't as if she couldn't lift herself onto the seat and back to her chair. On her good days. She just didn't have the capacity to hold it long enough to get herself there and situated sometimes.

Thinking of the struggle Nonnie had just managing life's most basic functions, Mark felt his frustration drain away. He waited to make sure that she made it back to her chair okay, and let himself out to run downtown for more motor oil.

CHAPTER TWELVE

"I SWEAR I'M NOT stalking you," Mark said in lieu of a greeting as Addy stepped out the door Thursday afternoon.

Sitting on the low wall in front of her unit, she watched as he slid a plastic box under her car, used pliers to loosen something up and guided the center of the box to catch the flow of used and dirty oil.

"I know you're not," she said, enjoying the break from the personnel files she'd been perusing all afternoon. Pleasingly boring files belonging to well-qualified people.

"I want to warn you, she's probably cooking up some plan to get you and me together."

"As long as we know it's not going to happen, there's no harm in her meddling. We both understand and accept it for what it is."

His grin warmed her more than the bright sun shining down on them. She should go in.

But she didn't feel right leaving him all alone to tend to her vehicle.

"I hate to think what she says about me when I'm not around to defend myself," Mark said, leaning back against his truck, which was parked in the driveway next to her car.

"I can tell you one thing she never mentions," she said. "Your grandmother never mentions any of your friends."

"She didn't think they were good enough for me."

"You don't agree?"

"No. I grew up with them. Some of them are like family to me."

"Any one more family than the others?"

She handed Mark the glass of tea from the tray she'd carried out and he sipped. "I was closer to some than others."

"Did you have a woman you were closer to than others?"

It wasn't her business. Absolutely not her business.

But if she knew, she could stop obsessing about it. Could stop wondering if there were late-night phone calls. If some afternoon she might come home to find a strange woman on their shared doorstep.

If she knew his heart was taken, she could stop imagining him naked.

He crossed his ankles, studied his flip-flops. "I did."

"As in past tense?"

Squinting in the sunshine, he looked at her. "I asked her to marry me. She turned me down."

Was the woman daft? "I'm sorry."

"Don't be. I'm not sure that I was ready to marry her. I just didn't want to leave her high and dry."

"Not much of a reason to marry."

"I was deciding whether or not to come out here," he said. "We'd been seeing each other a couple of years. I'd reached a turning point. I wanted her to know that I hadn't just been using her until something better in life came along."

"Like a scholarship offer."

"Like anything."

"Do you love her?"

"I care about her, yeah."

She needed him to love the woman—so much that there'd be no chance for anything to develop between them.

So much that she could go to dinner with him as they'd planned and know that this was the only meal they'd ever share.

"Obviously you care or you wouldn't have spent two years with her. But do you love her?"

She was watching him. Waiting for an answer to a question she had no right to ask.

"I don't really have anything to compare it to," he finally said. "But if I had to swear on the good book, I'd probably say no. I'm not pining away for her and it seems like I should be if I were in love with her. If there is such a thing."

"You don't believe in love?"

"Not in society's prettied-up version of it. Television, romance novels, even the classics would have you believe that there's some magical feeling that's going to descend upon you and sweep you away to a place where the feeling will never fade and it will sustain you through all things and at all times."

"Yeah."

"It's a fairy tale. And before you ask, I don't believe *Cinderella* is a true story or that there's a Santa Claus, either."

"What do you believe in?"

"Loyalty. When you commit to someone, you follow through on that commitment."

"Like you do with Nonnie."

"Like my grandmother has always done for me." His tone was sharper than usual.

Uncrossing his ankles, Mark straightened, handed her the glass of tea and buried his head beneath her hood.

Taking the hint, Addy told him he could leave her keys in the mailbox and carried her tray back inside.

MARK CHANGED THE OIL on both vehicles, cleaned up, got ready for work and, after kissing Nonnie on the cheek while she napped, slipped out of the house half an hour early.

The smart thing would have been to head straight for the truck, but he didn't even make it down the steps. He knocked on Addy's front door and handed her back her keys.

"I'm sorry," he said as she took the key ring from him. "I'm not used to talking about myself."

"Why would you need to? Everyone in Bierly has known you since you were born."

She had a point.

"Nonnie told me that you had it rough. She said your mother left home when she was sixteen and came back a year later, nine months pregnant with you."

The skin on his face tightened. Just as he'd feared, his grandmother was spilling all his secrets.

"What else did she tell you about my parents?"

"Nothing."

"I have no idea who my father was...." The truth stuck in his throat. He'd been sired by a male so irresponsible he hadn't bothered to wait around to see if he'd been a boy or a girl. Or even born alive.

And if Addy was going to hear about it, he wanted it to be from him. She stood hugging her door and the empathetic look in her eyes drew him right in.

"Nonnie got pregnant with my mother in high school," he said. "Her dad had been killed on the farm and her mom didn't have anything extra to give her. It took all they had to live and pay taxes on the farm once it was no longer being farmed. Nonnie had to quit school and start cocktailing to make ends meet."

"Nonnie said she was a bartender."

"Mom grew up in the bar."

"Did you, too?"

"Nonnie never let me inside the place. The one time I disobeyed and marched in the front door demanding to see her, I got a butt whipping that I've never forgotten."

His face completely serious, he shook his head.

"Nonnie felt responsible for every bad choice my mother made, and made certain that she made up for every one of them with me."

"How old were you when you went to the bar?" she asked softly.

"Seven."

He had to get to work. To quit thinking about this woman and focus on the business of building his temporary life in Shelter Valley. To concentrate on getting good grades and earning the money they needed for Nonnie's co-payments and general care.

"And your mother. Do you still hear from her? Does she know you've moved? Has she ever helped with Nonnie?"

"She wrapped her car around a tree when I was twelve. Drunk driving. She died instantly. Thank God she didn't take anyone else with her."

Adele's silence eased the constriction inside him. Until she said, "This woman you left in Bierly, what's her name?"

"Ella."

"Are you still in touch with her?"

This was not front porch conversation.

"Depends."

Frowning, she asked, "It depends? Either you're in touch or you aren't. What does that depend on?"

It occurred to him that for someone who didn't want a relationship, she was showing a good bit of interest in his love life.

"Depends on how you define 'in touch.' I text her. She doesn't answer."

"How long has it been since she answered?"

"Since the night I asked her to marry me. More than a month ago."

"You think she's holding out, hoping you'll miss her enough to come home?"

"Nope. She was seeing someone else before I even decided I was for sure coming to Shelter Valley."

"You don't sound broken up about that."

"What's the point? If she wants someone else, she wants someone else. Not her fault. And there's not anything I can do to stop it, either."

"Maybe if you told her you loved her…"

"Then I wouldn't be being me, and she'd know that, too."

"But you still text her."

"It's the right thing to do."

"Why?"

"Because I told her that I wasn't going to desert her."

She nodded and shifted against the door as though she was only halfway in the conversation. As though, at any minute, she could step back inside, close the door and sever their connection. "I'm just trying to understand," she said. "You propose. The woman not only turns you down, she breaks up with you. She's seeing someone else. And you're still planning to be available to her because you told her you wouldn't desert her. Am I right so far?"

"Pretty much."

"Most guys I've known would have moved on."

"I'm moving on."

"So the not deserting her...that's as in friends? You're going to stay friends with her?"

She was asking questions he didn't have answers for. Questions he hadn't asked himself. "Ella and I... We've been a couple for a long time." He had no idea why he was answering her. Or even thinking about the question. "I don't think of myself as free. At the same time, I don't find it wrong that she's seeing someone else. I don't expect her to remain true to me. She told me point-blank that she wasn't going to. She doesn't just want to get married, she wants to have babies right away."

"And you don't?" There was no judgment in her tone.

"Not right now, I don't. I can't speak to the future. I just don't know."

"You've got a lot on your plate. With school. Your grandmother. Work…"

What was it with the women in his life always trying to do his thinking for him?

"Life in Shelter Valley is temporary. My time here is limited. I won't take on fatherhood until I'm in a position to be a father."

Some things he just didn't question.

ADDY WAS ON her way home from the store Friday afternoon when she saw the red lights in her rearview mirror. And recognized the man driving the police cruiser behind her. Pulling to the side of the road, she waited.

"At least you didn't use the siren," she greeted as Greg Richards approached her car.

"I didn't stop you on your own street, either," the forty-seven-year-old sheriff said, coming up to her door with his pad in hand.

"I appreciate that, but you could have just called my prepaid cell."

"I didn't want to take a chance that you'd be with someone who might ask who'd called. Or overhear our conversation. I'd rather we appear to be complete strangers until we know who's behind the threats. I don't want to give anyone any cause to suspect you're anything but what you say you are."

The last time she'd seen the sheriff, when he and Will had met her at her Phoenix hotel right after she'd arrived from Denver, he'd been driving a ten-year-old Ford pickup and wearing jeans and a polo shirt.

"Do you really think someone is out to hurt Will?" she asked. "Maybe this was just a random act from a coward who was unhappy with a grade or something." A drastic way to express disappointment, to be sure, but it would let her off the hook so she could get the hell out of Dodge.

"We've had another letter. That's why I stopped you. I wanted you to know." With a uniformed arm on the top of her opened window, he leaned in toward her, and the intensity in his green-eyed gaze made her aware of the seriousness of the situation.

"It was left under the door of Will's office again. Same type of envelope. Ordinary copy paper from a common ink jet printer. It warned Will that he should be making plans to get a sum of money together."

A car passed. And then another. She'd been on her way home from the big-box store outside of town and hadn't yet reached city limits so they were surrounded by open desert, devoid of curious onlookers.

"Weren't the first threats against Will *and* Montford?" They'd shown her the letters. She didn't have copies. Her job didn't require it and she didn't want this initial review tainted with too many suppositions. Didn't want to go back to the letters, look for clues there. She had to keep her mind open to every possibility so she didn't overlook some instance, occurrence or behavior that could open Will up to a lawsuit because she'd been focusing somewhere else.

"They were vague, but yes, the implications included Montford. And this one could, too. It doesn't say how much money. Or from where."

"What does Will think?"

"His first instinct was to resign immediately rather than put the school in jeopardy."

Addy shook her head. "That's wrong on so many levels. You can't let a bully win, just in principle." Unless Will was guilty of the charges. "Second, his resignation in no way stops the perpetrator from suing him personally or going after the school if he or she really believes they have a case. In fact, his resignation would most likely make him look more guilty in the eyes of the court or a jury."

"Which is what I told him."

"Until formal charges are brought there's nothing he can do but continue on with his daily activities as though nothing is wrong. The less guilty he acts, the less confident his accuser will be. And the less chance they'll have some questionable behavior to report as evidence against him in court."

Nodding, Greg said, "I'll pass that on to him."

"And in the meantime, I keep looking. The first thing to do after receiving a hint of a threat is to get legal counsel. He's done that, albeit unofficially. The most we can do at this point is to be prepared."

"And find whoever the hell is behind this. That's my job."

"That, too. Because whoever this is, is now a criminal," Addy said. "It's officially become blackmail since the mention of money is actually attached to the threat."

"I don't expect it to end there, do you?"

Addy was naturally mistrusting. She knew that. It made her good at her job—kept her mind open to assessing both sides, always. She had to be able to jump into her opponent's mind-set if she was going to beat him.

And to see the facts clearly in order to ascertain if her client was guilty. She could only defend those she truly believed were innocent.

"Adrianna?" The sheriff shifted his weight on the edge of her car as a truck drove by, showering them with a burst of dusty air.

"If whoever is behind this has no real basis for the threats," he continued, "if Will is completely innocent, then I would expect the ultimate goal here would be money. It's no secret the Parsonses are a wealthy family."

"And Will's stellar reputation can work against him. Anyone who knows him knows that he'd sacrifice himself, or pay any price, to protect those he loves. Those he considers his own. He considers every single student at Montford one of his own."

"My theory is that whoever is behind this knows Will personally, or at least has personal knowledge of him. This probably isn't someone from somewhere else who tried to get into Montford and didn't make it and was left with sour grapes."

"I agree, in theory. At this point the vendetta appears to be personal as opposed to something being enacted by a stranger just looking for a way in to the Parsons fortune. I'm assuming there were no fingerprints on the third letter, either?"

"One. It wasn't in any database."

Arizona's vibrant afternoon sun was behind them. Addy longed for its warmth.

"Have you looked into the possibility that someone is vying for Will's job? Is there someone who would be next in line? Someone with a grudge who would use Will's goodness against him to get him to step down, leaving an opening for his job?"

"We've talked about that. I've done some quiet checking. We can't rule anything out at this point, but I'm not finding any likely candidates to fit that scenario."

"So the most obvious conclusions are that either someone is out for money…or Will did something that someone really believes was wrong, and this person is looking for justice in the form of monetary compensation."

"Wouldn't you think, if there was some real incident or incidents attached to this that the letter writer would give some indication as to the actual alleged wrongdoing?"

"Possibly. Unless whoever we're dealing with has more than a layperson's knowledge of the law. He's being very careful not to reveal his evidence, thus not allowing Will to build any kind of defense against the charges, either physically or emotionally. It's the strategy I would recommend, though not for purposes of blackmail, of course. If this guy is really intending to press charges, the less he says at this point, the better. Of course, if he's intending to press charges, he's making a grave error with this blackmail attempt."

"We knew we were dealing with someone making a grave error the moment the first letter arrived," Greg said, straightening. A black town car passed and he watched it drive all the way down the road.

"You know them?" Addy asked.

"No. Which is why I'm watching them." Greg grinned. "I want to know when I've got a stranger in town."

"Because of the threats against Will?"

"Because I take my job to protect the people of Shelter Valley very seriously. Don't get me wrong, we welcome strangers. With open arms and open doors. Ask my wife, Beth, about that. Or any number of our other citizens. We just like to know who's in our midst."

Had Greg known the fire marshal who'd covered up her dad's hideous crime? Not that making what he'd done public would have brought any justice. James Keller had died in the fire. There'd been no one to arrest for arson.

Only a little girl's life to try to preserve.

But the exposure of an insurance settlement erroneously paid could create a mess she didn't need. She hadn't had any culpability in the situation, but she'd benefited from it.

Greg watched another car go by and turned to wave. The sheriff had probably still been in high school when her house burned down.

What would any of them, the Parsons family included, think of her if they knew the truth? That she was the daughter of a murderer? Of a man so unstable he'd lost all sight of right and wrong.

Would they understand and agree with the fire marshal who'd taken fate into his hands for the greater good?

Would they be willing to bury wrongdoing if it served their purpose?

"What do you know about Tory Evans?" Addy couldn't let Greg Richards walk away without expressing her concerns. They'd hired her to do a job. She had to do it. She hoped, for Will's sake, that the sheriff knew more than she did about the Evans situation.

Knew something that would protect Will if his blackmailer was tied to that situation.

"Tory?" Greg Richards stood with his hands on his hips, facing her. "Why do you ask?"

"Because she taught classes under an assumed identity, putting Montford in jeopardy of lawsuit, at the very least, and as far as I can see, no charges were ever pressed."

"First, Tory is a friend. A good friend who's had a tough life and given more to Shelter Valley than the town will ever be able to give back. Anytime anyone needs anything, Tory is quietly there, providing. Food, clothing, a helping hand…"

"I'm not out to get Tory, Sheriff," Addy interrupted quietly. "I'm looking for possible lawsuit opportunities against Will Parsons. I read the article that was published in the newspaper regarding Tory's…indiscretion. I'm asking you if there was more to it than what was written in that article."

"Tory's mother died when she was ten, leaving the girls in the custody of their stepfather. I can't speak to all of the man's sins, nor would I speak of Tory, period, but because you've been given access to records, I will tell you that Tory's stepfather married her off at seventeen to a man with connections. Ties to the underworld. Anytime she tried to leave him, anyone she associated with was in danger. She hid her true identity more to protect those around her than to protect herself. And she didn't steal an identity so much as accept the one given to her when she woke up in the hospital after the accident."

"Mitigating circumstances, I understand. A grand jury might not have charged her, a jury probably wouldn't have convicted her. I'm not questioning that. I'm questioning Will's culpability, or apparent culpability, in the situation. As far as I can tell, he didn't press charges or sanction her in any way. Tory is married to a Montford. She's a close friend of Becca's. That doesn't look good. It looks like he played favorites."

"She'd only been in town four months when Will made the decision not to press charges against her. And no one knew that Ben Sanders was a Montford back then. Sam Montford, his cousin, was long gone and Sam's parents, the only other living Montfords, were in Europe for an extended stay. None of the Montfords or Sanders family had even met."

That would help if Will were ever taken to court on discrimination charges. Help, but not necessarily exonerate him.

"Will weighed the decision heavily," Greg said, his arm on the top of her car again as he leaned down to look her straight in the eye. "The first thing he did after Tory presented herself in his office and confessed what she'd done was arrange to have tests administered to every single student who'd taken her classes. It's a test given to any student who believes he or she has surpassed the requirements for a given class, but who needs the credit hours for their degree. As long as they pass the test and pay for the hours, they get credit for the class. Every single one of Tory's students passed and Will was able to award them the credit hours, which meant that, in theory, no students were hurt by her indiscretions. He visited with me and with his board and the university attorney who, by the way, doesn't know about the current threats.

"After much discussion it was agreed that it was in Montford's best interests not to press charges. To do so could have affected Montford's reputation and, in a domino effect, the university's academic rating, as well, which could then affect our alumni and the several thousand students who were currently enrolled. A diploma from Montford has external economic value. ..."

Greg's tone was not quite defensive, but close. And Addy respected him that much more for the heart he obviously put into his community.

"I know and that's a valid argument," Addy told the lawman. "One he could feasibly win with if it ever went to court. Still, we need to be aware that the situation exists and is potentially flammable."

"You're saying that thing with Tory could be a valid basis for charges against Will?"

"Yes."

"Shit." Sheriff Richards stood back, turned to the road and then spun around to face her again.

"We don't know that the letter writer even knows about Tory."

"There was an article in the university paper, as well, after the board made its decision. Will insisted on complete disclosure."

"I know." She'd found that article, too. "And if he has to answer to charges, that article will be to his benefit. I just wanted you to know my opinion based on what I've found."

"You want me to tell Will?" Greg was to be their go-between if Will or Addy needed to relay messages to each other.

"I leave that up to you," she said. "For now, I'm a researcher looking for possible lawsuit opportunities against Will. I can't think beyond that."

Adrianna Keller had always been good at emotionally compartmentalizing.

She hoped to God that Adele Kennedy was equally adept.

CHAPTER THIRTEEN

NONNIE WAS STILL UP, sitting at the computer, when Mark walked in the front door just after eight that evening.

"Who's winning?" he asked. Judging by the poker hand on the screen, it wasn't her, which was unusual.

"I'm waiting for the river." She continued to watch the screen. "The River." A draw card in Texas Hold 'Em, Nonnie's current game of choice. "I'm up two tokens for the night." She had to win ten hands to earn a token.

"Which brings your overall token account to, what, nine hundred and forty-six?"

"One thousand and sixty-two." He could barely hear her.

"What?"

"One thousand and sixty-two," she said, somewhat breathlessly.

"Don't pull that with me, old woman," he said, coming closer to watch as she won the hand. "Don't go lowering your voice like you're out of energy just so I can't hear you."

"I wouldn't do that." She didn't look at him. And her cantankerous tone didn't put him off a bit.

"Yes, you would."

"Don't you have homework to do?"

"How many tokens, Nonnie?"

"One thousand and sixty-two." He'd heard her correctly.

"That's over eighty hands of poker in three days!"

"Winning hands," she pointed out. "I've still got my touch."

He didn't doubt that. And hoped she kept it forever. But he wanted more for her than a life spent playing poker against other lonely people online.

ADDY WASN'T GOING to set one foot outside her house Friday evening. To prove that fact to herself she pulled on the pair of cutoff black sweat shorts she wore for cleaning, and her favorite T-shirt. The one she only wore in private because she figured she was the only one who'd appreciate the saying emblazoned across the chest: I Live in My Own Little World, But That's Okay—They Know Me Here.

The threat against Will had escalated. She had so much to do, so many personnel files to get through. Scholarship recipients to investigate. Athletic programs to look at. Clubs to join on campus so she could see how they operated.

And homework to complete. Her cover would be blown if she failed out of her classes.

Pouring herself a glass of wine—something she allowed herself about once a week—she sat at the kitchen table with her laptop, leaving the desk in the living room for the next occupant of the duplex to use. The desk faced a wall and it was too far from the kitchen window and the sliding glass door—she couldn't hear the fountain.

She opened the secure server, typed in her user name and password, and opened the faculty files. She was still in the first half of the alphabet. The *P*s weren't far off. Where she would find Will's personnel file. His hiring information. Any formal complaints. Performance reviews.

She prayed to God she wouldn't find anything suspect among them. Prayed she could protect the man whose family had taken her in such a long time ago. She wasn't nearly as sure now, as she'd been when she'd taken this job, that she'd be able to do so.

The people of Shelter Valley lived by their own code. A good code. One that worked. But not necessarily one that would fit into today's court system where only the law—case law—mattered.

She needed a pen and got up to get one from the desk drawer where she stored her supplies.

She caught a glimpse of the front window through her peripheral vision as she bent over the tray of pens—one slot for red, one for black and one for blue. The window overlooked the front yard, the driveway and the road beyond. The houses across the street. Straightening, a black pen in hand, she moved to the window, just to check on the state of the neighborhood like any reasonable person living alone would do.

Mark was home. She'd heard him come in. And yes, there was his truck parked right next to her car in the driveway. His and hers. The sleek, big black truck and the small, older, tan-colored sedan.

Male and female. Side by side.

She had work to do.

She was not going outside that night.

Mark was as temporary as the duplex. He had a bit part in the life of Adele Kennedy. He could not mean anything to Adrianna Keller.

And it was Adrianna Keller who sat down at the kitchen table, and proceeded to take notes with her black pen as she peered at the files in front of her. Personnel records for an Amanda Kingsley. She'd been a professor of music at Montford for thirty years before her retirement five years ago.

The sliding glass door opened next door. And shut again. She was not going to look up. To see Mark sitting in his chair close to her side of the patio. She was Adrianna Keller. An attorney with a job to do.

She didn't hear him sit down. Had he seen that her chair was empty and gone back inside?

Had he needed to tell her something?

Addy dropped her pen. Picked it up. Her stomach was fluttering, her nerves on edge. Her heart was going to start pounding soon, too. She knew the signs. A panic attack.

She had nothing to panic about.

Closing her eyes she focused on the calming sound

of the fountain and made herself forget the man who might be sitting out there all alone.

MARK HAD TO WORK all weekend, split shifts with time off in between. But he was still up before dawn on Saturday—woken by the sound of Nonnie's chair whirring by his door on the way to the bathroom. Out of bed and down the hall before his eyes were completely open, he bent to look inside the refrigerator. If he didn't get the bacon frying, she'd do it herself. Because a good day started with a good breakfast and a good breakfast consisted of bacon and eggs. Every single day. Health experts might say that the cholesterol and fat was bad for you, but Nonnie was over eighty in spite of it.

"Adele had dinner with me last night." Nonnie wheeled herself up to the table half an hour later, a jar of grape jelly, napkins and silverware on her lap. "She brought over a pot of kielbasa and red potatoes with fresh green beans."

He'd sat outside and had a beer the night before, hoping she might join him, but she hadn't. So he'd spent the rest of the evening with his tablet, trying to focus on his art history reading while his thoughts kept painting visions of his neighbor undressing, getting ready for bed...getting into bed.

He'd texted Ella twice.

"It was good," Nonnie said, draping Mark's napkin across his knee and stuffing the tip of her own beneath her collar.

"Good."

"She's a looker."

"Who?"

"Who? Who are we talking about? Adele, that's who. Don't you think she's sexy?"

His head was bent over his plate as he shoveled eggs into his mouth. "She's all right."

"There're bound to be lots of men calling on her once they realize she's here."

"Bound to be."

"Why ain't you one of them?"

He knew where this was going. And knew better than to fight it. He lifted his chin. "Who says I'm not?"

He wasn't. But he managed to shut down his nosy, matchmaking grandmother, which made the false implication worth uttering.

SATURDAY MORNING, Addy attended a meeting for students interested in writing for the school newspaper. She listened while the student editor, a long-haired, bearded senior named George pontificated about truth in reporting, about upholding university standards without hiding facts, about full disclosure and university pride. The paper's adviser, a Professor Nancy Litchfield, reiterated most of the same.

Nothing was said about needing to have articles vetted by university staff before publishing.

With an article about border patrol in mind—just

as an excuse to infiltrate their little group—Adele Kennedy signed up to be one of the year's two new reporters.

"DID YOU GET that kid a job?" Nonnie asked as she and Mark sat over empty breakfast plates, drinking coffee Sunday morning before work.

"I got him an interview," Mark said. He'd asked management to give Jon a chance, and offered to train the kid on his own time. Entry-level line jobs were hard to come by. The kid might end up cleaning bathrooms to start with. But at least he'd be in the door. "It's up to him to get the job."

"They know he's in school?"

"Yeah."

"And they'll work around his hours like they do with you?"

"Yeah."

She grunted. And Mark took the praise equably.

"You don't talk about school much."

He shrugged. "Not much to tell."

"You just don't want me knowin' I was right."

"About what?"

"You. The scholarship. Or rather, you don't want me knowin' you know I was right. But I do. Whether you admit it or not."

Mark cocked his head, half grinning at her, half perplexed. "Why is it so important to you that I admit fault?" he asked.

"Who says it's important to me?"

"Isn't it?"

"I'm right, aren't I?"

"My point exactly."

She nodded. He smiled and finished his coffee.

"Pssst."

Addy was on her front porch, locking the door behind her Sunday morning, when she heard the familiar sound.

Why Nonnie didn't just call out to her, she didn't know. Hiding her smile, she turned toward her neighbors' house.

"Pssst," Nonnie said again.

"Nonnie? You need something?"

"So long as you're not busy," came the frail voice from just inside the door. And then, "Come in, girl," she said with more gusto. Mark's grandmother was sitting at the computer. "I got a favor," she said.

"Of course." Addy had stopped in twice the day before to say hello. The woman had been on the computer both times.

"Next time you're at the store, could you pick me up a bottle?"

"I'd be happy to," Addy said, watching over Nonnie's shoulder as she won a game of backgammon against someone from Sweden. "A bottle of what?"

"Skunked him!" Nonnie exclaimed, putting her chair in reverse. "Be right back," she said as Addy moved quickly to get out of her path.

Nonnie occasionally made rapid trips to the bathroom. But that morning, she whizzed right past it and on to her bedroom, returning a minute later with an empty bottle of whiskey on her lap.

Stopping her chair in front of Addy, she held up the bottle. "This. Can you get me some of this?"

"What about your medications?"

"Pooh them," Nonnie said. "I don't drink enough for it to make a difference. Just a nip at night sometimes when I can't sleep. Been workin' on that bottle for most of a year," she said.

Still, Addy couldn't agree to something that could put the woman's life at risk. "I'm sure Mark would pick some up for you. They sell alcohol right in the grocery stores in Arizona."

"I ain't askin' him."

Because she shouldn't be drinking alcohol? "Why?"

Backing up to her spot beside the small table that held Kleenex, bottled water, Nonnie's phone and everything else the woman might need, Nonnie looked Addy straight in the eye.

"Because that boy seen enough whiskey in his life. I ain't ever, ever going to make him see me with a bottle."

Addy noticed the woman's hands were shaking as she gripped the bottle in her lap.

"Mark drinks," Addy reminded softly, not completely sure Nonnie was bluffing. The woman had missed her calling—she'd have been better suited to the stage.

"Beer only," Nonnie said. "And never more than

two a night—one when he's driving. And I ain't talkin' 'bout him, anyways. I'm talking about the women in his life."

Women. Was Ella a drinker? Was that why Nonnie hadn't liked the woman? It wasn't her place to ask.

"He ever tell you about his mum?"

"Just how she died," Addy said, remembering. That's when she realized that Nonnie was being completely sincere. Wishing she could fade through the wall, back to the safety of her house, Addy just stood there. She couldn't get any more emotionally involved with these two. Helping an old lady on occasion was no different than volunteering with meals-on-wheels like she'd done in Colorado. But this…sharing their lives…

"My daughter didn't just die drunk, she lived that way, too," Nonnie said, her voice filled not so much with disgust as with pain. And regret. "My fault. I raised her around the stuff and didn't see till it was too late that she'd been sneaking sips behind my back. Lots of them. Got to the point she'd do anything for a drink. I thought, after Mark came along, that things'd be different. She loved him more than anyone. Just not as much as she loved the bottle."

Nonnie paused, breathing hard. Tears pricked at Addy's eyes and she felt the need to bolt but was physically unable to move.

"I did what I could, but when I saw her drinking around the baby, I told her to git. She could see the boy whenever she wanted, but only if she was sober.

The courts tried to take him away from her, away from me, but in the end, I won. She'd come back every now and then, mostly for money. And every time, that boy thought his mom was home to stay. He never quit believing that she'd get sober and they'd be a family—the two of them...."

Addy's heart cried for that boy. And ached for the wonderful man he'd become.

"I can't afford the sleeping pills the doc prescribed," Nonnie said. "He told me that a little nip at night, on the hard nights, wouldn't hurt if it'd help me sleep. My friend Doris used to buy it for me. I been rationing, but I'm out and..."

Without another word Addy took the empty bottle from Nonnie, and got the hell out of there.

CHAPTER FOURTEEN

AFTER CLASS ON MONDAY, instead of waiting for Addy outside her building, Mark left school right away, intending to get a five-hundred-word essay written for his English 101 class. He went to Harmon Hardware and Electronics instead to drop off a toaster he'd fixed and to pick up some solar lights.

He hadn't seen Addy since Friday. But he'd heard about her. Incessantly. Knew that she'd had pasta salad for dinner Saturday night and eggplant on Sunday. That she had gone shopping in Phoenix and had picked up some chocolates for Nonnie.

She'd been in his thoughts. Far too much.

"Mark, good thing you stopped in." Hank greeted him with a smile from behind the old-fashioned counter—one that resembled the counter in the drugstore on Main Street in Bierly. "I've got a vacuum cleaner I need you to look at if you've got time."

"Sure, Hank, leave it by the door and I'll take it on my way out." He made a beeline for the outdoor lighting and found what he was looking for almost immediately. The lights cost a little more than they would have been at the department store out by the highway, but the owners of independent shops needed support. He knew. Jimmy's dad had owned the drugstore back home.

"How's your grandmother doing?" Hank asked as Mark brought his lights up to the counter.

A sixtyish woman was perusing the paper towel holders in the center aisle. He'd noticed someone in the paint section, too.

"She's fine," Mark answered.

"Some folks have been wondering what she does all day while you're at school and working. We haven't seen her out and about."

"She spends a lot of time on the computer, Hank. She did at home, too, but people were always stopping by to interrupt her so I didn't worry about it as much."

"Well…" Hank paused and the woman he'd seen earlier came forward. "This is Veronica."

"Hello." The woman smiled.

"Hello." Mark shook the hand that she held out.

"I'm sorry for butting in, but a few of us have been talking over at the diner and we were thinking that, if you don't mind, we'd like to stop by and meet your grandmother. If you think she'd like that, that is."

"I'm sure she'd love it."

"I understand she's in a wheelchair."

"That's right. She has MS."

Veronica frowned. "I'm so sorry to hear that. There's a gentleman at Big Spirits, that's a drop-in center for the elderly here in town, connected to Little Spirits, the children's—"

"The day care, yes, I know," Mark told her. "I have

a…friend…who's new to town and just started taking his son there."

"Oh, you must be talking about Jon. He and Abe live around the corner from me. He's such a nice young man. And that baby. I told him to call me any time he needs a sitter, but he doesn't seem too keen on leaving the boy with strangers. Anyway, I'd be happy to stop by and introduce myself to your grandmother. Maybe we'd have something in common. …"

"Maybe." If nothing else, the two could talk themselves to sleep. Stifling a grin, he couldn't wait to tell Addy about the woman.

"Anyhow, there's a gentleman at Big Spirits who has MS. Maybe your grandmother could come to the center sometime and meet him. Or she can just come and play games and eat with us."

"Thanks for the suggestion," Mark said, easing his wallet out of his pocket. Nonnie needed people in her life.

"Oh, dear, here I am talking a blue streak when you're such a busy man," Veronica said. "Just tell your grandmother I'll stop by sometime tomorrow afternoon. Does she play cribbage? Maybe we could play cribbage. She shouldn't be sitting there all alone. Especially not with MS."

Veronica was still talking as Mark paid Hank and made his way to the door. Smiling, he loaded the lights and the vacuum into the back of the truck. Nonnie, meet Veronica. Veronica, meet Nonnie.

Thankfully he'd be at work tomorrow afternoon.

ADDY WAS WORRIED. She hadn't seen Mark in three days. She'd thought about him all the way through her botany lecture, planning the nonchalant way she'd greet him when she saw him outside class.

And she'd been inordinately disappointed when he hadn't been there.

But she was worried about more than her ridiculous obsession with her next-door neighbor. Over the weekend, she'd found something else in the Montford faculty files that bothered her. Which was why she set off for the physical education building to look for Randi Foster's office.

Randi Foster, who, before her marriage to the local vet, Zack Foster, had been Randi Parsons.

Will's baby sister.

She'd known Randi was back in Shelter Valley, working at the university. She'd purposely steered clear of the physical education department until now. Until she'd reached the *P*s and had reason to look through Randi's personnel file.

She hadn't seen Randi in person for twenty-five years. Hadn't spoken to her. But she'd watched her play golf on television.

Would she still have that blond hair? She'd always thought Randi beautiful with her combination of light hair and dark brown eyes. Randi had been, what, ten when she'd lived with the Parsonses? Just a kid, herself.

She looked at the room numbers along the top of the wall. She was almost there.

The woman wasn't going to recognize her. Will hadn't even recognized her. But Addy remembered Randi. The older girl's room had been right across the hall from hers during the six months she spent in the Parsonses' home. There were many nights that Randi had come into that room to rescue little Addy from her nightmares.

The door to Randi's office was open.

A woman sat at the desk, writing.

Her hair was still blond. And very short.

Addy took a deep breath. She thought about Will Parsons on trial. Out of a job. Thought of all the people who would be hurt. Unless Addy could formulate an airtight case against anyone who had a score to settle with him or the university. She had to know what they might be up against.

"Ms. Parsons?" Randi, a former golf pro, still used her maiden name at work.

Addy had known she worked at the university. She hadn't known that Will had promoted his baby sister to women's athletic director.

"Yeah." Sounding distracted, Randi didn't look up right away.

"I…need to speak with you," Addy said, slowing her heart rate with even breaths. "Your office hours were posted so…"

"Yes." Randi finally dropped her pen and jumped up. "I'm sorry. I am holding office hours now." She pointed to the chart on her desk. "Class schedules. They drive me nuts but have to be done."

At the beginning of the semester? Wasn't that leaving it a little late?

"I'm supposed to predict how many students I'm going to have in my second-semester classes while I'm still checking numbers to see which classes exceeded enrollment for this semester! What can I do for you?"

"I, um, was wondering…well, I heard that you helped Susan Farley." Addy's hesitation was only half put on for the sake of her cover. Seeing Randi, acting as if the woman meant nothing to her, was proving much more difficult than she'd expected. Next to Will and Becca, Randi had been Addy's lifeline at a time when her emotional and mental health had been extremely fragile.

She'd thought herself well past any vulnerability she'd felt toward them.

Randi came around to rest her backside against the front of her desk. Her arms were crossed. "Helped her?"

"Financially. I…have a little sister. She's a star tennis player in Colorado.…"

Addy knew a star tennis player in Colorado. She'd defended the girl when her high school wasn't going to let her play in a critical match because she'd be missing class to do so. In Addy's mind, it wasn't a question of whether or not school athletes should be permitted to miss class to play sports, but a question of inequality due to the fact that football players at that same school missed class every single time there was an away game during football season.

She'd won.

She named several of the tournaments the girl had played in. "Our folks can't afford to pay college tuition but with the money my dad makes, we just miss the cutoff criteria for her to qualify for a student loan," she said.

She'd concocted a scenario similar to a case she'd come across in her research where Randi Parsons had been over budget, having even spent the overflow funds from the alumni athletic account and yet, after school had started, had managed to find funding for Susan Farley, a basketball center who'd gone on to play in the pros and currently had major sponsorships, including commercials on national television. Where the money had come from, she had no idea, but after learning about the situation from Randi's files, she'd gone on to read articles about the woman who'd credited Randi Parsons with helping start her career. There'd been a reprimand regarding the overflow account expenditures in Randi's personnel file. Which had spurred Addy to begin an hours-long investigation to uncover the rest of the facts.

And now she needed an incident with which she could counteract an allegedly discriminatory action.

The nepotism—the fact that Randi, who'd obviously taken liberties with school money, was working for her brother—wasn't something she could do anything about. At least, not right then.

Addy couldn't talk to Will. And she had to look into every possible reason someone could have to blackmail him. Nepotism as a basis of discrimination was a big one—if he'd hired his sister over other equally qualified applicants. Or kept her on staff in the face of blatant overspending when others had been let go for similar wrongdoing.

If he were charged, the prosecution's investigation could very easily locate the same case Addy had found, and they could foreseeably establish a "test" of sorts to see if they could catch Randi in the act of misusing school funds as a means of strengthening their case. It was what Addy would have done.

"I'm currently a freshman here at Montford," Addy said slowly, not having to fake the nervous hesitation with which she spoke. "It took me ten years to save for this, but my sister's tennis can't wait the four years it will take me to finish if she hopes to have any kind of career with it. If she attended Montford she'd be able to stay with me, which would alleviate her living expenses, but the tuition here is so steep. I was just hoping that maybe there would be something you could do."

The whole scenario—her in Shelter Valley, there with Randi, pretending to be someone she was not— was making her physically ill. Her head throbbed.

"There are funds designated for scholarships. And

some alumni money is available each year, too, but that's all been promised for this year."

"I figured that." Addy glanced down, thinking about what she'd discovered the day before. Susan Farley had started school after the semester had begun. On full scholarship plus living expenses. The largest athletic scholarship the university had awarded to date—in both men's and women's athletics. It had come at a time when all scholarship funds had already been designated for the remainder of the year.

The woman had gone on to fame and fortune. And anyone who'd been turned down in similar circumstances could sue.

"I used to watch you golf," Addy said, effecting a shyness that was not natural to her. "You were really good."

Her arms still crossed, Randi lifted one foot to the chair in front of her desk. "That was a long time ago, but thanks. I'm into in-line skating now."

Because skating didn't take a lot of upper-body strength?

"I read about your car accident. I'm sorry." Randi had been at the top of her game, in Florida to participate in a tournament she'd been expected to win, when she'd been involved in an accident that had crushed her shoulder—and ended her golf career.

Addy had received a phone call from Will shortly

after the accident. She'd sent a card to Randi, with no personal note attached. She should have called.

"Like I said, it was a long time ago." Randi reminded Addy of herself. Compartmentalizing to contain the things that could not be controlled.

"Susan is playing pro basketball now, isn't she?" she continued. "She's sponsored by one of the big tennis shoe companies. I saw her ad on TV. Montford's women's athletic program is the best."

"Susan did make it to the pros. She's doing quite well. Has your sister applied for tennis scholarships?"

"She didn't have to apply. They came to her. My father met with the colleges, chose the one he thought would be best, but when my sister got there a couple of weeks ago, the scholarship offer was only good for tuition and books, not living expenses. And the tennis coach won't let her work her first year while she acclimates to the team, to competition and studies. My parents can't afford to keep her there and it's too late to apply anywhere else."

And ten years ago Randi had mysteriously come up with funds for a late-in-the-semester scholarship offer for a promising basketball player.

"I heard what you did for Susan and so I thought, maybe, on a long shot…"

Randi shook her head. "I called in some favors on that one," she said, and Addy's stomach sank. "My brother is the president of the university and I've already pissed him off as many times as I can afford and still keep my job," she continued with a self-deprecating grin. "But let me see what I can do."

"I'd really appreciate it." Addy pulled a piece of paper from her satchel and handed it to Randi. "My name and phone number are on there."

Calling in favors wasn't necessarily wrong—or even inappropriate. But granting special funding if others who were similarly situated had been turned down would definitely be cause for a lawsuit.

"What's your sister's name?" Randi asked as Addy was about to leave. "You said she's played in tournaments, maybe I can find some video on her. ..."

Addy was prepared. She gave out her client's name, having already received permission from the girl's family to do so, telling them only that she was working on another case, and added to Randi, "We have different fathers," to explain the different last names.

"Can we please keep this between us for now? I don't want to get her hopes up. Or get my folks involved until I know for sure that there's a chance we can work something out."

There was only so much she could ask her former clients to do.

"Sure." Randi held out her hand. "Thanks for stopping in. Your little sister's a lucky girl."

Addy took the other woman's hand and prayed that Randi didn't do anything that could get either her or Will in trouble.

And then she prayed that God didn't strike her dead for the lie she was living.

Whoever had coined the phrase about "one lie leading to another" had been completely, one hundred percent correct.

It felt like hers were leading her straight to hell.

CHAPTER FIFTEEN

SITTING OUTSIDE ON the patio with a beer late Monday night, Mark sent Ella one of his nightly texts, wondering how long he was going to keep it up. She wasn't answering. At some point, that let him off the hook, didn't it?

He'd given his word that he'd be true to her. That he wouldn't bail.

He was not his old man.

Addy's light was on. After midnight. It had been three days since he'd seen her, but it seemed like three weeks.

Hell, he hadn't even known her for three weeks.

But every night, when he climbed between the sheets alone, he thought of her sleeping right next door.

And he liked having her there.

What was the harm in that?

They were adults. Fully capable of being friends without taking things too far.

Crushing his empty beer can, he opened a second.

He wasn't going to knock on her door. It was past midnight.

He'd seen his schedule that evening. After working eight days in a row he was finally going to have a day off Wednesday.

Her light was on. And the window was open. She was moving around in there.

"You okay?"

He heard rustling and wondered if she'd join him under the stars. They'd shared a drink once before. He should have put on a shirt with the sweats he'd pulled on after his shower....

"Mark?"

"Yeah."

"I didn't realize you were out there." Her voice came from the kitchen window over his right shoulder.

He sipped, but didn't turn around. "I worked late. I was too wound up to sleep."

"I thought you were off at eight."

God bless Nonnie. He could sure count on her to let everyone know every detail about him.

No, that wasn't fair. Not everyone. Just those she approved of.

"A guy called in sick. I covered for him until they could get someone else in."

She didn't respond. He wasn't sure she was still there.

"How've you been sleeping?" He peered up at the sky, seeing only a couple of stars, waiting to see if he'd get an answer.

"Fine."

She was still there. Was she not dressed? Was that why she wasn't coming outside?

"No more nightmares?"

"No."

He wasn't sure he believed her.

And he didn't like that they were becoming strangers again.

"You free Wednesday night?" Veronica What's-her-name was stopping by to see Nonnie after Bible study—maybe with another lady or two in tow—to share that week's spiritual message.

"Yeah."

"Want to have dinner then?"

"Sure."

"Okay. Well, good night."

"'Night."

Hot dog! He had a nondate with the girl next door.

Rustler's Roost in Phoenix was everything the guys at work had assured Mark it would be. Named after the early Phoenix cattle rustlers who'd supposedly built the mountain hideout, the restaurant boasted a slide, by which patrons accessed the dinner tables, set one floor below the entrance.

More uptight patrons, or those with disabilities, used the stairs. He slid down the slide. Addy opted for the stairs. She claimed she'd made the choice based on the calf-length black cotton skirt she was wearing with black wedges and a black-and-red ruffled blouse. He didn't buy the excuse. She could have tucked her skirt under her. The wedges and blouse had no bearing on slide proficiency.

In black jeans and an off-white button-down shirt he used to wear the couple of times a year he had to look nice for church, Mark was about as dressed up as he got. He'd tried to leave his sleeves buttoned at the cuff but hadn't made it out of the house before he'd rolled them up his forearms.

Sitting there at the rustic, but somehow still very ritzy, window table overlooking the Phoenix valley with one of the most beautiful women in the room, he felt like a testostcrone-fueled kid his first time off the farm.

"We're going Dutch," Addy announced, perusing the menu in front of her.

"No, we aren't." There were just some things a man did. To show respect.

With the top half of her long hair held back with a black clip, she looked as refined as the prices on the menu when she gave him the blue-eyed stare he was coming to recognize as her "I mean it" look. "Just friends," she leaned forward to say. "You agreed."

"I asked you to dinner and I picked the place so I'm paying. It's the decent thing to do. If it makes you feel any better, I'd pay if you were Nonnie, or my fifth-grade schoolteacher, too."

Those rose-tinted lips smiled at him—and food was the last thing on his mind. Paying for it, *or* eating it. "You'd take your fifth-grade teacher out to eat?"

Picturing Mrs. McDougal—short, plump and just a

few years younger than Nonnie—he shrugged. "If she was hungry and I was there, sure, I guess I would."

"But you never have?"

"No, why?"

"Because." Still smiling, folding her pale-pink-tipped fingers together on the table in front of her, she leaned toward him again. "Your life is just so different from mine. I can't even remember my fifth-grade teacher and I'm pretty sure I never saw her again after leaving elementary school. Where I come from, you don't usually run into your teachers or your doctor when you're out and about. Too many people, too many neighborhoods."

He felt sorry for her. And slightly backward at the same time.

"Don't get me wrong," she continued. "I love hearing about your life. I find it fascinating."

Like a bug under a microscope? Or…

"I've wondered sometimes, what my life would have been like if I'd been raised in a smaller town."

Resisting the urge to cover her hands with his, he said, "You'd have had people like Nonnie in your life every minute of every day."

"You make that sound like a bad thing."

Shrugging again, he looked at the menu. "Sometimes it is and sometimes it's not."

"There's good and bad in everything."

"Right."

"So when is it a bad thing?" The edges of her lips

still tilted upward, but her eyes were serious. Searching. Curious.

A combination that hit him right in the center of his pants.

"YOU BUILT A RAMP out of aluminum siding from the town dump and attempted to fly across the creek on your bike?" Addy laughed so hard she almost choked on the steak she'd put in her mouth. Addy couldn't get enough of his childhood stories. And couldn't remember ever having so much fun.

She'd enjoyed herself before, of course. Been happy. But…fun? It wasn't something she was good at.

"I was eight," he said, jabbing his fork into the rattlesnake he'd ordered for dinner—because it was on the menu and he'd never heard of anyone eating it before. "At least I didn't put on a red cape and try to fly off a roof."

Addy stopped laughing and looked at him, the rugged, gorgeous features that were taking up way too much head space these days. "You know someone who did?"

His nod was accompanied by a smile—and sadness, too. "My best friend, Jimmy. Now there was a boy who couldn't turn down a dare. Unfortunately, he didn't always take the time to think before he acted…."

She wondered if Jimmy's death at the plant the year before had come about due to lack of forethought.

Wondered, too, if Mark had been responsible for getting Jimmy a job at the plant in the first place. According to Nonnie, he'd been the first of his friends to have a full-time job. And while he'd worked other jobs on the side, he'd been at the plant for most of his life.

"Jimmy was the one who had the bright idea of filling an old milk jug with rotten eggs and leaving it outside old biddy Buchanan's bedroom window."

"Old biddy Buchanan?"

"That woman was old when she was young," Mark said, attacking his potato with the same gusto he'd shown his rattlesnake. "She hated kids. Any of us happened to laugh or raise our voices anywhere near her yard and she'd be out there telling us to shut up. She put up fences around all of her flower beds, too, afraid one of us might stumble and fall off the sidewalk and trample them. Never put them around her yard, though. No, that would have meant she'd have no reason to yell at us."

"Maybe she was sick. Or lonely. Or in pain."

"She was a pain." He grinned. "I don't know about lonely, but she wasn't sick. She was just mean. Even Nonnie said so."

"So Jimmy put a jug of rotten eggs in her yard."

"No, it was Jimmy's *idea*."

She was smiling again. So much it hurt her face. "You did it."

"Yep."

"What did Nonnie do to you that time?" She'd already heard about his punishment for skinny-dipping in the lake during a Bible school outing. He hadn't been in Bible school. He'd just been around the bend in the lake when the kids who were in Bible school had shown up. His grandmother had made him wash his own clothes, by hand, for a month—giving him an awareness of the importance of having clothes, and being clean. And of keeping clean clothes on.

"Every meal for a week she put a hunk of bread with Limburger cheese spread on it on my plate. I had to eat it before she'd serve me anything else."

"That stuff stinks!"

But the memory didn't seem to be affecting his appetite at all. "Yeah, well, what you might not know is that it stinks more the older it gets and it takes three months for the stuff to age enough to be creamy and spreadable."

One look at the scrunched-up, little-boy expression on that handsome, masculine face and Addy was laughing so hard she had tears in her eyes.

"WHERE DID ELLA fit in to all this?" Their plates had been cleared away. Mark was having a cup of coffee, and Addy was still nursing the raspberry iced tea she'd had with dinner.

She couldn't stop thinking about the woman who'd won Mark's loyalty, if not his heart.

Had Ella fit right in with Mark's wild side? Addy had never been the kind of girl who'd been turned on by bad boys...

"Ella came later," he said. "I liked another girl, but her parents were strict, and then I quit school and we rarely saw each other."

It was the first time Mark had intimated that life in Bierly might not have been as small-town idyllic for him as he preferred to let on. She'd heard about white-trash remarks from Nonnie. About Mark being shunned by the "uppity" folks until it came time to need a favor.

Seeing Mark from a different perspective, as, say, the parents of a young girl might have seen him—the son of an alcoholic mother and being raised by the local barmaid—Addy wondered just how hard he'd had it growing up. As far as parents were concerned, Mark's quitting school had probably sealed his reputation as a loser that nice girls would be warned to stay away from.

Tears threatened and Addy shook herself. What was the matter with her? Mark was only a friend. Someone she hardly knew and wouldn't know for long. Besides, he could take care of himself. Had come out the other end just fine.

Better than fine. As Mark stood to move his chair so a large man seated at the table behind them could get out, his denim-encased thighs were directly in Addy's line of vision. Thighs that came so perfectly together at his fly.

Her lower body tingled and she swallowed. Glanced outside.

She was losing it.

HE'D TOLD HER they were going to dinner as friends. He'd given her his word and meant to keep it.

She'd been up front about the fact that she didn't want a relationship. Neither did he.

But as he drove back to Shelter Valley with Addy sitting at his side, Mark was hard and horny—and not sure what to do about, either. Addy was hardly the first woman who'd ridden in his truck. Ella had ridden right where Addy was sitting almost every day for the past two years. He'd never found the experience particularly sexy.

The thought of Addy's butt against his leather was doing him in.

Like he was that kid fresh off the farm again. Instead of a thirty-year-old mature man who'd been responsible for others since he was sixteen years old.

The woman affected him like no one else.

"Did you ever get in trouble as a kid?" They'd spent the evening talking about his antics. He wanted to know about hers. To know her better.

He wanted her to feel as vulnerable as he was feeling....

"Not that I can recall."

"You have to have done something wrong. No one's perfect."

"I didn't say I didn't do things wrong!" She chuckled. "I said I didn't get in trouble for them. All Gran had to do was call me by my full name and I'd practically break out in tears. I hated disappointing her."

"Because you were afraid she would leave you?"

He would've sworn she stiffened next to him. "It's a natural reaction," he said, softening his tone. "I figure you got the same spiel I did as a kid from your counselor."

"You had counseling?"

"Just at school. After Mom died. Another hazard of living in a small town. Everyone knew her. And they thought, after she'd died, that I'd have a problem dealing with the mixed emotions of hating what she did, but grieving because she was my mother."

From what she'd said, she'd loved her father. Before she'd hated him. Their situations were different, but some of the childhood processes would have been the same.

Watching the road in the pitch darkness as they sped through the desert, Mark said, "I didn't like counseling and I certainly didn't think I needed it. I can't say I participated, but apparently the things the guy had to say found a way in. It didn't take me long to figure out that they thought my acting up after Mom died was due to some subconscious need I had to test Nonnie—to push her until she finally shipped me off. The guy—I can't remember his name—suggested that I had a fear of being abandoned. Because from my first days, I had been.

"I assured him that I had not been left. Nonnie had been with me from the moment I was born and she wasn't going anywhere."

"Was that true? You really weren't afraid of being left?"

"Looking back on it, I'm not sure. I know I didn't

think I was. Mostly I remember being pissed that the guy suggested such a thing. He wasn't from Bierly and I figured he just didn't know Nonnie."

And she'd very expertly turned the conversation right back to him.

He needed to know about her.

ADDY WASN'T EAGER to get back to Shelter Valley and the work that awaited her.

She'd written a controversial article about border guards that made her stomach churn and dropped it off at the school newspaper office that afternoon. If they printed it, they'd put the university in a tough political position. If they didn't, they'd be taking away her freedom of speech.

All institutions faced the challenge at one time or another. She had to know how Montford handled it.

She also wanted to know more about Mark Heber and she already knew too much. She was spending too much time with him—and wanted more. It was like he'd deposited a part of himself inside her and that part was breeding. Rapidly.

"There's a casino with a quiet bar not far from Shelter Valley," Mark was saying as they neared their exit. "It's out by the cactus jelly plant, right off the freeway. Some guys from work told me about it."

"I don't gamble."

His chuckle had her turning to look at him. She'd been trying to avoid the temptation to soak up any more of him. At least for the night. "I don't gamble, either," he said. "In fact, I've never been inside a casino. Never saw the point. If I have extra money to spend, which I never have, I'd invest it in something a little more stable than a game of chance. I was going to suggest that we stop in for a drink. Unless you'd rather get straight back."

If he wanted to spend more time with her as badly as she did with him, she had to get straight back. But what if he just needed a little more time out in the world before he went back to the home he shared with his grandmother?

"A glass of wine sounds good," she said, afraid of just how good it sounded.

She only wished it was the wine compelling her to agree. But she had half a bottle chilling in the refrigerator at home.

Adele Kennedy's home.

But she wasn't really Adele. And now more than ever, she'd better not forget that.

"You said you've never been engaged."

The little round table separating her and Mark didn't put enough distance between them. She could still make out the flecks of darker blue along the rims of his irises in spite of the dim lighting in the bar. She could see him so clearly she felt as though she was slowly becoming a part of him.

Or he was becoming a part of her.

Either way, this had to end. "I haven't been."

"What about friendships? Have you had any that were long-lasting?"

She'd asked for this by asking him so many personal questions over dinner. Going out with him had been a bad idea.

She thought of Will Parsons. She'd kept in touch with him for twenty-five years. She'd come running when he'd called, saying he needed her.

"Yes, I've had long-lasting friendships."

"In Colorado?"

Her chest tightened. "I'm not sure what you're asking," she said, more because she didn't want to answer than because she wanted clarification. "I had a best friend in high school, Trudy Whalen. She's in Florida now, married to a cop, and we keep in touch."

"I was referring to male-female friendships. You know about Ella. I just wondered if there'd ever been anyone special in your life."

"Not really."

"Why not?"

His eyes were only inches away—seeing far more than was safe. "I don't know. I'm not a virgin, or anything," she assured him, telling herself the conversation was no big deal. "I just...I don't know. There's always been a bit of a disconnect. I'm sure it's me."

She could admit it to him. They weren't a couple. And weren't going to be one.

"I'm not."

She sipped her wine. In too big a gulp. Her head was already spinning, although she hadn't even finished half a glass. His beer wasn't finished yet, either. "You have no way of knowing that."

"Probably not, but you're so compassionate, so… open…to accepting me and Nonnie into your life. That doesn't sound like someone with a disconnect."

"Being neighborly is very different from being… intimately…attached."

"Of course it is, but the ability to connect comes from the same source."

He was confusing her with his odd conversation. Probably because she knew she couldn't engage on a real level. "Maybe."

"I have to be honest with you, Addy. I think I'm falling for you."

No.

"I don't mean to scare you, or make you uncomfortable," he said, his gaze locked with hers. "It doesn't change anything. I understand you aren't looking for a relationship and neither am I. I just need you to know."

She nodded. And a little bit more of her gave way to a little bit more of him.

CHAPTER SIXTEEN

MARK COULDN'T SLEEP. Home from his nondate, not long off the one glass of beer he could have while driving, he'd hoped to fall into bed and catch a few hours of shut-eye before he had to be at the plant.

Thursday was Jon's first day of work. Mark wanted to be there. Not that he had anything to do with the janitorial department, or would oversee Jon in any way. He didn't need to be present, but he wanted to make sure the guy had no problems getting his locker and learning the lay of the land.

After tossing and turning for a long time, Mark got up, tiptoed out to the kitchen, got a beer out of the fridge and quietly let himself out the back door. Nonnie was a sound sleeper, but she also woke up many times during the night. He didn't want company.

Or, more accurately, he didn't want Nonnie's astuteness poking around his psyche.

He noticed the body occupying the chair on the other side of the wall too late to retreat.

SHE'D COME OUTSIDE to get away from Adele Kennedy. To think.

And then the object of her thoughts was standing there—in nothing more than a pair of basketball shorts and a sleeveless undershirt. Almost as though she'd conjured him up.

That was the problem with falling for your neighbor. He was always right there.

"I'm sorry," Mark said in a near whisper. "I thought you'd be in bed."

"It's no problem, I can go in." She started to rise and remembered that all she had on was the short terry-cloth robe she'd belted around herself when she got out of the shower.

"No." He glanced at her, and then away, uncapped his beer. "Please, stay. I'll go in." But he didn't.

Holding up his bottle, he said, "I hope I didn't blow things between us, with my pronouncement tonight. I just had to be honest in case you don't feel safe around me, or something."

"Of course you didn't blow things." She'd spoken too quickly. "You were being honest. I admire that."

"A lot of people say they do, but real honesty makes them uncomfortable."

"I'm not one of those people. I prefer to know where I stand."

For her, honesty meant that she wasn't her father's daughter. She was mentally and emotionally strong. And morally determined to choose right.

So what was right? Helping Will in the only way possible, which, at this point, meant living a lie? Or being honest with Mark Heber about who and what she was?

He sat down.

In her world, complete honesty was rare. By nature, lawyers tended not to say anything at all if the truth would hurt their case.

There were those in her profession who didn't seem to care about right or wrong, truth or justice, at all. To them the world seemed to revolve around winning. It was all about having the best argument. The ability to read and manipulate a jury.

Not that she could tell Mark any of that.

He sipped his beer. She held a cup of decaffeinated hot tea.

She must be a better lawyer than she thought, the way she was lying to Mark.

But what choice did she have?

She already knew the answer. She just didn't like it. There really wasn't a choice to make. She'd given Will her word. She'd known him a lifetime. Owed him.

She'd only known Mark a few weeks. And she'd soon be leaving...

"You ever think about going back to Bierly?" She didn't know the place, but it wasn't Shelter Valley. Maybe, if he went back, and wanted to get to know an educational lawyer from Colorado, she could be friends with him in real life.

Maybe even more than friends. Sitting with no underwear on so close to Mark, Addy couldn't deny certain things. Uncomfortable things. She crossed her legs, pulling the edges of her robe together, and her arm brushed against her nipple. She practically jumped out of her skin. Since when did touching her own nipple send shards of pleasure down below? She clasped her hands tightly around her cup of tea.

"I plan to go back," Mark said slowly, softly. "We have a home there—the house where I was born. And Nonnie, too, for that matter."

Oh, God. No, they didn't. That secret wasn't hers. But it was being kept from Mark.

A man so honorable he'd confessed that night that he was falling for her.

She needed to confess, too. So badly.

And to find out what would happen if he touched her like he'd implied he wanted to.

"Is there a college there you can transfer to?" She was grasping. But if he qualified for a scholarship at Montford, surely he could get one at a state school in West Virginia.

She had to look up his scholarship. But not until she looked at the others. In the order she would have normally looked at them. She was splitting hairs, but somehow the distinction mattered. She was going to look Mark up, but only as though he was a normal scholarship student. *Not* as if she'd found out something about him because of their friendship and was acting on that. "I can't transfer," Mark was saying while Addy was busy thinking about all of the people he'd grown up with—about Ella—and wondering how long it would be before someone said something to Mark about Nonnie's house being sold.

Nonnie had sworn her to secrecy, but there was no way an entire town would keep her secret.

More likely, as soon as the new owners took possession, Mark would find out, just as everyone else in town did.

In the meantime, Nonnie had told her the house stood vacant with a For Rent sign still out front. "I can't quit school, either," he continued. "A condition of accepting this scholarship was that if I fail or drop out, I have to pay back every dime already spent, so that there's a full scholarship available to offer to someone else. Just with this semester's expenses, I'd owe more than my truck is worth."

He'd be in Shelter Valley for at least four years. Adele had a year—at most. Probably more like another month or two—if the escalated threat was anything to go by.

"I don't know if I'm going to be able to afford to stay long enough to get my degree." The words flew out of her mouth. Adele again. Lying. In a lame attempt to warn him.

He'd said he was falling for her. Her body was falling for his, too. Like tipping over the edge of the highest peak on a roller coaster.

"You could get a job. You're studying horticulture—have you checked at the nursery outside of town?"

"Not yet. I'm fine for now." She'd already told him that she'd saved enough so that she didn't have to work.

Oh, what a tangled web we weave, when first we practice to deceive.

Mark didn't deserve this.

"I like you more than I've ever liked a man before in my life." Adrianna, Adele, it didn't matter who was talking. The words were the absolute truth. And they felt right.

His glance was intimate. She could feel it clear to her toes. And everywhere else, too.

"That sounds promising."

"I'm just not ready for anything more than friends." So true. And he'd be in Shelter Valley for a long, long time. She was out of there as soon as she was done with Will. She had to be.

In her psyche, Shelter Valley was synonymous with her father. She'd gotten that much out of counseling. And her recent nightmares, the visions haunting her, the breakdown she'd had out here on the patio with Mark, were all proof that she was not psychologically healthy here.

Shelter Valley was not a shelter to her. The town imprisoned her in a past that could debilitate her.

"I'm not asking for more than friends." Mark's reply was slow in coming, like he was choosing his words carefully.

"But tonight you said—"

"I said that I'm falling for you. Not that I'm asking you to do anything about that."

"I just..." *Be honest where you can. You have to give him that.* The little voice inside of her blared inside her mind. To keep her word with Will, she had to lie to Mark. Except where it didn't involve Will.

"I'm…not opposed…to something between us," she said carefully, growing moist in intimate places as she revealed herself. "I also know that I can't get involved in a relationship right now. I don't want to lead you on and then not be able to follow through."

"Define relationship."

Holding the edges of her robe together at her throat, she stared at him.

"You said you can't get involved in a relationship," he repeated her words back to her. "But we already have a relationship. We're two people who are relating—even if it's just as neighbors."

She frowned. He was confusing her. No, he was asking for a clarity she didn't have. And there was so much she couldn't say.

Addy thought about after Will's trouble was resolved. She'd be hightailing it out of Shelter Valley. Could she and Mark have a long-distance relationship? Would he want to? Would she?

Would he ever want to speak with her again when he found out she'd been lying to him? He was a man of honor. Honesty was so important to him —as it was to her.

Would he understand that she'd been honoring Will?

And what happened if he didn't?

The answer became clear to her.

"I can't promise anything more than this moment," she told him, and felt something settle inside of her.

"Fair enough. I can't, either."

"What about Ella?"

"I haven't heard from her."

"Are you still texting her?"

"Not since you agreed to have dinner with me."

"I'm not always going to be living next door to you, even if I keep going to Montford. This place is kind of expensive and…" No, she wasn't going to weave a more tangled web than she absolutely had to.

"I have no idea what my future holds," he told her. "And no money or time to date."

"Okay. Good. No promises or commitment."

"Just an understanding that we mean something to each other in the here and now."

"Right." Could she do this? Was it right?

She'd already shared more of her true self with Mark than she'd ever given to anyone else. He knew her deepest secrets.

Just not her surface one.

Surely that would be enough. If and when he found out the truth.

"So…not to be crude, but does the here and now include sex?" He hadn't been kidding about that honesty.

She was so hot. Her body throbbed.

"We're mature adults. With…natural…needs," he added.

"Could we, um, take that under advisement?" Oh,

hell, she was talking like a lawyer. Because she was one. Because he was talking about sex and Adele couldn't have sex. Only Adrianna could.

"I'd advise us to go on another date," Mark's tone was low, sexy. He was half grinning.

"And see what happens?"

"Yes."

"When?"

"Tomorrow night? I'm off at eight. We could meet right here. Have a late picnic…"

Her stomach filled with exquisite butterflies, and she nodded.

His gaze held hers.

They didn't need to see what was going to happen. They both knew.

MARK WAS SITTING on a rock in the courtyard of the cactus jelly plant on Saturday, eating his lunch alongside his lab partner who sat, mostly silent, on another rock. There were tables. Mark just preferred the rocks—they seemed to fit with the mountains towering around them in the distance.

"So I tell Abe I'm going to work, and he starts to cry," Jon said, breaking the silence that had allowed Mark to fantasize about the night ahead.

"Did you take him to Little Spirits?"

"Yeah."

"I thought you said he likes it there."

"He loves it there. Except on Saturdays. He threw a fit last Saturday when I tried to drop him off for a couple of hours. But the woman who runs the program, Bonnie Nielson, is the greatest. She held him and he calmed down pretty quick. I've found most of the women in Shelter Valley are pretty phenomenal."

"You got a girlfriend?" It wasn't a topic they'd gotten around to in class.

"Nope. No time. No takers, either.

"Anyway, Abe's crying, so I tell him I'm going to school and he stops. Instantly. Like how does a two-year-old know the difference between work and school? And why would he care?"

He had no idea. Hadn't spent a lot of time around kids. "Maybe he just didn't like the change," he said, thinking that Addy would make a great mom someday. Kids needed someone soft-spoken and nurturing to guide them through the minefield of temptations and disappointments that were part and parcel of growing up.

"Yeah, maybe." Jon bit into his second bologna sandwich and Mark went back to pretending that he wasn't giving every single spare thought to his new neighbor.

The ring of his cell phone interrupted him this time. Dropping his sandwich back in the brown paper sack Nonnie had put it in while he'd been in the shower that morning—after he'd made the requisite bacon and eggs for breakfast—Mark pulled the phone from his belt clip, checking the caller ID as he did so.

He'd expected to see Nonnie's number, but the screen displayed an Arizona area code. Nonnie's pay-by-the-minute cell was still a West Virginia exchange. Addy's was Colorado. "Hello?"

"Mark Heber?"

"Yeah. Who's this?"

"Shelter Valley EMT, Mr. Heber. I'm sorry to inform you that we have your grandmother…"

His phone beeped, signaling another incoming call. Briefly pulling the phone away from his ear, Mark checked to see who was calling him.

Addy.

"Where are you taking her?"

"She's refusing to go anywhere, sir. But her blood pressure is dangerously low and—"

"Put her on," Mark interrupted, his tone harsh.

"Markie-boy?" Not two seconds had passed.

"Go with them, Nonnie."

"No, Markie-boy…" He heard short, quick breaths. "If I'm going to die…" More breaths. "I'm doin' it right here. …"

Standing in the direct sun, he stared at the mountains, his free hand clutched around his lunch bag. "You are not going to die, Nonnie. It's not time. I'm not there. You go with them, do exactly as they say, and I'll meet you at the hospital."

"I'm…not afraid…"

"Give me your word, Nonnie. You can't die without me." He wasn't yelling, but it was as close as he got to it with her. His heart pounded and he felt frozen to the ground.

He'd get to her. He'd fix this.

"Nonnie?"

"Mark? It's me, Addy."

Instant relief flooded him. And then the fear was back. Mark spoke in rapid staccato. "Make her go with them, Addy. They can give her something for her blood pressure."

"I'm going with her, Mark. I left the room long enough to call you and that's when she started refusing to go to the hospital. I'm back now. They're already carrying her out. I'll ride in the ambulance and meet you there."

He squinted, dropped his lunch into the trash and reached into his pocket for his keys. "Where are they taking her?"

She named a hospital in Phoenix. He had no idea where it was but knew that the GPS on his phone would get him there by the quickest route.

He told Addy so, thanked her for being there and ran for the parking lot. He'd call his boss on the way.

The last thing he remembered as he turned the truck toward Phoenix was Jon wishing him good luck.

Luck be damned. He and Nonnie had been through low blood pressure before. As long as her brain still sent signals and her heart still ticked, they'd sail through this challenge, too.

He never should have listened to her, though. Never

should have moved her across the country. She was eighty-one years old. With multiple sclerosis. The trip had obviously been too much for her.

CHAPTER SEVENTEEN

By the time Mark got to the hospital, Nonnie's IV had been pumped with enough medication to get her blood pressure back to normal. Her heartbeat was steady and relatively strong. Her blood work had come back okay. Addy was smiling as she greeted him at the door of the emergency room, waiting to take him back to the cubicle where Nonnie was dozing on and off.

"She's waiting for you to take her home," she told Mark, relieved almost to the point of giddiness to be able to tell him that his grandmother was all right.

"She's been released already?" he asked, his gaze seeming to devour her face, as though searching for any sign that she was hiding bad news.

"No, they'd like her to stay overnight, but she's insisting on going home."

He nodded. "I'll talk to the doctor…"

"He already told her that if she has someone who's willing to sit with her all night, and to check her blood pressure every hour, he'll send her home. You're going to have a hard time changing her mind now."

Addy had decided that she'd be the one to stay up all night if necessary. She knew how to read a blood pressure gauge. And she didn't have to work the next day.

"I have no intention of changing her mind," Mark said. "I just want to know if I'm changing her medication at all before we get her out of here."

Addy didn't know why she was surprised. Of course Mark would go the extra mile for Nonnie.

He'd give up his life for her.

Because he was that kind of guy.

"YOU DON'T HAVE to stay," Mark said. It was two in the morning and he and Addy had been sitting on his couch, watching Netflix and taking turns checking on Nonnie every fifteen minutes. Except when they woke her to check her blood pressure, his grandmother had been sleeping the whole time.

"Of course I'm staying," Abby said. "You nap for an hour, and then I will, just like we said."

"Seriously, I'm used to this. I won't fall asleep."

"You've done this before? Sat up all night? Checking on her every hour?"

He was tired, but fine. The important thing was that Nonnie was out of danger. "I was sixteen the first time her blood pressure dropped. She was unconscious at first, but as soon as they got her back up and running, she refused to stay at the hospital. She insisted that I was too young to be left home alone. Too many temptations."

"Like you'd have gotten into trouble with her in the hospital sick."

"She wasn't really worried about me getting into trouble. She was worried that the state would come and take me away from her if she wasn't well enough to care for me."

"So what did you do?"

"I charmed a young nurse into showing me how to use a blood pressure cuff, and then marched into Nonnie's room and showed the doctor that I was fully capable of taking care of her at home. I was already nearly six feet tall and clearly able to lift her. It didn't hurt that I had my driver's license in case of an emergency."

Addy was sharing the couch with him, but she hadn't touched him. He hadn't touched her, either. He knew better than to play with fire.

"I'll never forget the look on Nonnie's face when I proved to the doctor that I knew what I was doing. It was the first time there was a switch in our roles, and as a guy who'd been fighting to prove his manhood, the moment was sweet. I also think that day was the first time she realized that I would always be there for her, able to take care of her, no matter what."

"Was that when she was diagnosed with multiple sclerosis?"

"No, her blood pressure problems aren't directly related to the MS, although both can be triggered by stress. The MS diagnosis came about three months later, after a lot of tests that didn't turn up anything else."

That had not been a good day. The day he'd sat

with Nonnie and heard she had an incurable disease had been the first time he'd realized he was going to be alone in the world someday.

Completely alone.

BY MONDAY, NONNIE was back to her usual self—maybe even a bit better, since she'd been forced to rest for forty-eight hours. Though Addy hadn't known the woman a long time, she felt pounds lighter as she let herself into her side of the duplex that afternoon after coming home from class and spending the next hour visiting with Mark's grandmother.

Thoughts of the night ahead were turning her joints to jelly and she had work to do. She also had no idea whether she'd even see Mark that night. He was off work at eight and probably had homework to do.

But if she did see him…

Would he…?

She'd driven out to the big-box store after class and purchased birth control. Every time she thought of it nestled in the bottom of her purse, her nerves got a bit more jittery.

Oh, she'd had sex before. But none of her lovers had moved her to the point of fantasizing about them nonstop.

Time to focus. To work.

So far she'd neither experienced nor witnessed any sign of preferential treatment in any of her classes, at the Montford library, the computer lab, or with campus food services. She'd signed up for the drama club, which was due to have its first meeting later that week, and she was considering rushing a sorority. She'd heard from the editor of the school newspaper. They were going to publish her article, right next to one with an opposing viewpoint.

Handled professionally.

Just as she'd have advised.

But the Randi Parsons Foster situation could be a problem. A baby sister who called in favors for athletic scholarships didn't look good on a university president's record. Nor did gross overspending without more than a written reprimand attached. Not when accompanied by a promotion to a head position before the age of thirty.

She still had files upon files to weed through. The rest of the personnel files. Financials. Student records.

She'd made it as far as the *S*s in the personnel files and was determined to make it through the whole alphabet before she'd allow herself to head outside for a nightcap.

Matthew Sheffield. He was right after Barbara Schmitt. Hired at thirty-two as technical coordinator for the performing arts center thirteen years before, Sheffield was currently listed as the center's director, a position he'd held for nine years. The quick promotion for a man in his early thirties was unusual enough for her to want to look into the situation more closely. The fact that his file was sealed had her even more curious.

Because she worked only the cases she handpicked and because she had her own practice rather than belonging to a firm, Addy couldn't afford paralegals to do her research for her. Which meant she paid for access to secure information sites.

Signing on to a secure site where her law degree allowed her membership, she quickly found Matt Sheffield's birth certificate and his known addresses. From there she moved on to other legal documents. The man had been married only once, to his current wife, Phyllis Sheffield, sister of Caroline Strickland, all of whom currently resided in Shelter Valley. Caroline Strickland—her landlord?

There'd been another Sheffield on the employee roster. Flipping quickly between documents, she confirmed that Phyllis Sheffield, formerly Phyllis Langford, was a psychology professor at Montford. And she remembered something else, too.

The file she needed was somewhere…on the right-hand corner of the table. Tory Evans Sanders's file. The woman who'd impersonated her older sister and taught English for a semester before confessing what she'd done—the woman who'd never been charged—had lived with Phyllis Langford when she'd first come to town. Phyllis and Tory's older sister, Christine, had been close friends. Phyllis had been responsible for Christine getting the job at Montford—all according to the newspaper article Will Parsons had written for the campus newspaper the semester following Tory's tenure there. A follow-up to the original article published when Tory's duplicity was first discovered.

None of which meant anything…

Phyllis Sheffield and Becca Parsons were friends—another fact she'd learned through numerous local articles regarding social functions involving the town's mayor.

Sheffield's file was sealed for a reason. On a hunch she called up criminal records. Three Matt Sheffields came up in response to her search. The first was eliminated by age and race. The second by age and location. The Matt Sheffield she was looking for wasn't twenty-seven and living in Alaska.

The third listing fit.

Addy's heart sank.

INTENDING TO STAY home from work Monday afternoon if he needed to, Mark pulled into the driveway right after his last class. Nonnie was in the living room sitting at the computer.

"What're you doing home?" she asked.

"I live here." Her color was good. And she was wearing one of her favorite dresses—a tie-dyed cotton thing. She and a couple of her friends had gone through a tie-dye faze about ten years ago. She'd made some T-shirts for Mark, too. They went straight into his drawer, and more recently into storage in Bierly.

"You're supposed to be at work."

"My shift doesn't start for an hour." He paused. "Will you be okay here by yourself?"

He bent to kiss her cheek. She lifted her face and then said, "Don't worry so much. And don't be bothering me right now. This is the first time I've had all week to play and I'm up two tokens."

"What do you want for dinner?"

"The leftover chicken salad that's in the refrigerator."

"Chicken salad?"

"Addy brought it over. We had it for lunch."

Addy. His body got a little hard just hearing her name. And he was standing in his kitchen talking to his grandmother.

Would he see her tonight?

"And if I didn't want the chicken salad twice in a row, which I do, I'd have some of the goulash that Veronica dropped off this morning. Or the vegetable soup Becca Parsons left," Nonnie was saying, without any signs of breathlessness.

"Becca Parsons?" He tried to focus on the conversation at hand, not the one going on in his brain. "Why do I know that name?"

"She's the mayor of Shelter Valley. Can you beat that? The town mayor bringing soup to an old barmaid like me?" Nonnie chuckled. "I called Bertie and told her. She cackled so loud she 'bout burst my eardrum."

Bertrude Green had been one of Nonnie's best friends for as long as Mark could remember. And he didn't share his grandmother's humor. "Why shouldn't the mayor serve you, you old bat? You're royalty. And as far as I've seen, Shelter Valley doesn't have any railroad tracks for you to get on the wrong side of so I suggest you don't try." But if she did try, he'd be right there, cleaning up the mess. Nonnie's fire was a part of her.

"Nah, we're starting a new life, boy. I told you that. In Shelter Valley, the Hebers are respectable folks."

"They're respectable in Bierly, too." To anyone who mattered.

She turned from the computer. "You worked your ass off to make it so, Markie-boy, but it's not right. You having to try so hard to prove what most people just take for granted—that you're an honorable man."

"I don't work harder than anyone in Bierly. Times are difficult."

"You did and you know it. Just to prove you was good enough. And you was better than all of 'em."

Inside he cringed. On the outside, he smiled and helped himself to a glass of chocolate milk.

"Like I said, Nonnie, you're royalty."

"Good thing you ain't as dumb as you are blind," his grandmother snorted. "Now get off to work and leave me be for a bit. A girl can't get any peace around here."

"You're sure you're okay?"

"Do I look okay?"

"Yeah. But that doesn't mean anything other than you're a great actress."

Flinging out her arm she asked, "You want to take my blood pressure? Just to make sure I'm not lying?"

She was fine. Or she wouldn't have offered. He pulled his keys out of the pocket of his jeans. "You win, crotchety old lady, I'm out of here," he said, kissing her on the head as he passed.

And prayed all the way to work that he wouldn't be subjected to a repeat of the last time he'd been there. A guy could only take so many of those calls.

MATT SHEFFIELD HAD been in prison. Found guilty of statutory rape by a jury in Flagstaff, Arizona, and sentenced to ten years.

As she scrubbed the shower stall in her bathroom, Addy wrapped her mind around what she knew and tried to work off the tension that the knowing had caused. Water wasn't just for listening to. It was for cooking, providing nourishment. It was for drinking, quenching thirst. And it was for cleaning. Taking away the grime of the world.

The kitchen was already sparkling. Faucet, a shiny silver without a single smudge. Beige sink looking like new. Formica counters smooth and spotless. Floor grout off-white, as it should be.

And Nonnie was fine, too; she'd checked on her every hour on the hour.

Spray from the shower splashed against the walls she'd scrubbed, filling the floor until it could slide down the drain. It splashed her hair and arms. The front of her T-shirt, the thighs of her jeans. She didn't feel cleaner.

Mark's front door closed. She felt the vibration and heard the muffled slam over the sound of the shower.

She'd heard him come in minutes before, so he must be leaving again. He'd be on his way to work.

Would he be joining her outside that evening? Was he wondering if she'd be there?

Hoping that she'd offer him more than tea?

Down on her hands and knees, she scrubbed at the tile. Rinsed and moved toward the garden tub a couple of feet away. She'd never had a garden tub before.

She liked it. And had already begun thinking about the remodel she'd do on her bathroom when she got home. It would be her present to herself for having made it through her time in Shelter Valley. With what Will was paying her, she could afford a new bathtub.

Statutory rape. Before coming to Shelter Valley, before going to prison, Matt Sheffield had been a junior high and high school theater teacher. One who, in his second year of teaching, at age twenty-four, had been convicted of having sex with a fourteen-year-old student in his office after hours. The girl had gotten pregnant.

Addy's tub was clean. She wiped it out every time she used it and wished she hadn't. She needed more to scrub. The toilet didn't take long. The double sinks were wiped clean each morning, as well. Her old toothbrush in one hand and a bowl of clean, hot water in the other, Addy moved on to the grout on the bath-room floor.

Six months after the girl's baby was born, a boy, a paternity test proved that he was not Matt Shef-field's son. It didn't prove that Matt had not had sex with his student.

Sheffield's attorney motioned to appeal the con-viction against him. Based on the new paternity evi-dence, a new trial had been granted.

Addy was a lawyer. She knew how these things worked. With a couple of phone calls and a pleading for expediency, she already had the trial transcript downloaded on her computer. She'd read the perti-nent parts.

Sheffield had spent a lot of time alone with the girl. According to the girl's testimony during the trial, Sheffield had told her that any man would be hon-ored to have her as his wife. He'd praised her often, telling her that she had more to offer than most of the people he knew. He'd led the child to believe that he found her desirable. She'd told him she had a headache. He'd given her some pills. Told her she could use his office couch to take a nap. When she'd woken up, he'd been on the couch with her. Holding her in his arms.

The story itself, while sickening, wasn't shock-ing to Addy. She worked in educational law and the reality was that teachers behaving inappropriately with their students was not as uncommon as people would like to believe.

Matt Sheffield was found not guilty at his second trial. The man was set free. But his getting off did not in any way mean that he hadn't had sex with his young female student. It only meant that the prosecutor, given the fact that the girl had lied about previous lovers during the first trial, had been unable to convince a jury beyond reasonable doubt that Matt had sex with her. There'd been no evidence, only her word against his. And she'd admittedly been unconscious through the alleged act.

Matt Sheffield would never be able to teach in the public school system again. But he'd completed the education required to teach at the college level and moved to Shelter Valley. Addy scrubbed the floor until her nails were broken and her knuckles were scraped.

Montford's hiring policies required that Will Parsons verify a criminal check on every single employee at the university. Will had to have known about Matt Sheffield's criminal history, the exact charges that had been filed against the man. The years he'd spent in prison.

Yet he'd still hired the man to teach eighteen-year-old girls.

Addy sat up on her knees, her soapy hands holding a toothbrush in midair.

Wait a minute…

Dropping the toothbrush, she hurried from the bathroom, wiping her hands on her T-shirt as she made her way to her computer. A few quick keystrokes, a couple of returns, and she was back to the university's personnel files, looking up Phyllis Sheffield's history at Montford. The psychologist had been hired to start the fall 2001 semester. She'd given birth to twins, Calvin and Clarissa, in early June 2002. A few more clicks. Matt Sheffield was the father of twins, Calvin and Clarissa, born in June 2002.

He'd fathered Phyllis's children less than a month after the woman had moved to Shelter Valley from the East Coast. Which sounded to Addy as if the man hadn't learned how to be circumspect with his fly, although he'd chosen a conquest who was of legal age this time. The criminal charges should have been enough to prevent Will from hiring the man. Fathering children with a coworker he hardly knew should have, at the very least, been further cause for concern. But it was at that time that Will Parsons had approved a promotion for Matt Sheffield from technical coordinator to director of the performing arts center.

Addy added another task to her list. When she showed up at drama club later that week, she was going to come as a femme fatale, ready to give the club's adviser, Matt Sheffield, anything he wanted.

CHAPTER EIGHTEEN

THERE WAS A MARKED energy in Mark's step as he made his way to his car after his shift Monday evening. Jon's supervisor had looked Mark up to let him know the man he'd referred was performing beyond expectation. He hadn't received an emergency call regarding his grandmother. He had, in fact, had a call from the woman herself to tell him good-night—and not to bug her with a pressure check when he came in from work. She'd also told him to drive safely on his way home—Nonnie's version of "I love you."

And…he was heading to the chair on his back patio.

After a shower. No way was he showing up smelling like cactus jelly. Or sweat.

It was too hot for jeans, too, he decided as he climbed into the truck and rolled down his window. September in Arizona might not be as hot as August or June or July, but it was still close to eighty degrees—and that was after the sun went down. He hoped he'd thrown his basketball shorts into the washer with his work clothes. And a T-shirt that matched would be nice, too.…

The peal of his cell phone broke the peacefulness

inside his truck. Tensing, he grabbed the phone off the holster on his belt, his gaze going instantly to the caller ID flashing on the screen. He'd heard from Nonnie less than an hour ago. If she'd failed to put on her nighttime undergarments before bed she could have tried to get herself to the bathroom and had problems....

Nonnie wasn't calling. Nor was it the paramedics, or Addy. He pulled off to answer, anyway.

"Ella?" Holding his phone to his ear, he tried to ease the dread seeping into his gut.

"Hey."

That was it after all this time? "Hey"? Not that it had been years. It just felt like that to Mark. So much had changed. He'd changed.

Just as she'd known he would.

Guilt fell like dead weight over him.

"How are you?" Lame. But he didn't know what else to say. Why was she calling?

Because all she'd needed was for him to quit trying? Playing hard to get worked sometimes. But he hadn't been playing. And wouldn't. Thoughts tumbled one after the other. He wasn't a game-playing type of guy, Ella knew that....

"I'm okay." She didn't sound normal. "I wasn't sure you'd even speak to me."

"Why wouldn't I?"

"The way I treated you there at the end. Before you left. Going out with Rick. It wasn't right."

"Sure it was. You told me what you were doing.

If you'd done it behind my back, that wouldn't have been right."

Two minutes ago he'd been heading home, to his new home, hoping like hell that he was going to make love with his new neighbor.

"I ignored all the texts you sent."

"You told me you didn't want to talk to me." And he hadn't wanted to harass her. He'd just wanted her to know that he wasn't leaving her. That he'd be there for her if she needed him. He'd wanted to honor the promises he'd made to her. "Anyway, what's done is done." Or was it? God, he hoped it was. "Tell me what's going on. How's everyone doing? How's work?"

He stopped short of asking her how she was doing, personally. It made him ashamed as hell, but he didn't want to know.

"I'm… I don't know how to tell you this."

It sounded as if she was crying. He stiffened, his free hand wrapped tight around the steering wheel.

"You can tell me anything, Ella, you know that."

Was she getting married? And feeling guilty? How did he tell her he was fine with that?

"I know. And I will tell you. It's just that, it's so good to hear your voice and…"

She *was* crying. Because she was suddenly missing him? Doubting the decisions she'd made?

Ella had always come to him first before deciding anything major. Which was fine with him. Even now. The crying…that was new. …

"Are you drinking, Ella?"

"No."

"Not even one or two?"

"No! Of course not! I just...talk to me, Mark. How's school? Are you working? What do you think of Arizona?"

She didn't ask how Nonnie was doing.

"School's fine. I got a job at a plant here. Arizona's different, but not bad." The desert was growing on him, but he didn't think Ella would understand if he told her so. The way the shades of brown took on life was something you had to experience. And he was certain she didn't want to hear that he liked his new life. "What's up, Ella? I'll help if I can, you know that."

Was she in some kind of trouble?

He glanced at his watch. Almost nine o'clock. Would Addy wait for him? "Is it work?" he asked. "If there's a problem at the plant I can make a few calls. You in trouble there?" She'd been late a couple of times. Once more meant a write-up.

Ella wasn't the type to cry over a write-up. Or even over being fired. She took life in stride. Didn't get real worked up about anything.

Like him leaving. She just found someone else. Even before he was gone. Life always had options.

"Work's fine. What kind of plant are you at?"

"Cactus jelly. I'm doing the same kind of work I was at home." Home. An odd term for a place that seemed so far away.

"You're supervising?"

"Yeah."

"How's the weather? Is it really hot?"

"Not too bad, eighties and nineties, but it really is a dry heat like they say. Nineties seem like seventies back home. You wouldn't believe the difference it makes not having all that humidity weighing you down." Cars whizzed past on the highway leading into town and a new wave of guilt assailed him at his eagerness to be among them. So he kept talking.

"From what I hear, getting here in September was a good thing. It never dropped below a hundred the entire month of August." He pictured Addy, sitting in her chair, watching her fountain. Had she noticed that his truck wasn't in the driveway?

"Maybe I should come out. For a visit. I've got vacation time coming…"

Ella, here? "Sure, Ella, if that's what you want to do." Ella staying next to Addy? Even more outrageous, Ella and Nonnie in the same house? "I'm busy with classes and work so I wouldn't have a lot of time to show you the sights, but you could do some exploring on your own."

He supposed she could walk to town and back, maybe get a bike… A month ago he would've been happy enough with the prospect.

Or at least, not as unhappy about it.

"You think Nonnie would give us hell if I slept in your bed with you?"

"I'd take the couch." For his sake, not his grandmother's. Nonnie was no prude. Still, she was eighty-one years old. It wasn't right to flaunt sex in her face.

Sex. He wanted it with Addy. Not Ella.

"Why the sudden change of heart, Ella? I thought you wanted nothing to do with Shelter Valley. Bierly's your home, you said." She'd been willing to toss him aside because of it.

She hadn't even seemed to consider the idea that there might be some benefit to him getting an education. Not that he could blame her. He hadn't believed it, either.

Who'd have guessed that he, Mark Heber, would ever take to schooling? He was the dropout.

"I'm pregnant, Mark."

Traffic disappeared. The night disappeared. His dash lights were all that were left.

"Did you hear me?"

"Yeah, I heard you." He could barely keep the phone to his ear. He just wasn't processing.

"I want to have this baby."

Of course. That was a given. Ella didn't need and wouldn't want an abortion. She wanted to be a mother. Wanted a family.

"A couple of months ago you asked me to marry you. Does that still stand?"

Ella…having a baby.

"I can't leave Shelter Valley." The air in the truck was suffocating. He couldn't see the mountains. Couldn't see a way out. "I'd owe too much money."

Money that he was going to need.

"You haven't asked if the baby's yours."

He didn't want to know. "Is it?"

"Of course it is. I'm two and a half months along."

They'd gone tent camping. She'd forgotten her pills. He hadn't had a condom. She'd said she was safe. That missing one pill wouldn't matter.

He couldn't remember if she'd had a period after that.

I want kids now, while I'm still young enough for them to think I'm cool. Ella's words came back to him. From the night she'd broken up with him. The first time he'd ever heard them.

But maybe she'd been planning this all along—from the camping trip on. Even before they'd found out about the scholarship.

Someone should really turn the air conditioner on in the truck.

Had she known that she was pregnant the night she'd told him she was going to the pig roast with Rick? Or at least suspected?

"What about Rick?"

"We broke up."

Because she found out she was pregnant with Mark's baby?

"Did you sleep with him?"

"Yes."

So he could still sleep with Addy. No—what in the hell was he thinking? He didn't know what to think.

Or do.

"Does anyone else know?" Was he pond scum for

doubting her? For thinking that the baby might not be his?

"Just my mom."

Dot and he had gotten along. Mostly because Dot liked anyone with pants who'd take care of her daughter. "What's she think?"

"She's excited about having a grandbaby. She's been waitin' a long time." Ella's drawl sounded odd. Unfamiliar.

"And the doctor thinks it's okay for you to fly?" Were his doubts about the baby's paternity wishful thinking?

"I was going to take the bus out," Ella said. "It'd be fun, like a road trip. But I'll need you to drive me around when I get there. Lord knows Nonnie and I can't be spending all day together in that duplex you texted about."

Ella had lost her license to a drunk-driving charge before she and Mark had started dating. She had to make it through another year of sobriety before she could get it back.

Biting back a retort, Mark stared out of the windshield into the darkness, as though the desert he couldn't see would have answers he couldn't find.

"You have that much time off work?"

"I can take that family medical leave thing, can't I?" Things just kept getting worse and worse. "It's not like I'll be able to stand up all day as I get bigger, or even be able to reach the rods."

Ella worked at a machine that required adjusting

rods in quick succession. But that didn't mean she couldn't learn something new.

Not that he wanted the mother of his child doing manual labor while she was carrying his baby. But they weren't financially prepared. They had to have money coming in.

And it might not be his baby.

His baby.

Not too long ago he'd thought that was all he wanted out of life. His Ella. Them to get married someday. To grow old in Bierly.

And, eventually, in the distant future, for her to have his baby.

How could all of that have changed in such a short time?

"I don't like the idea of you traveling out here on a bus all alone."

"Mom said she'd come with me. If she don't like it there, she can fly back."

"What about her job?" He could give up his bedroom to Ella and Dot. Move out to the couch. They could stretch the food budget.

He just didn't want to.

"She can take a leave. She'd have to, anyway, once the baby comes, to help out for a bit. But with hairdressing it's not that big a deal. She can always do her regulars from home. Or go in after hours. It's not like Gilda would care. We could get assistance if we needed to. Food stamps and all."

Ella's mom had had the same chair at Gilda's Hair Salon since he and Ella had been kids.

"And if we stay in Arizona, she can get a job out there. Everyone needs haircuts. That way Mom can drive and we can drop you at work or school."

He couldn't picture Dot at the Valley Salon and Spa a couple doors down from Harmon Hardware and Electronics. He'd never been in there, but even from the outside, with its pretty curtains and fancy gold lettering, he could tell it was nothing like Gilda's.

But there was always Phoenix.

"When were you thinking about coming?"

"I'm not sure. I have another doctor's appointment in a few weeks. They're going to do an ultrasound."

A test to look at the baby. His baby? It was someone's son or daughter. He should identify with it. Care.

"Is everything okay?" he asked, more because he thought he should than because he wanted to know. He wished the child Ella carried good health. He just didn't feel any ownership of it.

"Yeah. It's standard now to do the tests."

Standard tests. They were covered by insurance. Mark sat up straighter, drawing a long breath of air into his lungs. "Your insurance will cover the pregnancy."

She had to stay in Bierly at least until the baby was born. Had to stay employed at the plant. What a relief.

"I know."

"You can't quit until after the baby comes. We

aren't married yet and my insurance benefits won't cover you until we are. Even then, they won't cover pregnancy until after you've been on the policy for a year." He'd been able to switch from his old plan to the jelly plant's group insurance plan.

"It's okay, Mark." Her voice softened. "You don't have to do all your worrying and planning up front. I'm not going to quit. Maybe later I will, but not now. I've got over a month's vacation saved up and then I'll check with HR to see about that leave thing."

"FMLA is only for twelve weeks," he said slowly, his mind coming out of its deep freeze. The Family Medical Leave Act. He'd had several employees take advantage of the government program.

"Bonnie took off almost her whole pregnancy and two months after, too, because she breast-fed."

"HR approved the leave. I'm not saying you can't get it. Just that the family leave you're talking about only covers twelve weeks. So you can get more time off, if the company approves, but you probably would only get paid for the three months. The rest would be without pay."

"But they'd hold my job, right? They did Bonnie's."

"If they approve the leave, then yes, they'll hold your job. The family medical leave through the government is a given."

"That'd be okay, then. Wouldn't it? I mean, it's not like I make a ton. Mom already said I should give up my apartment and move back in with her."

The back of his neck throbbed. He'd worked a

machine for most of the night, making up for production time lost by a new hire who was struggling. Mark saw potential in the older man and wanted to give him a little more time to catch on.

"Giving up the apartment's probably a good idea," he said now. As he remembered it, the lease specifically disallowed children. "And then we can talk about you coming out here."

"You don't sound angry."

"I'm not angry." How could he be? If she really was pregnant with his baby, he'd done this to himself.

"But you ain't happy."

"I... There's a lot to think about, Ella." More than she knew. Way more than she knew. "I'm just hearing about this for the first time. You've got to give me some time to let it sink in."

"I just...I thought...I knew you'd be shocked, and all, but I thought, once you knew, you'd be happy. It's our baby, Mark. Yours and mine. We made him."

Him. She couldn't know the sex yet, but that child could very well be male. A son.

He tried to picture it. To think about holding a child. There was nothing there. He should feel something.

"I have to be able to support a child, Ella," he said. Finances were the only thoughts he could focus on. "I've already used up a full semester's tuition and there are no refunds on that. I've paid the lease for the first semester and accepted a check for living expenses. If I quit school, I'd owe all of that back immediately. I just don't have the money." Not even if he cashed in his 401K retirement plan. Not after he took the hits for early withdrawal and taxes. They'd have some left, but not nearly enough to sustain him through an emergency with Nonnie...

He'd emptied his savings account getting him and Nonnie out here and settled in.

He wanted to sleep with another woman.

"I thought about what I said that night you asked me to marry you." Her tone was back to the one she used at work now and he wondered what she was hiding. "About loving Bierly and never leaving. I was wrong. I can move there, Mark. For us. For the baby. As long as I know it's only for the time you're in school and then we can come back here."

She hadn't asked how Nonnie was. Still.

Nonnie. Oh, God in heaven, Nonnie. Ella said only her mother knew about the baby, but if that was even true, it wouldn't be for long. *Telephone. Telegraph. Tell Dot.* He remembered the joke he'd heard around town more than once after he started dating Ella.

And once people in Bierly knew, Nonnie would find out. Between Facebook and email, Nonnie still knew everything there was to know about everyone in the town where she'd been born and raised. The woman and her computer were a dangerous combination.

"I need some time to think this through, Ella." He tried to relax the tension radiating through him. "There's a lot to consider."

"You taking back that offer of marriage, Mark?"

"You turned me down."

"Well, now I ain't. Please, Mark. Don't leave me in the lurch here."

He'd told her he'd be back. No matter what. Even after she wouldn't answer his texts, he'd told her he'd be back.

"It's late there, Ella." Almost midnight by his calculation. "Why don't you get some rest and I'll call you tomorrow. We can talk about everything then." His own drawl sounded loudly in his ears. Did he always sound that way? Did Abby think he was some backward hick?

Did he think that of Ella?

Growing colder and sicker by the second, Mark felt like a fool for ever thinking that he could really change his life. He was a high school dropout from Bierly. Always had been. Always would be.

And that was okay. Only problem had been him thinking that he could escape.

He'd been happy before. He would be again.

CHAPTER NINETEEN

ADDY FINISHED HER TEA. Took the glass into the kitchen for a refill and just happened to make it from the counter to the refrigerator by way of the living room window.

Mark's truck was still not in the driveway.

Working late? It wasn't impossible. With the time he'd missed that weekend, he'd want to make up hours if they were available.

And she had no right to be disappointed. They didn't even have plans to see each other. She'd just assumed.

Which was why she'd showered and slipped into a lacy white peasant blouse and her favorite jeans. And left off the bra she normally wore with the outfit.

Back in the kitchen, she poured herself half a glass of wine. Just enough to make her sleepy. To take the edge off the nervous tension running through her.

She'd been counting on seeing him. On giving in to the desire that had been haunting her every waking moment.

She'd been the one to insist that they could only exist in the moment. Because she was Adele.

Her emotions were strangling her tonight. Creating a dichotomy within her that had to be soothed so she could sleep. Or work.

Work. Her head hurt when she thought about work. What was she going to do if it turned out that Will had committed litigable acts? How could she help him if she knew he'd done wrong?

How could he have changed so much?

Or had he? She'd been six the last time she'd seen Will Parsons. He'd been twenty-eight or twenty-nine. What did she really know about his character? Other than the fact that he'd been kind enough to spend time with his ten-year-old sister and an impressionable orphan?

If only she could talk to Will's wife—not as Adele, but as Adrianna, the little girl who'd convinced herself that the childless couple would see how much she adored them and want to adopt her.

Water. She needed her fountain.

Its flow was endless. Even in the desert. Water sustained life. A nearby mine was flooded with it. Water recycled. It got dirty and came out clean.

Staring at the fountain from the patio doors, she remembered the day she'd brought it home. The first day she'd met Mark. The sight of those muscled legs walking across the couple of feet of lawn toward her. His low, half-amused rumble as he'd offered his help. The way his upper arms had tensed when he lifted the rock basin out of the box…

A door closed.

Her heart pounding in her chest, Addy moved only to take a small sip of wine. Mark was home.

HE WAS NOT GOING outside. He couldn't trust himself to do so. All the way home, Mark had talked to himself, preparing for the moment when he'd unlock the door to the duplex and step inside.

Check on Nonnie. That was his first responsibility. The old woman lay flat on her back in bed, her chair at the edge of the mattress beside her. Her cell phone lay perched on the empty pillow next to her head.

He'd told her to keep it close and she had. He smiled.

She was a good woman. Deserved the best he could give her.

Closing the bedroom door softly, he stood outside for a long minute, fighting with himself.

Take a shower. That was second on his list. A long shower. First hot. And then cold. He was in no hurry. Had no place to be and no desire to lie in a dark bedroom and stare at the ceiling.

Dressed in silk basketball shorts and a clean T-shirt—presents to himself purchased with the small portion of his Christmas bonus he'd slated for savings the previous year—he left his flip-flops in his room and wandered barefoot to the kitchen. He wasn't going outside. Didn't need shoes.

He needed a beer. And poured himself a glass of milk instead. White, not chocolate. No caffeine.

A baby?

Him, a father?

He had to do the right thing. Had to make damn certain that he was the best dropout Bierly had ever seen.

Unlike his old man, the world would be a better place for him having lived in it.

Life didn't hand out happiness. A guy had to make his own.

Movement from the patio caught his eye.

Addy was out there.

Waiting for him.

Amazing, how her mere presence compelled him to want to talk to her. As though she could somehow make a difference to the news he'd just received, the mess he'd made. And to go to her under the circumstances, when he might be committed to another woman, was pure selfishness.

There was no point in making matters harder on himself by giving in to temptation. Sitting outside with Addy, sharing his distress, would be a small-picture choice—and make life harder in the long run when he had to shut her out to open the door to Ella.

He watched Addy lean forward on her chair toward the fountain, her forearms resting on her knees. She rubbed the back of her neck.

Talk about selfish…he'd been so wrapped up in his own woes, he hadn't even thought about what Abby might need. What if she'd had a bad day, too? Needed to talk to him?

What if she was hurting because he'd come on to

her and was now leaving her sitting out there without any explanation? She'd know he was home. Probably knew he was standing right there, just a few feet away from her, aware that she was outside. She'd have seen the light go on in his kitchen.

His milk glass in hand, Mark opened the sliding door.

HE'D GIVEN HER enough time to reassess. To analyze, overthink and talk herself out of the advisability of entering into any kind of intimate relationship with her kind and incredibly sexy neighbor.

She hadn't done so.

Her nipples hardened against the white cotton of her blouse. Mark's hands had been gentle, his touch assured, as he'd assembled the small tubular pieces of her fountain. Would they be as attentive to her body?

Would he want her tonight? Or be too tired after a long day of classes and work.

She took in his glass of milk. And then, raising her gaze to his face, crossed her arms over her chest. Her outfit was completely modest to the eye, but she felt far too exposed.

"Bad day?" she asked, wishing her wine wasn't on the table between them, signaling the more libatious evening she'd envisioned.

He stood looking at her for a few very long seconds before picking up his chair and setting it down next to her. "Long day." The way he said it, his reply sounded like an understatement.

"You didn't get a lot of sleep this weekend."

Looking slightly morose, he stared out at the yard. Of course, it was dark and most of the yard was in shadows.

"How's Nonnie?" It had only been an hour since she'd been next door.

"Fine. Asleep and breathing normally."

"She ate a good lunch. Even had seconds."

"Thirds," Mark said, sending her a weary smile. "I just noticed that the leftover chicken salad is gone from the fridge."

Gran had taught her how to make it. The secret was in the grapes, and using leeks instead of onion. "I left out the almonds and water chestnuts," she said aloud, wondering what was wrong with Mark. "I wasn't sure she should have them."

"She loves nuts. And she doesn't have any real dietary restrictions."

She turned her focus to the stream of water sluicing over river rock a few feet away and asked, "Have I done something to offend you?"

"Hell, no!" Her head swung his way at the exuberance of his reply and their gazes met for the first time since he'd appeared. Met and held.

"What's wrong?"

"For the first time in my life I really, really want something I can't have."

An odd statement coming from someone who'd grown up so poor he couldn't complete his education. Who'd been a working man when most boys were still kids.

"What do you want that you can't have?"

Their gazes were still locked and his vivid blue eyes were cooking up her insides.

"You."

Throat dry, she asked, "Why can't you have me?"

He broke eye contact, and Addy tensed. Something was definitely wrong.

He'd heard about her. Her mind filled in the blanks he was leaving.

Somehow her cover had been broken. He knew she'd been lying to him. And he wasn't going to forgive her.

She didn't blame him.

"I got a phone call on the way home tonight...."

Someone had called him to tell him about her? Who? Nonnie? The older woman was as sharp as they came. And spent more time on the internet than Addy did.

But what could Nonnie have found? There were no pictures of her on the internet. Nothing to tie her to her practice in Colorado. She'd searched for herself on Google, just to be sure, after Will and Sheriff Richards had both told her that they'd performed their own internet searches.

She didn't know what to say. And as a lawyer, she knew that the best defense was silence.

It wasn't as if she could explain. The reasons for her silence were still valid. Intact. No matter what

Will Parsons had done, or who he'd become. Until she had a chance to speak with him, or prove that he'd actually done something criminal, until she told him that she was done, then she was under personal oath to him.

Even if the whole town found out who she was, she still couldn't tell them why she'd pretended to be someone else.

"It was from Ella."

She stared. "Ella?" He'd heard from his ex-girl-friend? Had Mark told Ella about Adele? Was the woman jealous? Had she set out to find everything she could about the woman who was stealing Mark away from her? And...

No.

Wrapping her arms around her middle, Addy looked away from the man who'd grown to mean far too much to her in such a short span of time. She wasn't thinking rationally.

Mark's unusual silence spoke of a huge upset, but it didn't have to do with her.

That's when she remembered the house. She'd doubted Nonnie's assurance that an entire town would keep her secret from her grandson. Nonnie must not have accounted for Mark's ex-girlfriend.

But why would the sale of the house mean that he couldn't have Addy?

Unless he'd confronted Nonnie already, and his grandmother had told him that Addy knew about the sale.

It could appear that she'd chosen to be loyal to Nonnie over Mark....

Feeling like a kid in the principal's office, but with the need deeply ingrained to have all the facts before speaking, she asked, "What did Ella say, Mark?"

"I..." She was looking at him and he turned back to her. "I have a question to ask you first, if I may."

The evening air was balmy. She was sweating. "Of course."

"In your opinion, if you told someone something that you meant at the time, are you beholden to the promise in the future?"

She frowned, but also welcomed the reprieve from her self-castigation. "Is this a rhetorical question?"

"For now."

It was a testimony to the state of her weakness for this man that she was so eager to accept the conversation at face value. "I think that depends on what you told and to whom. I mean, there's no way we can be accountable to everything we've ever said to everyone we've ever known. People change. Situations change. But if, say, you told someone in the past that you'd pay them back a loan, then yes, in my opinion, in the future you are beholden to that promise."

"I asked Ella to marry me."

"Tonight?"

"No."

"You mean the time you already told me about? Before you moved to Shelter Valley?"

"Yes."

"She turned you down."

"She wants to take that back."

"She wants to marry you?" No! She'd given Mark up. She couldn't just waltz back in and lay claim to him. He was Addy's now.

Oh, God.

"Yes." An unequivocal yes.

"Do you want to marry her?"

That was what this was about? Mark was getting back with his ex and felt badly for what he was doing to Addy? This wasn't about something she'd done?

"No."

Oh. Well, then… "You can't possibly think that you're beholden to a question asked in another place, in another time, Mark."

Maybe, technically, she shouldn't be the one discussing this with him. She had a definite conflict of interest.

"She turned you down. That ended the extent of the offer." In every legal aspect. But Mark was a man of honor, which was why Addy was so drawn to him.

"I told her that I'd be back."

"Back to Bierly. Did you promise to hold the offer of marriage open? Or say that you wouldn't see anyone else?"

"No."

Addy's shoulders relaxed while her lower body warmed in an entirely good way. "And you're sure you don't want to marry her?"

He looked her straight in the eye.

"Absolutely."

A smile started from deep inside of her and slowly infused its way through her being, driving Addy to act without thinking. Taking hold of his arm where it rested on the chair only a foot away from hers, she stood and leaned over him, planting her lips on his.

CHAPTER TWENTY

SWEET HEAVEN. Mark's body hardened and his mind shut down as his arms closed around the woman, settling her on his lap. She fit as if she was made for him. And not just body to body.

Her taste, her warmth, the tiny purring sound she made…this was what Hollywood movies were made about.

Like the rest of his life in Shelter Valley, the kiss was more than anything he'd ever experienced. Ever imagined.

Addy wrapped her arms all the way around his neck, pulling his mouth more fully against hers, darting her tongue around his lips and inside. He had to have her.

The sensation was animalistic. Instinctive. He kissed her hard and fast, and soft and sweet. Escaping into her, into the world they'd somehow created out of two chairs and a slab of cement.

Time didn't exist. Place had no meaning. There was Addy. And there was him. As she clung to him, he moved his hands up and down her back, her shape taking form in his palms, becoming a memory he would never lose. He was learning her, feeling her, because he had to know her in every way.

She wasn't wearing a bra.

He was hard enough to explode and he tightened some more. She was unfettered. For him. The invitation beckoned him beyond rational thought. With one hand supporting her back, he slid his other hand between them, running it beneath her blouse and up her side to the bottom of the swell taunting him. And then slowly up, feeling the softness, the heaviness, of her femininity until he finally reached her nipple. It was hard. He teased it with his fingers and his mouth ached to taste it.

Addy moaned. And moved, opening herself up more fully to him. "Please, Mark..."

Please, Mark. Words he'd heard earlier that night. They'd jabbed and left a wound.

Pulling his mouth away from Addy's, Mark stood and placed her back in her chair. "I can't," he said, his back to her as he stared into the darkness of the yard and willed his body under control. He wasn't turning around until he could trust himself to resist the temptation of the moments of pure bliss that Addy was offering him.

But they'd only be moments, she'd said so herself. She couldn't promise anything more than the moment.

And he couldn't give her anything more.

"I'm sorry."

He swung around. "For what?"

Shrugging, she motioned toward his empty chair. "Coming on to you like that. I shouldn't have… I don't know what came over me. I've never behaved like that before."

With his hands in his pockets holding the fabric of his shorts away from his erection, Mark walked out into the yard and then turned to face her. "Don't be sorry," he said, confusion and disappointment giving the words more passion than he'd intended. "Ever. For that," he added. "That was the best… It was a kiss I'll never forget."

"But you're going to marry Ella, aren't you?"

He had to tell her about the baby. He was an honest man. And had never known honor to cost so much.

"I have to."

"No, you don't. Not unless you love her."

"You know how I feel about love."

"Right, you don't believe in it."

"In the beginning people mistake lust for love. Kind of like the excitement and thrill of getting a new big-screen TV." He sounded like a moron. "And then the newness wears off and all that's left is disillusionment and disappointment. It's far better to be realistic. To look life head-on, see what's really there, and make the best of it."

"I don't agree."

He couldn't help that. You couldn't change what a lifetime of living had taught you.

"Love is something unseen. Something that exists

whether you acknowledge it or not. Whether you welcome it or not." She sounded pretty sure of herself.

"You know this, how?"

"There's no proof, Mark. Unless you look at people, at their actions, their choices. Love is evident in them."

"I meant, personally. You live alone. By your own admission, you've never been in a serious relationship. So how do you know?" Her own parents certainly had not been a good example of love.

"I loved Gran. My mother loved my father. And I know that love is the power that holds people together after the newness wears off. It's the need to be together no matter what comes your way. It's growing and changing together through life's challenges. Love is what lets a man look at his wife naked after twenty years of marriage and still find her beautiful. It's what lets an old woman look at her wrinkled and hunched husband and still want only him right by her side."

She lived alone. Always had. "How do you know?" She sounded like a dreamer. And he saw no evidence in her life to prove any different.

"I just do."

"So you think that if I don't feel this *love* for Ella I shouldn't marry her even though I gave her my word I wouldn't desert her?"

"I think that if you don't love her, it's not fair to her or to yourself to marry her. Now is the time to acknowledge that the relationship doesn't offer you what you need—not after you're married."

"How do you know it wouldn't offer me what I need?" He'd been with Ella a lot longer than he'd known Addy. Ella knew Mark Heber. And until he'd kidded himself that he could suddenly have a brand-new life, until he'd let Nonnie convince him that they could be something they weren't, he'd been completely content to marry Ella.

Addy joined him on the grass, placing herself directly in front of him until their noses were almost touching. "I know because of what just happened over there," she said. He couldn't look back at the patio. "If Ella had what it will take to keep you faithful to her for the rest of your lives, then you wouldn't have been able to respond to me like that."

"If I don't remain faithful, that is my fault, not the fault of the woman I'm with. It's a product of my own character. Something lacking within me. And I can assure you, when I marry, I will be faithful."

"I don't doubt that, and to an extent it's a reflection of who you are. But don't you see, Mark? If you marry Ella knowing that you don't want to—and you've already admitted you don't want to—then, in essence, you're lying to her. If it's any marriage at all, at some point she's going to sense that she doesn't do it for you."

I won't be good enough for you anymore. Ella's words from that night at the lake came back to him.

He'd denied her claim at the time. And he'd been certain he knew what he was talking about.

He hadn't met Addy yet.

"I don't know a woman who'd be happy knowing her husband didn't want to marry her, knowing that she didn't have his whole heart. She'd spend her whole life feeling like she wasn't good enough."

"You don't understand." But he wanted the out she was handing him. So badly he almost threw thirty years of right living to the side and took it.

"It's not fair to Ella, either, marrying her when you don't want to. You're robbing her of any chance of finding a man who'd adore her enough to still find her beautiful after twenty years of marriage."

Do you love me? Ella had asked right before breaking up with him. He'd said yes because he loved her as much as he'd ever loved anyone besides Nonnie.

He'd loved Ella as much as he thought it possible to love anyone.

Maybe he still did. His mind had the thought and his entire being revolted against it. He wasn't in love with Ella. At the moment, he wasn't even all that fond of her.

The way he felt about Ella was nothing compared to the way he felt about Addy.

The thought made him despicable.

And it wasn't fair to Ella at all. Addy was right about one thing. He couldn't marry Ella under false pretenses.

He had to tell her that he didn't want to marry her.

Addy stepped closer, lifting her face to his. And Mark looked deeply into the eyes of the woman who'd stolen a part of him without his even knowing what she was about.

"Ella's pregnant."

ADDY WOKE UP in a bad mood the next morning. She didn't want to be in Shelter Valley. She didn't want to know if Will Parsons was guilty of discrimination or nepotism. And she most certainly did not want Mark Heber to marry Ella from Bierly.

Thirty seconds after she opened her eyes she was on her feet. She was going to stay in Shelter Valley until her job there was done. She was going to do everything she could to either protect Will Parsons from wrongful accusation or prepare him for any defense he might need—though if he was guilty, she would be turning over her research to another attorney of his choosing.

And she was going to be the friend to Mark Heber that she'd told him she would be. In her shock the night before, she hadn't been able to put her heart back into the safe compartment where she'd kept it since the night her mother and brother died. She'd told him that she'd be around whenever he needed her. That, since they were two ships passing in the night, she'd be a good sounding board as he sorted through the choices he had to make.

Truth was, she hadn't been able to turn her back on him. She cared too much.

Not that caring was going to do her a damn bit of good. Mark knew her as Adele, not as Adrianna. There was no way he'd ever forgive her once he found out about her deception.

There was no possible future for the two of them.

But she cared. So much that her involvement with Mark wasn't about what he could give to her—it wasn't about the future. He needed a friend now. And for whatever reason, he'd chosen her. She had something that he wanted. Or needed.

And she had to give it to him.

Which was why, when he knocked on her door just after ten that morning, telling her that Nonnie had gone down for a nap and asking if he could come in, she opened her door wider and stepped back.

"You do your homework at the kitchen table." He nodded toward the computer and folders there, making her nervous. Her work for Will was done mostly on the computer and the evidence she was collecting was in secure folders, but she'd been collecting hard copy files, too.

"Yeah," she said, and added, "I can hear the fountain better from there."

Mark nodded again, obviously distracted.

"Did you get any sleep?"

He'd gone inside just a few minutes after delivering his bombshell.

"Very little."

She hadn't slept a lot, either.

Mark stood in the middle of her living room, his

hands in the pockets of his jeans, stretching the fabric of his jeans across his groin.

She wished she knew what to do for him. "You have to work today?"

"No. I told Nonnie I'd take her for a drive. She wants to see some town called Tortilla Flat. It's about an hour from Phoenix, straight up the mountain. One of the ladies who visited this week told her about it. Apparently the views on the way up are incredible." There was no enthusiasm in his tone.

Or on his face, either.

"It will be good for her to get out."

"You want to come along?"

"I have homework to do here." She motioned toward the laptop.

"If I hadn't told you that Ella was pregnant would you have come?"

Honesty, Adele. "Yes."

He dropped to the edge of her sofa, legs spread, elbows on his knees and hands clasped.

"I have to ask you something."

"Okay." Addy sat, too. In the chair perpendicular to him. She couldn't get too close to him. "If Nonnie's blood pressure hadn't dropped, if we'd gone out that night, would you have made love with me?"

"Yes."

"You don't take sex lightly."

"No."

"It's logical to conclude, then, that I mean something to you."

"Yes."

He looked at her. She looked back. His struggle was palpable. And she knew what she had to do.

"It wouldn't have gone anywhere, Mark. Even if we'd made love…"

"I know you think that, but—"

Shaking her head, she cut him off. "I don't just think it. I know it."

His grin had her wanting to crawl into his lap and make the world go away. Forever if she could.

A day alone with Mark, becoming one with him, might be worth giving up a lifetime of what she had to go back to in Colorado.

Or Shelter Valley was getting to her worse than she knew. She wasn't herself. Maybe her all-consuming attraction to this man was nothing more than a grown-up reaction to the memories the place stirred up. Memories of feeling alone and scared and clingy.

"You've got at least four years in Shelter Valley, Mark. I can't stay here."

"I know you talked about money issues…"

"There's that and…this whole small-town thing. I miss the city." It was lame, but it was the best she could do without jeopardizing her cover. She couldn't have him thinking, even for a second, that Adele Kennedy would be around long-term.

Especially now that he had Ella's situation to deal with, life decisions of his own to make.

"I'll be staying until the end of the semester, but that's it," she said, meaning every word. One semester of classes was enough to give her an idea about how various students were regarded and treated. She'd stay up all night for as many nights as it took to get through all the records and files and paperwork.

And then she had to get out of town before she lost every part of herself.

MARK SAT IN Addy's living room, feeling her words as though they were nails in his coffin.

"I'm sorry," she said, her eyes wide and moist.

"It's not as if I'm free, anyway." He said the words aloud. Having just come off the second worst night of his life—the first being the night after he'd learned about Nonnie's MS—he was prepared to face what he had to do.

"You've talked to Ella, then? Decided to marry her?" Addy's voice was calm, collected.

"I haven't talked to her, no. But I know that if she's carrying my child, I will do what's right by her. And the baby."

"What's right and marriage are not necessarily synonymous."

In Bierly they were.

"You said 'if.' You think there's a chance she's lying to you?"

"Yeah. But I don't put a lot of stock in the chance. More like wishful thinking."

"More like you're trying to save yourself from making the biggest mistake of your life."

"I'm being greedy. Wanting more than I've been given."

"It's human nature to want more. Healthy to want more. It's what keeps us working hard, contributing to society. Wanting more motivates us to get up every morning and do everything we can do to achieve our goals."

"One of the first things I do in the morning when I get up is shave. That requires looking in the mirror." He grinned at her. And wondered how he could be feeling so low and enjoying the moment at the same time.

Addy sat down on the other end of the couch. Close enough to touch.

"I paid a heavy price for my self-respect," he told her. "I don't negotiate with it."

"Paid how?"

"When I first realized I was going to have to quit school to take care of Nonnie because her care was going to require more money than we had and I was going to have to go to work full-time, I was angry. Bitter."

"Both understandable emotions. You were a six-teen-year-old kid with the world on your shoulders while most kids were worrying about what they were going to do to have fun in the next twenty-four hours."

"Nonnie insisted that I don't quit school, but back

then she was really sick. She couldn't stay out of bed for more than an hour. There was no way she could work. The co-pays were too much. She knew as well as I did that we weren't going to make it unless I got a full-time job."

He hung his head and then raised it again.

"I was also ashamed. Of Nonnie, my mother. Ashamed of who I was." Something about this woman was making him crazy. Or right for the first time in his life. Hearing his thoughts out loud, for the first time ever, he had a second's irrational thought that lightning might strike him down. "All my life I'd been trying to pretend that the town didn't look down on us. That the kids at school didn't make snide comments about us being white trash. I left the hospital the night that Nonnie was diagnosed and just kept on going. I didn't look back. More to the point, I didn't call. Nonnie was lying there in a hospital bed, unable to get up, let alone come after me, and I didn't even call to let her know I was okay."

"Where'd you go?"

"The woods at first. And then to Charleston. I had no cash, no food. I couldn't get a real job because I was certain the cops were looking for me as a runaway. I slept wherever I could find shelter and stole what food I had to eat. Eventually, I went to the only place I knew where folks would be friendly, maybe help a guy out—a local bar. I was also looking for an underground card game. My friends and I had been playing poker in our basements for years and I thought I was pretty good."

"No, Mark." Addy looked stricken. He looked away.

Minutes passed. And Mark knew for certain what he'd realized the night before. *You were who you were. You could move on. Move out. Move past. But the person you'd been, the things you'd seen and done, kept up with you.*

"When my grandmother couldn't reach me for a couple of days she checked herself out of the hospital and called a neighbor to come get her. She could barely walk but she was determined to find me."

"How long did it take?"

"A couple of weeks." He'd told himself that he'd had to leave. Nonnie had sacrificed everything for him. He couldn't be more of a drain on her now that she was ill.

He'd told himself a lot of things. Most of them bogus.

"She'd have found me sooner, but she was afraid to report me missing, sure that they'd take me away, put me in the system. So while I was hiding from the cops, afraid they'd haul me in as a runaway, the cops weren't even looking for me."

"Nonnie still wanted you with her."

The truth was he'd run because he'd been scared as hell that his grandmother wouldn't want him anymore, that she'd turn him over to the authorities and he'd have no say what happened to him, or what direction his life would take.

So he'd taken his life in his own hands and flushed it down the toilet.

Or would have if she hadn't found him.

"Thank God she knew me so well," he said. "She hadn't called the cops, but she'd told people she knew in the bar community about me in nearby cities. A couple of days after I'd hit that first bar in Charleston, someone spotted me and called Nonnie."

"I'm guessing you slept in your own bed that night?"

"With a very sore hide." And a sick soul. He'd run out on the one person who'd been there for him at her time of greatest need.

Nonnie had said she'd understood. She'd never blamed him. But he'd seen the sadness in her eyes.

"From that night on, I swore that I would not disappoint her, or myself, again. I am not like my parents. I don't run. I face the music, no matter how loud or bad it gets."

He'd learned that night to be grateful for what he had. And to spend his energy making the world around him better rather than always thinking about greener grass.

CHAPTER TWENTY-ONE

MARK WAS GOING to marry Ella. Addy was convinced, even if he wasn't. And since he couldn't leave Shelter Valley until he could either afford to pay back his scholarship, or until he graduated, he was going to be married, raising a kid, right on the other side of the wall from her.

There was no way she was going to live next door to a married man she had the hots for. That wasn't good, even as things stood in the present.

Knowing he was going to be a father had in no way diminished how much she wanted Mark Heber for herself. And she had absolutely nothing to offer him but the one thing he hated most. Lies.

Over the next several days she did her homework, attended classes and plowed through the rest of the personnel files, stopping when she found an *M* she'd missed. Todd Moore. She was pretty sure she'd met him. As she remembered it, he and his wife, Martha, had been Will and Becca's best friends.

And the Montford Board of Trustees, on recommendation from their president, Will Parsons had hired Todd as a professor of psychology straight out of college.

She perused the first couple of pages of the personnel file carefully. Todd's performance reviews were stellar. His professorial ratings in the top quarter.

And…

She read and then reread.

Todd had been terminated. By Will Parsons. For having an illicit affair with one of his students—a girl half his age.

Will had fired his best friend.

That was good.

And now she had to see who'd also applied for the psychology professorship that had been awarded, on Will's recommendation, to Will's best friend. Any one of those applicants could argue favoritism. And if they were bitter enough…

She visited Nonnie every day—always when she was certain that Mark wasn't home— and she stayed inside at night.

And on Friday morning, when she got out of the shower, she pulled on a pair of black leggings, something she usually wore under her exercise shorts, and a thigh-length blouse, belted it at the waist with black leather and finished the outfit with black wedged sandals. She kept her hair down, curled it and put on twice the makeup she usually wore.

Before leaving the house, she doused herself in perfume. And then she darted to her car.

She left botany class fifteen minutes early, too, checking to make certain Mark wasn't leaning against the building outside before hurrying back to her car and driving over to the performing arts center for the drama club meeting.

She sat at the front of the theater, right beneath the eye of Matt Sheffield, who was standing in front of them on the stage. When they broke up into small groups to role-play, she made certain that she was in the professor's group. And she stayed after the meeting, following him into the sound room under the guise of working on a theater article for the school newspaper.

She stood close to him. Too close. He backed up. She moved forward, touching his thigh with her hand.

He excused her from the drama club.

Maybe she'd come on too strong.

And maybe he was a decent man who'd been wrongly accused.

She went home and documented the event.

ADDY WAS SITTING in her living room, in jeans and a short-sleeved pullover with her computer on her lap, when Mark knocked on her sliding glass door Friday night.

She couldn't pretend she wasn't there. Her curtains were open, and her car was out front.

He was reaching out to her. And she'd promised herself she'd be there for him. For *him*. Not her. She opened the door.

"You're avoiding me." He looked her straight in the eye.

"Yeah."

"Please don't."

She felt her nipples harden just peering into those blue eyes that looked at her with such directness. She dropped her gaze and ended up staring at the black T-shirt stretched across his muscular chest.

"I'm here as a friend if you need me, Mark. But I don't completely trust myself around you. And I don't fool around with married men," she said.

"I'm not married."

"Engaged, then."

"I'm not that yet, either."

"Yet."

"I told Ella I didn't want to marry her."

She stepped outside. "How'd she take it?"

"About like I expected. She understood, but she's willing to try to make the best of things as they are."

"So, wait." She frowned. "Does that mean you are getting married?"

"It means that I don't know. I made the offer. She's trying to figure out if accepting it is the best thing to do."

"You told her you didn't want to marry her, but that you would."

"Yes."

She'd never heard of anything more bizarre. More destined for failure.

And she didn't doubt for one second that if Mark married Ella, if the marriage failed, it wouldn't be because of him.

She also knew that he deserved better—far better—than spending the rest of his life with a woman he didn't love.

"You curled your hair."

She'd forgotten. "Yeah."

"I like it."

Matt Sheffield hadn't been impressed. Thank goodness.

"People raise children together from separate households."

"I'm in Shelter Valley. She's in Bierly. It's a little far to commute." Taking her hand, he led her to their chairs, which were both still on her side of the patio. Sat down. "And getting married is the right thing to do. I'm not going to abandon my child. I know what it's like to grow up without a dad."

"You're staying here, then?"

"Yes." No doubt in his voice on that one.

"Have you told Nonnie? About the baby?"

"I just did tonight. I'm sure you're going to hear about it tomorrow. I work from two to eight, by the way, instead of noon like she told you."

"Your schedule changed?"

"No. She says she got the days confused, but she's lying."

"Nonnie lies?" Mark hated lying.

"Only when she's being conniving. But this time she came clean, which is why I know she lied to you to begin with."

Leaning back in her chair, Addy watched him. "She wanted me there when you got home."

His expression serious, he said, "She noticed that we haven't been spending much time together."

"She lied to me about your hours before you told her about Ella."

"Yeah."

"You still haven't told me how she reacted to the news." Nonnie had told her once that she'd love to live long enough to see Mark holding his own child in his arms.

"She spit."

"What? On the floor? Nonnie wouldn't do that. She's a stickler for clean floors." Addy had caught the old woman with a bucket and a mop moving slowly over the kitchen floor with her wheelchair earlier that week and discovered that mopping floors was one of the items on Nonnie's list of daily chores.

"I told her at the dinner table. Her plate was empty. And she spit on it."

"She doesn't like Ella?"

"Not any more than Ella likes her."

"Ella doesn't like Nonnie?"

"She's jealous of Nonnie's influence on me."

"Her influence on you? It's the other way around, I'd say. I can't tell you how many times I've heard Nonnie say, 'Mark doesn't want me to do this, or eat that, or try…'"

He chuckled. "Ella thinks I try too hard to please my grandmother."

"You have good reason to."

"Ella doesn't know that."

"How can she not? She knows you live with Nonnie. She knows Nonnie raised you."

"She doesn't know that I ran away. With the exception of a very few people, no one does."

Addy knew. Just like Mark knew things people she'd known for years had never heard. It meant something.

Maybe they just felt free with each other because they knew they'd be moving on soon and never see each other again.

"Ella thinks that a lot of the choices I make are due to Nonnie, when, in fact, they're choices I'd make regardless."

"Such as?"

"Putting work before pleasure."

"That's kind of a given, isn't it?"

"She always thought I worked too much."

"Did you?"

"Maybe. But we needed the money."

"What else?"

He shrugged. "Just lifestyle choices. She likes to walk a little more on the wild side than I do."

"Partying, you mean?"

"Just being irresponsible."

She was glad he'd come knocking. Hearing his voice again was good.

"What does Nonnie think you should do about Ella?"

"Ask her for custody."

She turned toward him. "Do you think Ella would

give it to you?" Visions of a single Mark living next door with Nonnie and a newborn flashed through her mind. A play pool, right there, just a couple of yards from her fountain. Little fingers reaching up over the edges of the rock bowl…

"If I paid her she might."

"You're kidding."

"It wouldn't be easy for her, but I think there's a chance, if she decides that she doesn't want to marry me, that she'll agree to give me custody of the baby. I know she's always been afraid of being a single mom."

"Afraid? Why?"

"Ella barely graduated from high school. There's not a lot around Bierly for her to do. Her job at the factory, there's no room for her to advance there. She could take sideway moves, but let's just say she's never going to get rich. Or even make enough, on her own, to buy a home."

"You'd pay child support."

"That would help with the child's expenses, but I'd also expect joint custody, which means she'd be equally responsible for half of the expenses."

He'd clearly given this a lot of thought. And was a lot more in control than he'd been four days before, when he'd first come to her with the news.

He had that sense about him. That he could handle anything. Including her deception?

"It's hard, being a single mom in Bierly, for another reason. There aren't a lot of options there, relationship wise. Even fewer when you're asking a guy to take on someone else's kid."

"You'd think, if someone loved her he would…and at our age, chances are he'd have kids, too."

"Having a baby will greatly limit her social life, which means that she'll have fewer opportunities to be out meeting people."

"Partying." She said it again, needing to not like the other woman.

"Yeah, maybe, but not like you might think. Ella doesn't do drugs. And she won't drink enough to get drunk."

"Still, she'd sell her kid so that she'd doesn't have to stay home at night?"

"Maybe not. She really wants a family and I think she'll make a good mom. As long as the situation is right for her. I'm just saying I don't know."

"Are you planning to find out?"

"I don't know that yet, either.…"

The statement hung there. As if he wanted something from her.

"I wouldn't do it," she blurted into the night. "Not for money or opportunity, not even if I thought my child would have a better financial future without me. I think a mother's love is more important than any of that."

"What about a father's love?"

"Of course." She was talking to a father-to-be. "The point is, a child needs love more than he or she needs financial security. And knowing that, I would keep my child with me at all costs."

She saw that little play pool again. And thought about giving her child away so that she'd have an easier life...

"Would you raise a child by yourself if it came to that?"

"I don't think I'd deliberately get pregnant, if that's what you're asking, but if I ended up alone and pregnant, yes, I'd raise the child."

At the moment, being a single mom was the only way she could see it ever happening. The only man she'd ever met who'd even tempted her to think about such things in a practical sense, opening her heart to the idea of having a family of her own again, was Mark.

And he was not an option.

MARK WORKED ALL weekend, making up hours from the previous weekend. Or so he told himself. The hours were offered so he accepted them. Ella used to accuse him of using work as an escape.

Maybe she'd been right.

At least he never turned to a bottle. Or split like his old man had done.

Nonnie was determined that he was going to buy custody of his child and she was doing better, physically, as though through sheer strength of will she could hang around to help him raise the baby. Several ladies from Shelter Valley were over on Saturday to teach her some kind of domino game. It sounded as if they played it on a board with little wooden trains. They'd had two tables worth of players and while he had no idea what dominoes and trains had to do with each other, he'd buy a houseful of both to keep the enthusiasm he heard in Nonnie's voice when he called home during his dinner break.

Addy was there when he called. She'd brought chili over for dinner. He wished he was there, too.

Instead, because Nonnie was tired and going to bed early, he agreed to stay and work until midnight, and when he got home in the wee hours of the next morning, his neighbor's lights were out.

He didn't hear from Ella. And he didn't text her.

He worked second shift Sunday, too.

It was for the best.

"THAT GIRL'S LYING."

"Pardon?" Addy stopped rolling the little ball of dough in her hands, staring at the older woman sitting next to her at the kitchen table, filling her cooking sheet twice as fast as she was.

"Ella." Nonnie practically snorted the word. "Trying to trap him, that's what she's doing."

Mark was Nonnie's boy. It followed that she'd blame the woman, any woman, for the situation he was in.

"What makes you think that?"

"She ain't no more pregnant than I am."

"How can you know?"

"I got my ways."

"Mark said Ella's been to the doctor."

"I don't believe it. Not in town. News would've spread quicker than fire."

"If she thinks she's pregnant and didn't want anyone to know, she could've have gone out of town." It was what Addy would have done.

Nonnie shook her head. "Ella ain't got her driver's license. It's why she lives in town."

"She doesn't know how to drive?"

"She knows how. She drove drunk and lost it."

Addy wasn't up on DUI law, but she knew enough to know that the woman must have done something pretty severe to lose her driving privileges.

"While she was dating Mark?"

"Before. She's got another year before she gets it back."

"Someone could have driven her."

"And then it wouldn't be a secret no more." Nonnie was clearly in denial. "Mark also says she told her ma about the baby," the older woman continued, "and if she did the entire town would know by now. It's not on Facebook, and Bertie hasn't heard about it, which she would've if Ella was pregnant."

"Ella asked her mom to keep quiet until she knew what she and Mark were going to do about the baby."

"Ha!" Nonnie's blue-veined hands didn't miss a beat as she completed a tray of what would soon be chocolate chip cookies, pushed it aside and pulled another one in front of her. "Dot ain't kept a secret since she was born. I've known that girl all her life and if she had any idea that her Ella finally got my Mark locked down I'd have been getting phone calls within the hour."

"But Ella hasn't decided whether or not she's going to marry Mark."

"'Cause she knows she ain't pregnant. If she was, that would be enough reason to spread it around. Everyone knows Mark would do the right thing and marry her."

"If you thought she was pregnant, would you expect that, too?" She was just curious.

And anxious to finish baking Mark's favorite cookies—a job she'd volunteered for so that Nonnie wouldn't be lugging trays in and out of the oven alone. She rolled a little faster so that she could get back to work.

"No, I would not," the woman said succinctly. "Much as I want that boy to settle down with a real family of his own, I know he wouldn't be happy with Ella, and a kid doesn't need to grow up in a household lacking joy."

During their morning visit, Nonnie had told her she was going to bake cookies. Mark had been working long hours and still had homework to do and a test to study for the next day—his first big exam according to Nonnie—and she'd wanted a treat waiting for him when he got home.

To give him energy to do his schoolwork, she'd said.

And Addy had volunteered to help.

"Don't you think Mark should be the one to decide what makes him happy?"

"Nope."

Addy didn't agree, but she wasn't going to argue, either.

"That boy is a rare one," the woman continued. "He makes one mistake in his life—an understandable one if you ask me—and he spends the rest of his life afraid to think of himself 'cause he's afraid to make the same mistake twice."

Addy's fingers slowed and then started up again. She didn't want those piercing eyes turned on her. Didn't want to become any more entangled with the Hebers and their challenges and their sense of justice that so closely mirrored her own.

Didn't want to feel as though she was a part of them. As though she'd come home.

But she couldn't help or change her feeling that what Nonnie had said was completely, one hundred percent correct.

She couldn't help believing that Mark Heber wasn't just being a gentleman, doing the right thing, by offering to marry Ella. He was martyring himself because he'd been a scared kid who'd run away from home when he'd found out his grandmother was sick.

"You got to stop him."

The soft ball in Addy's fingers flattened. Nonnie was staring at her. Not even blinking.

"What?"

"He's got a thing for you. Any fool could see it, and

where my boy is concerned, I'm no fool. You could stop him from ruining his life."

"Me? What can I do?"

"Sleep with him, that's what. If he sleeps with you, he'd have to give in to those feelin's he's got for you. Besides, once things get intimate, he'll feel beholden to you, too."

"Except that she's pregnant and I'm not."

"She ain't, either. He's just feeling guilty 'cause he slept with her and then left her high and dry."

Was there truth to that? Was Mark's conscience making him prey to an avaricious woman who wanted him at any cost?

He'd said he wasn't sure he believed Ella about being pregnant.

He'd also told her he wanted to make love with her. He told her with his glances, his body language, every single time they were together.

And she probably told him, too. Lord knew, she thought about it all the time.

Couldn't seem to stop thinking about it. Especially in bed at night, or in the shower, with the water sluicing over her skin in a trail his hands could...

If she slept with him, could she really save him from a lifetime of unhappiness?

"You like him."

"Yes, I like him, but—"

"You more than like him."

"Yes, but—"

"It's like I said. It's your job to save him."

"Absolutely not." Finishing the last one of her cookies, Addy wiped her hands on the moist paper towel beside her, pushed back from the table and carried two of the four laden trays over to the pre-heated oven.

"At least think about it."

"No, Nonnie." Turning, she pinned the woman with her courtroom stare. "I will not sleep with Mark just to keep him from marrying another woman."

"Then do it because you want to."

Addy excused herself to go to the bathroom, praying that Nonnie hadn't seen how badly her hands were shaking.

CHAPTER TWENTY-TWO

MARK WAITED FOR Addy outside her botany lecture on Monday morning.

In jeans and a white, button-down blouse, with her satchel over her shoulder, she could have passed for any one of the many students around them, except that she was the only one he noticed. Her particular gait. The exact color of her blond hair.

The set of her shoulders. The way she tilted her head. Didn't matter, he had her inside of him.

She walked right up to him, which he took as a good sign. She could have pretended not to see him standing there. "I miss you." His jeans and short-sleeved polo shirt were appropriate for the seventy-degree coolness, but he was sweating.

"I just saw you on Friday night," she said, but the light tone in her voice didn't match the way her eyes took him in.

"How'd your exam go?" she asked next, falling into step beside him.

"I totally aced it."

She grinned and nudged him. "Good for you!"

She'd touched him and he was on fire. How could

he contemplate marrying another woman when he wanted this one so fiercely?

"I never saw myself as a classroom type of guy."

He'd never seen himself as a guy wanting more than he could have, either.

"It doesn't surprise me at all." Addy's glance was personal. His body responded. "You just needed to give yourself a chance."

Ella would have made some comment about him being too good for her. Or asked him if he was going to move to a big city and work at some fancy job. She'd have wanted to know how his good news affected her.

Had she ever thought of what he wanted?

Was he being selfish now, only thinking of himself?

They reached the entrance to her parking lot. In silence, he walked beside her. And then she was pulling out her keys. Unlocking the door.

Before climbing in, though, she turned to him. "For what it's worth, I…miss you, too."

His hands in his pockets, Mark nodded. "I'll be home for dinner tonight so you don't have to worry about Nonnie."

"I know. She called out to me as I was leaving this morning."

He couldn't let it end. Not yet.

"So…will you join me outside tonight?"

"Yes."

He had to get to class. And she looked so damned

good, standing there with the reflection of the sun peeking through the trees to linger like gold dust in her hair.

He'd never known hell could feel so good.

ADDY STOPPED BACK in to see Randi Parsons Monday afternoon. She'd had a message on her machine the day before from the woman she'd once hoped would be her aunt. Randi wanted permission to check her "sister's" academic records for possible admittance into Montford.

Which sounded like Randi might have found some scholarship money. Was Will's baby sister a miracle worker? Or a softhearted woman with shady ethics?

Her heart hoped for the former, but her instincts were pointing toward the latter. She'd spent the night before going over the university's budgets while Mark had been at work. Starting back when Will had become president of the university.

She'd been nibbling away at the plate of chocolate chip cookies Nonnie had insisted she bring home with her.

And had lost her appetite when she got to the women's athletic budget from ten years before. Or rather, both the men's and women's budgets. The men's athletic budget, which was nationally understood in the educational world as an investment against revenue for the school, had been drastically cut to give more money to women's athletics. The person responsible for the budget request had been Randi Parsons.

It had been approved by big brother Will.

And while, on the surface, it seemed fair that both athletic programs receive equal funding, the reality could be seen in the financials. Women's athletics did not earn out its expenditures. And men's athletics, which used to bring in a sizable sum of money to help fund other university programs, had progressively, over the years, brought in less and less.

Everyone knew that athletics were a major source of support for many universities, Montford included. And it was also common practice to designate program funds commensurate with what they brought in.

It could be reasoned—it would be reasoned if anyone wanted to take cause against Will on the topic—that he'd put the entire university at financial risk by granting his little sister's request.

Randy wasn't in her office. Feeling pushed from the inside out, Addy started looking around for Will's sister, poking her head into an equipment room. The basketball gym. A dance studio.

All the while trying not to think about Mark Heber. She was in Shelter Valley to work. She had to get the job done so that she could leave.

The sooner, the better.

Before she did something stupid. Like sleep with a man she couldn't have.

The gymnastics gym door burst open, almost slamming into Addy as she reached to pull it open. Randi stood there, a horrified look on her face.

"Are you okay?"

"Yes." Addy attempted a natural smile. "I'm fine."

Dressed as usual in spandex shorts, matching top and spotless tennis shoes, Randi smiled back, her eyes opening wider.

"Adele! How nice to see you again. How's your sister?"

"Fine." Addy felt sick looking at the sincere smile on Randi's face.

She'd slept in the same bed as Randi more times than she could count.

"I'm glad you stopped in! Did you get my message?" Randi asked. "I'm still working on scholarship money. We have to be careful not to break any rules, but I think I might have found a private donor willing to help. ..."

"That's okay," Addy said. She'd been following the woman's progress, the online forms Randi had filed, all in accordance with policy. Randi hadn't pulled any strings where the scholarship admittance was concerned. If she'd played favorites ten years before for the basketball player, she'd apparently learned her lesson. There were no forms filed on that one. "I was just stopping by to let you know that she got another offer. She's going to be playing for a community college close to home her first year with the hopes of getting an agent."

Her former client was doing so. The words were only half lie.

"Well, if you're sure..."

Addy nodded. "She's made her decision."

"Tell her to keep us in mind for next year, then," Randi said. "I viewed her footage. She's good."

"I will."

"Let her know that it would be best if she applies by January."

Backing out the door, Addy nodded. She would pass on the information to her former client. She'd taken the girl's case gratis because the girl and her parents hadn't been able to hire an attorney. And if their allowing her to use their daughter's name for this, another case, could actually get the girl seen by Randi Parsons, if it could get her into Montford, then something good would have come from involving them in the deception. Not that they knew she'd used their daughter's name deceitfully. Just that she'd needed it for a case.

"Thank you," she said to Randi, and got the hell out of there.

One thing was for sure, if the threats against Will materialized into actual charges before they discovered who was behind the anonymous letters, his defense team would have an arsenal of information ready and waiting for them.

If nothing else, Addy was doing her job well.

Randi would forgive her the lies, if she ever found out about them, because Addy was working under direction from the older brother Randi adored. The question was, would Addy ever be able to live with herself again?

She was finding out that she was a good liar.

The fact that she was doing it for a good cause didn't seem to matter anymore.

MARK JOINED JON on his favorite rock about ten minutes into his afternoon break on Monday.

"Hey, man, I didn't see you around this weekend." And they'd had a test in class that morning so hadn't had a chance to talk then.

"Abe was throwing up all weekend."

So Jon, as his sole caregiver, had to miss work. On one level, he understood.

But from a work standpoint—which mattered since Mark had stuck his neck out to get Jon the job—they couldn't have a new hire calling off.

"I traded with someone on third shift and had a neighbor lady, Veronica, sleep over," Jon continued. "Abe's pretty clingy and the doctor says it's okay if I pander to that a bit, just so long as I also get him out and socializing. I figured puking was a good excuse for pandering. Anyway, the doc says it was just a twenty-four-hour thing. He's fine now."

Mark listened, and his mind wandered, too. What if Ella still wanted to marry him? Outrageous as the idea sounded, he was seriously thinking about asking for full custody of their child.

"If you worked nights, when did you sleep?"

"When he napped, mostly."

"How'd you do on your test?"

"Didn't ace it, but I'm sure I passed."

If a twentysomething guy could raise a kid alone, then he could certainly do it.

"You ever have time to go out?" he asked now, trying for a light tone as he felt out his own situation.

"Not much." Jon chuckled.

"That ever get you down?"

Taking half of his peanut butter sandwich in one bite, Jon shrugged. "Sometimes, but not as much as having no folks or family around. Now that's a downer."

Agreed. "Still, you're such a young man to be raising a child alone."

"It's better than not having my son at all," Jon said. "And really, he's a fun little dude. I like having him to come home to."

"Bet it puts a damper on your love life, though. No time to date, huh?"

Not that Mark cared a whit about that for himself at the moment. With Addy moving back to Colorado at the end of the semester...

"Nah. The problem is, I don't want to. What with school and work and taking care of Abe."

Something registered within Mark, a distant memory. Or understanding. He didn't give up school because he had to. Just like Jon wasn't giving up dating because he had to. He'd given up school because keeping him and Nonnie together had been more important to him.

He didn't see that the realization changed anything

about his current situation. He didn't know what it mattered. He just felt…different.

"You've got time," he told Jon, packing up the garbage left from his lunch. "When the right woman comes along, you'll feel differently. You'll know."

What the hell had he said that for? Like he knew what he was talking about?

Unless he did.

"In the meantime, I have a proposition for you." This wasn't about him. Life wasn't about him. Life was about perspective.

"What kind of proposition? You've already done so much for me."

"I live with my grandmother. She's in a wheelchair and doesn't get out much, and I'm looking for things to keep her off the computer. She loves kids and since we don't know too many people here yet, I was thinking maybe some night this week, when we're both off, you could bring Abe by to visit with me and Nonnie so you can have some time to yourself to do whatever you want to do."

"You'd do that for me?"

"You'd be doing me a favor."

"Then I'll bring him by, see if he and your grandmother hit it off, and we can take it from there."

Thursday night was the only night both he and Jon were off. He made a date.

And wondered if Addy would want to join them.

CHAPTER TWENTY-THREE

WITH PROOF IN HAND that Randi Parsons Foster followed protocol regarding scholarships—at least sometimes—Addy went straight back to her duplex, ready to take a look at a sampling of Montford's scholarship applications. Applicants who'd been accepted, those who'd been turned down. Anyone who applied and lost out to someone else could feel that they had a discriminatory lawsuit.

She started with the year Randi had found money for Susan Farley. Where had the money come from? And had anyone who was similarly situated been turned down due to a lack of funds that same semester?

Punching in a couple of key words, she ended up with half a page of female athletes who'd applied for money to play for Montford during the year Susan Farley had started there.

She printed off the page and added it, along with the names of the three other applicants who'd applied for Todd Moore's position, to the folder she was preparing to turn over to Greg Richards. Every single one of those names had just become possible suspects in the Will Parsons extortion attempt.

Or possible victims in the Will Parsons discrimination suit.

She looked at her blinking cursor.

She had computerized scholarship records from the past twenty years at her disposal. Could look up anything she wanted. But, ethically, she could only do so in accordance with her investigation. She compiled a list of applicants, rejections and awards for the twenty years. Printed it off, too.

Looking up Mark Heber's application wouldn't be in accordance with her investigation. But she'd done the right thing. Looked through the records that would be most likely to give rise to a blackmail threat—personnel files, classroom procedures—first. And she'd looked at the Susan Farley scholarship because she already knew there were some questions about that one. Susan had received a full ride, private funding.

No source named.

Addy had a question about one more. Yes, she'd found out about Mark's unusual scholarship situation because he'd confided in her as a friend. But the whole reason she was in Shelter Valley, posing as a student, was so that she could get in with students and uncover any possible instances of discrimination.

She had to take a look at Mark's file. Find out who'd applied for Mark Heber's scholarship on his behalf.

There was nothing there.

ELLA CALLED JUST before he got off Monday evening. Seven forty-five in Arizona made it almost eleven in Bierly. Another late-night call. Not a good sign.

He didn't rush out of the plant. Or call her the second he got to his car. He called Nonnie. His grandmother was just on her way to bed.

"I'm settling in for the night, Markie-boy, so don't come poking in my door when you get home. The light wakes me up."

"Since when?"

"I got my you-know-whats on, too, so I won't be needing the bathroom. I'm tired. And I want some time to myself."

"You've had hours to yourself this evening."

"Nah, the church ladies stopped by. They want me to show 'em how to do them Christmas chimes I made out of can lids—you know the ones that made the money for the church school a few years ago?"

"Yeah, I know." And he didn't have to wonder how the church ladies knew. Nonnie had been very proud of her invention while he'd had cramps in his hands for a week after bending all the lids just the way she'd wanted them. "I've got my drill in the back of the truck," he told her. "And my clamp and pliers, too. You start saving your lids and I'll get them ready for you."

"Good. I was gonna ask you tomorrow. Now, I'm off to bed. You drive careful and remember I have my phone on the pillow, and I'll call if I need anything, so you don't have to worry I'm gonna come rolling out into the middle of anything you might be doing tonight."

"You're welcome to roll out into my homework anytime."

"Addy's been home alone all night," Nonnie said. "Ain't right, a young girl like that, good-looking and sweet, spending so much time over there alone. I'd have invited her for dinner but the ladies was here."

"I'll check the patio when I get home," Mark said because he knew the conversation wouldn't end until he did. "If she's out there, I'll tell her good-night for you."

"She likes white wine."

"Nonnie..."

"You should stop on your way home and get some."

"Good night, old woman."

He was grinning as he hung up. And didn't immediately dial his next call.

He drove out to the desert instead. To a vista that overlooked the city lights in Shelter Valley. What was he going to say if Ella wanted to marry him?

The right thing. He had to do the right thing.

What was right? Nonnie had her opinion. Addy agreed with her—if for different reasons. Marrying Ella was wrong.

Neither of those opinions mattered. He had to do what *he* thought was right. The problem was, what he thought seemed to change by the hour.

This confusion was new to him, and he didn't like it.

So he focused instead on the mental checklist of what he knew.

The baby was as much his responsibility as hers. It wasn't right that just her life be disrupted.

He wasn't sure the baby was his.

If the baby was his, he wanted it.

He didn't want to marry Ella.

He couldn't choose his happiness at the expense of others.

He had to stay in Shelter Valley for at least four years.

Shelter Valley was beginning to feel like home.

He missed some of his buddies in Bierly.

He missed having his own home, filled with his own things—a place where he could knock out a wall if it would help Nonnie maneuver more easily.

Ella couldn't drive. She wouldn't be able to get around Shelter Valley.

He couldn't leave Ella and Nonnie home alone together all day.

Dot would drive both him and Nonnie nuts in no time.

He was in very heatedlike with Addy Kennedy. To the point of almost believing in people being meant for each other. And maybe even close to believing in love.

Ella didn't interest him anymore.

Could he help that? She'd worried that he'd move on and she wouldn't be enough for him anymore.

He'd assured her that would never happen.

And it had.

Angry with himself, filled with shame, Mark dialed Ella's number, hoping that she'd gone to bed and wouldn't pick up.

"Mark? I called almost an hour ago."

Her disappointment in him didn't even begin to mirror his own. He couldn't live like this. Feeling selfish and base. He had to make this right.

"I was at work, Ella," he said, his tone purposely soft. Intimate. "I'm not even home yet."

"You stopping off at the bar? Having a cold one with the boys?"

The Mark she knew would have done so. And she'd have met him there, too.

"No. Believe it or not, I haven't been to the bar here yet. Mostly I just go home and do homework."

"Mostly?"

"I've been working some extra evening shifts to make up for the hours I can't work because of class."

"That sounds like my man." Her tone had softened, too. He could almost feel the tension easing out of her. "Work before play."

"Always." At least that hadn't changed. There were parts of himself that were still familiar.

"How about you?" he asked. He had to care about her. She'd been his girl for more than two years. That mattered.

He'd known Addy less than two months and she mattered more.

"I made up my mind about us, and I had to call

you before I changed it again. I'm trying to be more like you, Mark, doing the right thing instead of the easy thing. That's what you always said."

"That's right, Ella." He was glad that she was trying to improve herself. Glad that he could help…

Dread filled his gut. He wasn't ready to sign on for a lifetime of…no passion. Wasn't ready to leave behind all of the possibilities he'd been exposed to over the past weeks.

For the first time in his life he'd started to dream—while he was awake.

"I'm not pregnant, Mark."

He was dreaming. Awake. "What?"

"I want to marry you. There's no one here who's ever going to be as good as you, but I'm not pregnant. I made my decision to be honest with you and so that's what I'm doing."

She wanted to marry him.

She was trusting him enough to be honest with him.

She wasn't pregnant.

He could only deal with one thing at a time.

"You lied to me?"

"No! At least not about the being pregnant part."

"You lost the baby?" She wouldn't have ended the pregnancy of her own accord. Another given.

And the thought of his child dying, even in fetal form, elicited a sadness he couldn't have predicted.

He hadn't been there. …

"No."

He frowned. The seesaw of conflicting emotions was getting the better of him in spite of himself.

"You said you didn't lie about the pregnant part. What exactly did you lie about?"

"The doctor part. I didn't go to a doctor. I did a home pregnancy test. It came back positive."

"So you *are* pregnant."

"No. I went to the doctor today. I took him the test results, and he did his own test. It was a false positive."

"You aren't pregnant." If he wasn't careful, he was going to fly right off the edge of the mountain and float down to the city below.

To the lights and school and his new friends.

To a patio where he hoped one new friend in particular would be waiting for him.

White wine. His grandmother had told him to buy a bottle. Good advice.

"Did you hear what I just said?" Ella's words registered, as did her hurt tone.

He'd heard her voice going on.

He was a jerk.

"I want to come out there for a vacation, Mark. I already put in for the time, thinking that I would be going on leave. I was taking vacation time first because I'd get full pay. I can take the bus out just like I said, but Mom wouldn't need to come with me. You can show me your new town. Maybe I'll like it better than I think. I mean, you've lived in Bierly your whole life, too, and you like it there."

"It's not a good idea, Ella."

She'd given him honesty. He owed it back to her.

Her pause was excruciatingly long.

"It's happened, hasn't it? I knew, when you quit texting, but I just didn't want to admit it. You've moved on. I'm no longer good enough for you."

"You're good enough for anyone, Ella, and don't you ever forget that. And I will never move past being your friend. I just don't want to marry you."

He'd already told her that. A few days ago. And what he'd promised her was that he'd be there for her.

"If you're ever in trouble, if you ever need anything, you call me and I'll be there for you. I promise."

"You really do mean that, don't you?"

"Yes." His breathing came easier.

"You're a good person, Mark Heber."

"I don't feel like one at the moment."

"Because you aren't head over heels in love with me?"

"Maybe."

"I'm not head over heels in love with you, either." Her words shocked the hell out of him.

And a lot of the guilt, too.

"You're too good for me…"

"Don't start that again."

"No, hear me out." He heard the clink of a bottle as she paused and knew that she'd started drinking. "You are too good for me, Mark. As in too Goody

Two-shoes. It's too hard living up to you. I like to let loose, have fun, forget about other people sometimes."

He knew that about her. He'd always admired her ability to let go. "You don't ever hurt anyone," he told her.

"No, but I don't bend over backward for them like you do, either. I've tried, but it just doesn't come naturally to me. And I'm tired of trying so hard. I just want to be me."

"Then why did you say you wanted to marry me?"

"Because you're hot. And you're going to be the greatest husband to whatever woman you marry."

"You still planning to stay sober?"

"Of course. Rick don't drink. Remember, I told you he took me to a church thingie?"

"You still seeing him, then?"

"I was till I thought I was pregnant. He's not you, but I have more fun when I'm with him."

"Do you love him?"

"I don't know. Maybe I will once I get you out of my system."

"Does he love you?"

"Yeah. He tells me almost every night. Or he did until I ended things."

"You think you'll be able to patch things up?"

"I don't know. You got any advice?"

Resting his head against the back of his seat, Mark spent the next half hour staring out at the lights in the valley below and helping his ex-girlfriend get her new man.

A man she'd already slept with. Several times.

Even if Ella had been pregnant, there'd been no guarantee the baby had been his. She'd just wanted him to be her baby's father, so she'd tried to make it so.

He understood. Accepted her for what she was.

And moved on down the road.

CHAPTER TWENTY-FOUR

NOTHING WAS AS IT should be. Not her investigation of Will Parsons. Not the life of deception she was living. And not the compulsion to be with Mark Heber.

She didn't go an hour anymore without thinking of sex. And her thoughts always included Mark. She'd been dreaming about sex, too, and waking up crazy in need.

But it was about more than sex. Physical desires she could fight. She was an adult, capable of abstaining. She could lock her doors and stay inside.

She could just tell Mark that she didn't want him to touch her. Ever. He'd abide by her wishes.

Sex wasn't the issue. No matter what Nonnie asked of her, Mark was not going to make love with one woman while another was carrying his baby. Nor would he share his body with one if he'd promised to marry another.

Both were reasons why she loved him.

Jumping up from the table, not even sure what folders she had open on her laptop, Addy went to the spare bedroom, as far away from Mark as she could get without leaving her place.

She'd said she'd meet him outside. She'd been waiting half an hour. He was late getting home.

The spare bedroom felt foreign. She never used it.

She loved him.

That was the issue.

The truth had followed her into the room. She couldn't stay in there with it.

Hurrying back down the hallway, Addy grabbed her car keys and rushed to the front door. She'd go for a drive. Get away.

She just needed a change of scencry.

To find perspcctive.

She pulled open her front door.

And found Mark.

HE'D GONE OUT the back door first. A bottle of wine and two glasses in his hands, he'd approached her chair, some corny words about toasting to a celebration on his lips.

When she hadn't been there, he'd glanced at her window, seen lights on and taken a seat. To wait.

He'd listened to her water. Thought about Ella. She was going to be all right.

If not, she'd call. And he'd help her in any way he could. They'd spent a couple of good years together. They'd always have that.

At some point it had dawned on him that Addy wasn't coming out. Maybe she'd already been out.

He'd purchased the wine chilled.

He needed to see her.

He'd walked through his half of the duplex, past his homework and out the front. And then he'd knocked on her door.

"MARK!"

Did he know that she loved him? Could he read the truth in her eyes?

"You're on your way out." He glanced at the keys suspended in her hand.

"Yes, I…I…" She what? What could she possibly say to this man that wouldn't make her sound crazier than she was?

I'm an impostor who's in love with you?

She couldn't be. She'd just been out of her element too long. She needed to get out of Shelter Valley. Needed to be able to believe that Will Parsons was as perfect as she'd always believed him to be.

She'd agreed to meet Mark outside on their patio and now she was running away.

"What's wrong?"

His frown was filled with as much compassion as concern. And something far more personal, too.

It was the personal that got to her. Inside her. And she noticed the bottle of wine in his hand. The two glasses in the other.

"I… Nothing's wrong," she said. Another lie because everything in her life was wrong.

"I was just heading out for some…milk." He knew she didn't drink milk. They'd talked about it the first time Nonnie had shared his chocolate chip cookies with her. "For cooking."

"What are you cooking this time of night?"

"Pudding." The lies rolled off her tongue. And with every word she hated herself more.

Or, at least, hated the predicament she was in.

"Could I interest you in a celebratory glass of wine instead?" He held up the bottle.

"Of course." Her mouth answered before her brain had a chance to process the question. She stepped aside.

Letting him into her living room. Only her living room.

"You want to go out back?" she asked.

"If you'd like."

"Or we could stay in here." She motioned to the couch. And the chair next to it. She was acting like a schoolgirl. An idiot.

She was acting like Adele Kennedy.

Unfortunately, Adele had given away Adrianna Keller's heart.

ADDY WENT FOR NUTS. A bowl of them. To go with the wine. She couldn't afford any chances that the sweet white liquid would go to her head. Dull her inhibitions any more than they'd already been dulled.

She needed something to do with her hands.

And a moment to herself, as well.

She was not going to fulfill Nonnie's request. Regardless of what the older woman thought, it would not do Mark any good at all to tempt him to sleep with her while he contemplated fatherhood and marriage. It wouldn't save him. It would make him hate himself.

And hate her, too, when he found out that she wasn't who he thought she was.

She wasn't in love with him, either.

She was tired. And lonely for someone who knew her. Really knew her.

Mark was the closest thing there was. Her fault. So many people in Colorado had welcomed her into their lives.

And she'd kept her distance.

She wasn't going to do that anymore. As soon as she got home she'd throw an open house. Get involved in some civic organizations. Meet her neighbors. Find someone to fall in love with.

Her resolve firm, she picked up the little glass bowl of salted cashews and joined Mark in her living room.

"I took the liberty of pouring the wine," he said, indicating the bottle with the screwed-off top on the coffee table behind two full glasses of wine.

He was sitting on the couch.

"Come, sit down," he said, his smile so warm she felt it clear to her womb. "Toast with me."

"What are we toasting?" she asked, sitting a foot away from him on the couch and picking up her glass. She smiled, glad to have him there.

Happy that he'd come to her to celebrate whatever good news he'd brought with him.

"Did you get a promotion?" It was a little soon for a promotion, considering that he'd only had the job for a month, but the guess was the best she could come up with.

He shook his head and held up his glass.

"Here's to me not getting married." His grin was infectious and she played along, clinking her glass against his and taking a long sip.

"Ella turned you down?"

"Not exactly." He held up his glass again.

"Here's to false positives." His grin grew. She sipped some more.

"Wait a minute." Lowering her glass, she held it with both hands on top of her knees.

"Ella isn't pregnant?"

"No."

"But the doctor…"

"She didn't go until today. She'd only done a home pregnancy test. It was positive."

"And she's not pregnant?"

"No. Her doctor did a blood test today and confirmed that she's not."

Nonnie hadn't been in denial.

She'd been right.

ELLA HADN'T BEEN pregnant, but she could have been. Mark had had a narrow escape and was more aware than ever that every single action he took came with consequences.

"This past week has been a real eye-opener for

me," he told Addy as they sat together on her couch sipping wine. In leggings and a long blousy white shirt, she looked sexy as hell.

And so much more.

It was the more that he wanted.

"How so?" Her lips curved into a natural smile.

"I realize how much this education means to me. In Bierly, I was content. I'm not content anymore. In Bierly, I was willing to settle for whatever life gave me. Suddenly I want more."

Her blue-eyed glance warmed him dangerously.

"You are part of the more that I want."

She sat straight up, setting her glass on the table, and Mark froze, thinking she meant to lean over to him, to initiate the lovemaking he was aching to have with her.

His body throbbed. Grew. And she sat with her back half facing him, her elbows on her knees, her hands clasped.

"I want that, too, Mark. So badly I shake with it, but…"

He sat forward, as well, covering her hand with his. "The time's not right," he said, "I know."

Turning her head, she gazed at him, her eyes filled with need—and a curious sadness, too.

"When we make love—note the *when,* not *if*—it will be when it's just you and me focused on you and me." He told her what he'd realized on the drive home that night. "Both of our lives are in flux. We're adjusting to major changes, major moves."

The words sounded better in his head.

But he meant them.

Even as a part of him hoped she'd talk him out of waiting.

ADDY COULDN'T DO it anymore. She couldn't let Adele have Mark. And she couldn't tell him about Adrianna.

She took a sip of wine. "I'm moving back to Colorado." There just wasn't any other choice.

"Now?"

"Soon."

His dismay was written all over his face. And hurt her more than he'd ever know.

"How soon?"

Turning her hand over, she threaded her fingers through his, knowing that this was probably the last time she'd ever touch him. "Before the end of the semester. I…I can't justify the expense of being here when I know I'm not staying—I miss the city too much." Lies. Lies. Lies. And then…truth. "I want you to know that I care for you more than I've ever cared for anyone in my entire life," she said, and looked him straight in the eye. And then she did what she promised herself she wasn't going to do. "If—when I go home—you want to come to Colorado, even just for a weekend, I want you there. Please know that." Just in case, when he found out who she was, he still wanted to see her.

"Okay."

"Will you think about it?"

"Coming to visit?"

"Or more. When you finish school." She was killing herself. Dangling hope when it wasn't the smart thing to do.

"Yeah. Okay."

"Promise?" *Let it go, Adrianna. Let him go.*

"I'm not sure what you're asking." He was just kind of there. Not pulling away, but not engaging, either. "I can't promise what I don't know."

"I…I'd just like to think that sometime in the future, there will be a future for us."

"I'd like that, too."

She had no idea what the words meant, but they felt good, just the same.

CHAPTER TWENTY-FIVE

SHE HAD TO GET OUT. Addy was at a breaking point and she knew it.

She was in love with Mark. Adrianna Keller, a woman he didn't even know existed, was in love with him.

She might have been able to carry off sex without commitment but she couldn't make love with duplicity.

And still…she needed Mark's arms around her—needed to feel complete as only his body melding with hers could make her complete.

She needed him to be in love with her.

He didn't even know who she was.

And when he found out…

Would he even give her a chance to explain? Mark, who prized honesty above all else, would feel as though she'd betrayed him. And she couldn't blame him.

After spending a miserable Tuesday fighting with herself, she moved through the duplex Wednesday morning as if on autopilot. She'd missed class but hadn't seen that there was any reason for her to attend.

Two of her four suitcases were packed with the

winter clothes she'd brought just in case she'd be staying through Shelter Valley's cooler season. She'd brought in the plastic bins from the storage shed assigned to her unit on the side of the building and put them in the spare bedroom. They'd hold the linens, toiletries and kitchen utensils she'd brought with her.

If Mark did let her explain, would he even like Adrianna? He'd befriended a woman in his same position—a first-year college student living in a rented duplex—not a juris doctorate graduate with her own law practice and a home in a nice neighborhood in one of the country's premier cities.

She cleaned and packed and planned, and waited for Greg Richards to contact her. With a prepaid cell phone she'd called his number and hung up twice in a row—their prearranged signal to let him know that she needed to speak with him.

He'd find a way to get in touch with her without compromising her cover. If she'd had an emergency, her cover be damned; she'd dial 9-1-1.

She noticed the sheriff's car in front of their house at a little past ten. And again a second time just after eleven. Figuring that he wanted her to drive outside of town again, she grabbed her keys and her purse, slipping her folder for Greg inside an oversize bag, stepped into her sandals and headed out.

"Psst." Nonnie's front door was open, leaving only the screen between her and the outside world.

The older woman was sitting at the computer not far inside.

Addy couldn't pretend she hadn't heard her. "Did you need something?" she asked, peering through the screen door.

"You missed class."

"Yes, I had some things to do here."

"You sure you're not sick? I made some chicken soup. I was planning to call in about half an hour 'case you was sleeping."

An eighty-one-year-old woman with a debilitating disease had made her chicken soup because she thought she was sick. Tears sprang to her eyes and she blinked them away.

"I'm not sick," she said. "But I would love some chicken soup. I've got an errand to run—can I stop in when I return?"

"Sure you can." Nonnie turned back to the computer. "Did you sleep with him?"

She already had her back to the door. Almost didn't turn around. But she suspected she'd just hear the question again when she came back for soup. Preferring a screen door between them, she simply said, "No," and hurried down the steps.

MARK WAITED FOR Addy outside the science building again. Waited so long he was almost late for his second class. Between his second and third class, he remembered that he hadn't mentioned Thursday night with Abe to her and gave her a call.

She didn't answer.

And when he stopped in at home between school and work, Nonnie told him that Addy hadn't been back for her soup, either.

ADDY DROVE BY the sheriff's office on her way out of town. She hadn't been on the road ten minutes when he passed her. She followed him, and he led them past the cactus jelly plant where Mark worked to a turn-off on state park land. Pulling in, he stopped his car and came back to her.

Rolling down her window, Addy frowned up at him—partially because the sun was in her eyes and partially because she was just plain not in a good mood.

"Sorry for the all the clandestine hoops we're jumping through here, but until I know for sure what's going on I don't want to take any chances."

"It's okay," Addy said, understanding Greg's concern.

"You want to get in, Sheriff?" she asked, motioning to her passenger seat.

Maintaining his stance leaning over her car door, he shook his head. "I apologize for my paranoia, but I want this to look like an ordinary stop. I'm guessing Will didn't tell you about my dad."

The question came seemingly from nowhere.

"No, he didn't," she said, needing to hand off the folder in her bag and deliver the rest of her message. She needed to leave town as soon as they thought they could be done with her services. Sooner if possible. She'd been in class over a month, had poked all over campus and had found nothing untoward. Not in class, extra-curricular programs, campus housing, campus work studies, or even in eavesdropping at the student center.

Almost unanimously, students at Montford appeared to love Montford.

She wasn't surprised.

And she felt confident that she could do the remaining research from her home in Colorado.

Greg had been speaking about his father having been on his way someplace.

"He was carjacked," she heard him say.

Her heart lurched and the sheriff had her full focus as he should have had all along. "Where?"

"Not five miles from here," he said. "He'd been on the freeway…" The sheriff broke off then.

"Was he hurt?"

Sheriff Richards nodded. "He lived another nine years, but only with assisted care. He never resumed any kind of a life. It took me that long to find out who'd killed him. Turns out it was kids—part of a gang initiation. It involved the little brother of a member of the sheriff's department in Shelter Valley. He covered for him. This was a man I trusted with my life."

"So you don't put anything past anyone." Which made her feel better about what she had to tell the sheriff about Will Parsons.

"People do what they have to do given the situations handed to them," he said. "I have no idea who is behind the threats to Will, but I don't count anyone out, either."

"I understand."

She could turn over the file and be done here. Get back to Nonnie and her soup and packing. Back to avoiding the man who could very well have been the love of her life until she could get safely out of town.

People do what they have to do given the situations handed to them, Greg had said. "That sheriff or deputy who was responsible for covering up the crime that eventually took your father's life...did you hate him when you finally discovered what he had done?"

"Hard to hate a guy who was looking out for a kid brother who'd been sucked into a gang against his will," Richards said.

"But wrong is wrong."

"Yes. And there are mitigating circumstances."

True. "Mitigators can lessen sentences, but they don't suspend guilty verdicts."

"They might not suspend guilty verdicts in court," Greg Richards said, standing up straight and peering down at her. "But I know for a fact that they have been used to prevent charges from being filed in the first place."

They were. She couldn't deny his claim.

"So, as a cop, you think it's okay for someone to do something wrong if they do it for the right reasons?"

He frowned, assessing her for a full minute before

he answered her. "The question you asked is irrelevant to me," he said slowly. "You seem to want there to be a clear line between right and wrong in all matters."

"Isn't there?"

"You surprise me, counselor. You're making law the only factor in life and we all know that the human element carries as much or more weight than the law does. A person's reason for doing what he does is sometimes as important as what he does."

He had her full attention. Because she needed the absolution he seemed to be offering.

Was it possible that Mark would apply Sheriff Richards's leniency to her when he learned why she'd been lying to him from the moment she met him?

"Self-defense in court is based largely on motive," she agreed. "I uncovered some questionable circumstances involving Will Parsons," she told the man.

"Tell me."

"I already told you about Tory Evans."

"Yes. I've been following every angle I can think of regarding that incident but so far nothing has clicked."

"It could be something as simple as someone having read the article, seen the potential for a lawsuit and trying to get rich quick."

"Of course there's that possibility. And if that's the case, there might not be much any of us can do until an actual attempt at extortion is made. What else have you found?"

"Will hired Matt Sheffield in spite of the man's prior criminal history."

"Matt told Will about his past. When in possession of the full facts, Will didn't deem the man's past a threat to Montford or his students."

"Yet, within a month of starting at Montford, the man had impregnated one of Montford's professors.

"He also had an accusation of sexual impropriety made against him by one of his students." There'd been nothing further in the file except that the charge had been dismissed.

"An internal investigation was conducted and the student, who had an eating disorder and was looking for validation of her physical attributes, admitted to her problem and got help," Greg said. "She's married now to an attorney and they have a child together."

She wanted to hear this. Needed to hear it. And yet, her lawyer's mind couldn't ignore facts.

"But what about the initial charges against Sheffield? He was convicted, did prison time."

"The victim is now in prison. She admitted to falsely accusing Sheffield."

"And is still in prison for that?"

"No, she's in prison for abducting Sheffield's son after her own son was killed."

"The type of student that teachers fear," Addy said, fully understanding now. Just because she was an educational attorney who fought for the rights of students didn't mean that she wasn't aware of cases where the students were in the wrong. "A child who is mentally off, but still a child, and thus deserving of empathy and compassion." She told the sheriff about her failed attempt to get the drama adviser to show any sexual interest in her.

Another potential strike against Will had been erased. Or, at the very least, was arguable enough in a court of law that it would be tossed out the window if anyone tried to bring him up on charges.

"Just FYI, Sheffield sent the girl in question a check every single month from the time he got out of prison until she abducted his child and went to prison herself."

"Guilt money?"

"Absolutely not. Strictly compassion. The girl came from a rotten home and really showed potential. Sheffield believed in her right up until she threatened his wife and children. He's a great guy. I hope you get a chance to get to know him while you're here in town." She nodded, but she had to get to the point of why she'd summoned him. "I'd like to leave town, actually," she told the sheriff. "But we'll get to that in a second. We've got another problem."

"What? Or should I say, who?"

"Randi Parsons Foster."

"Will's sister?"

"Ten years ago, she awarded a full scholarship to Susan Farley after the semester had started and after all scholarship funds had already been allocated." Pulling the file she'd brought for him out of her bag and handing it over, she said, "Here is a list of names of female athletes who'd applied for scholarships that year but were turned down due to lack of funds. Any of them could claim discrimination or unfair advantage, most especially considering that Susan Farley has now moved on to such fame and success, which could certainly be attributed at least in part to her Montford education and connections. That's where the external economic value inherent in a Montford education actually hurts the institution. It makes the institution—and Will—a target for lawsuits."

"Do the records show where Randi got the money?"

Addy shook her head. "It came from a private source." She told him about her subterfuge and Randi's potential offer of a scholarship resulting from her bogus request, based on her "sister's" academic records.

"At least tell me Susan Farley met Montford's entrance qualifications."

"I don't know that yet. In a court of law it won't just be a matter of whether or not Montford found her acceptable. I have to research the types of test scores they use, assess the testing agencies, look for case law involving any of them."

The type of work she could do from Colorado. Work that would really only come into play if they went to court—for Will's defense—which could be completed at a later date.

"Let me know when you have some answers."

She nodded. "I found something else odd," she continued. "I came across a student who's here on full scholarship, but there's no record of an application. I befriended the applicant, got friendly enough to ask about his scholarship and he claims that the award just showed up in his mailbox. Prior to that, he'd had no intention of attending college anywhere. I looked up his tuition and it says it was paid with cash."

With a dry throat, Addy gave the sheriff Mark's name. "I'll ask Will what he knows about this," Greg said.

"I'm worried about something else, with Randi. There were budget changes, requested by her, that pulled funds from men's athletics and gave them to women's athletics, the end result of which netted the university little change in the amount of money women's athletics brought in, and diminished the men's athletics monetary contributions by thousands."

"I'm assuming Will approved the budget changes?"

"Yes. And there's one more. Todd Moore."

"Will fired him as soon as Moore's intentions became clear."

"I know. That's not the problem. The liability comes in having recommended him for hire in the first place. Moore was his friend."

"He wasn't qualified for the job?"

"He was, but maybe not as qualified as the three other applicants— all out-of-towners. But what really hurts is that Moore proved to be a poor choice. It could be argued that if Moore hadn't been Will's friend, his lack of moral character might have been recognized during the interview process. In the end,

Moore's fall from grace is proof that he wasn't the best choice and any of the three other applicants could have cause for suit against both Will and Montford. All three of their names are there."

"Okay, we've got some potential problems here. But at least we're on top of them. And that's why we needed you."

"I have to tell you, I hate every aspect of what I'm doing."

"I understand. I also know that Will is sleeping at night because you're here."

"I wonder if he'll still feel that way when he knows that I've found some things that could cause potential trouble for him."

"Of course he will. You didn't make his choices for him. You're just giving him a heads-up on any choices he's made that could potentially come back to bite him. Believe me, he's incredibly grateful to you and even more fond of you than he is grateful. To listen to Will you'd think you were his kid sister or something."

The tone in the sheriff's voice, when he made that last comment, told Addy that Will hadn't spilled the secrets from her past. She should have known he wouldn't.

She longed for an evening in his company. His and Becca's. She was living only a few miles from them, from their sweet and miraculous children whom she'd never even met.

She'd wept when Will had called to tell her that

after twenty years of trying he and Becca had finally given birth, in their forties, to a healthy little girl. She had a picture of Bethany on her refrigerator. The beautiful child was twelve now.

"So what's this about you needing to leave town?" the sheriff asked. "How long do you need to be gone?"

"Permanently," Addy said. She told the sheriff about her immersion in campus life. "I suppose if I stayed longer something could present itself," she allowed. "Wrongdoing isn't immediately obvious, but I haven't seen or heard of even a hint of impropriety in all the time I've spent on campus. And the historical research I'm doing, the computer work, could just as easily be done from my home in Colorado."

Home. With the drive out to the desert, followed by a conversation that was much longer than she'd expected, she was way past soup time. After Nonnie had made the soup especially for her.

"I'm not sure that's true," Sheriff Richards said. "By your own admission, the case against Randi grew stronger after your meetings with her."

"That's true, but—"

"And you collected evidence to counteract a possible suit involving Matt Sheffield.... I'll do this," Richards said, straightening. "I'll talk to Will and get back to you."

Addy nodded, wanting to leave immediately, but not willing to jeopardize her relationship with Will Parsons to do so. She might have given Mark Heber her heart, but she'd given Will her word first.

CHAPTER TWENTY-SIX

ADDY HAD NOT YET returned by the time Mark had to go to work. Leaving Nonnie with instructions to call him if Addy showed up, he climbed into his truck and headed out. He was overreacting, he was sure.

It just wasn't like Addy to tell Nonnie she'd be over and then not show up. It wasn't like her to skip class, either.

At least not in the weeks he'd known her.

Before that, he had no way of knowing if Addy was the reliable sort or not.

What did he really know about her at all, except what his gut told him?

Out on the freeway, heading toward the cactus jelly plant, he pressed his foot to the gas pedal until the needle was teetering over the eighty mile an hour mark. He didn't usually get so worked up. About anything.

The move across country had messed him up, or his next-door neighbor was doing so. Either way, he didn't like it.

Going as fast as he was, he almost missed the little old sedan pulling out of an entrance into the state park. He'd never seen the driveway in use—

the scenic views, picnic tables and facilities were located at two other entrances. But he knew Addy's car—looked for it in the drive next to his truck every single night and every single morning, too.

He had driven past before he could think to wave, or in any way acknowledge that he'd seen her. But he watched her pull out onto the freeway from his rearview mirror.

And that was when he also noticed the sheriff's car pulling out directly behind her. Two cars, one right behind the other, on a drive that had been otherwise deserted every time he'd driven past it for weeks.

Addy and a cop.

Which meant trouble no matter how you looked at it. Either she'd had to call the police. Or she'd been pulled over.

Pulling his phone out of the holster at his belt, he started to call her. And stopped. She had his number and wasn't calling him.

He wasn't going to trespass where he wasn't wanted. No matter how much he cared. It wasn't right.

Clearly she was fine enough to drive. Or dial her cell if she needed him. Knowing that, he turned his focus to the things he had in his control.

Like work.

MARK WAITED FOR Addy's call while he worked—not that she'd ever called him at work before. The only time his cell vibrated was when Nonnie phoned just after he'd clocked in to tell him that Addy had pulled in the drive.

By the time his first break came around, he'd talked himself into making a friendly call. Just to put his mind at rest. If she didn't want to hear from him, she didn't have to answer. She picked up on the first ring.

"Are you okay?" He didn't mean to sound territorial, but damn it, they had a future. Sometime in the future. She was a friend—one of the few he had in this town.

He was one of her few friends, too. She'd told him so. It was his job to look out for her.

"I'm fine, Mark. I'm sorry I missed your earlier call."

"And Nonnie's soup." Not a big deal, except that it wasn't like Addy. Which was why he'd been concerned.

And then he'd seen the cop car right behind her.

"No, I got the soup. Ate it at your kitchen table, actually. Nonnie wanted to chat."

If she could sit and chat with his grandmother, she must be all right.

Leaning against a wall in the break room, he slid down to the bench beside him, breathing easier. "I'll bet she did," he said. Based on the not-so-subtle inquisition he'd been subjected to that morning, pertaining to his late-night visit with Addy the previous night, he cringed at the thought of what Addy had been put through.

"Who was the victor?" he asked.

"I'm not sure," she said. "I think that remains to be seen."

"When?"

"Sometime in the future." That future they'd talked about the previous night?

"I passed you on the way to work," he told her because he approached life from the front line. Always. "You were pulling out of the state park land."

"You did?"

"Yeah, but I noticed you too late to honk."

"I didn't see you."

"There was a cop car right behind you."

"Oh."

"Everything okay?"

"Yes. Everything's fine." Was it his imagination or did she suddenly sound different?

"You're sure?"

"Yes."

"Okay." It wasn't like she owed him any kind of explanation. It was just odd.

He didn't think for one second that Addy was seeing someone else. There'd be no reason to lie to him about that. Or any reason to ask for a future with him if it were so.

"Are you in some kind of trouble?"

"No." She didn't give him any more.

MARK WAS A SMART man. He knew something was up.

Which meant that she was either going to have to engage in more lies, or tell him the truth.

The idea made her blood run cold. She'd lose him for sure.

Or would she?

If he really cared, he'd know that Adele was only a cover, like a piece of clothing she had to wear for a short time—that the woman he cared for was Adrianna. Once he got past the initial shock, Mark would forgive her for the betrayal.

Or not.

Either way, she had to finish this job so she could have her life back.

Montford entrance qualifications were steep. Greg was waiting for them so, sitting at her table later that afternoon, she read through them, studying the various methods by which they measured academic proficiency. She visited websites of private institutions that issued accredited testing opportunities. Compared them to accepted public scholastic exams.

If acceptance into the university was behind the threats against Will, an attorney defending him in court would need to have the statistics she was compiling.

She had to have them in order to fairly compare the specific entrance qualifications of individual applicants.

Addy knew from experience that any one of the names she'd given Greg Richards could easily file suit against the university. Especially with athletics involved.

These days, courts were looking closely at the things universities covered up with regard to their athletes.

Her search engine stalled briefly between sites. Addy listened to her fountain.

The website for the testing facility she was looking at declared that it had been founded by college professors from Yale and Georgetown. Their tests were administered under strict supervision at secure sites during regularly scheduled intervals. They appeared to be valid and legitimate, so she moved on to the next facility.

Several hours of research later, Addy had found nothing of concern regarding Montford's entrance exam practices.

She moved on to scholarship applicants. She performed a search of their student records and compiled various testing and GPA data into a spreadsheet. From there she made three lists: applicants who'd been denied entrance due to lack of scholarship funds, those who'd been denied due to lack of qualifications and those who'd been granted scholarships and entrance in spite of the fact that they lacked the entrance qualifications.

Looking up only specific names might have gained her the information pertinent to the question at hand, but any prosecutor or civil attorney would search out all possible incidents of discrimination. Just because one person sued didn't mean there'd only been one who'd been wronged. And the case would be much stronger if there were more.

Thinking like an attorney was what Addy did best. It was why Will had hired her.

She wasn't there to think like a woman—about the man next door.

She looked over the scholarship applicants who were turned down due to lack of qualifications. Six of the names she'd given to Greg Richards were listed among the more than two hundred applicants who'd been turned down for scholarships due to low test scores the semester that Randi Parsons Foster had privately accepted Susan Farley into the basketball program.

Which gave rise to a fourth search. Students who'd been *admitted* to the university without meeting academic standards. On scholarship and not, at any time in university history. Will Parsons and Randi Parsons Foster needed that spreadsheet to be empty.

Addy held her breath, expecting it to be empty.

It wasn't.

Eleven names were on that list.

There were eleven times in the more than one hundred years the university had been in existence that students had been admitted without the proper qualifications.

Skimming the list quickly, Addy wanted first and foremost to assure herself that Susan Farley wasn't named there. The female basketball player posed the biggest risk to the university based on the perceived benefit her time at Montford had provided to her. She had measurable assets, which meant measurable damages to those who'd been denied the opportunity she'd been granted.

There it was. Second on the list. Farley, Susan. The girl's high school grade point average had been a full point lower than Montford's minimum acceptance score. Looking further, she noted that Susan's collegiate GPA had been above minimum by the end of that first semester, and according to official records, the girl had maintained an average that met Montford guidelines through graduation.

All bad news to Addy. The point could be argued that Montford's superior tutelage had fostered the girl's higher scores, which could then be argued in defense of the external economic value theory that would award damages against Will and the university if charges were pressed.

The worst-case scenario would be if there was proof that Susan's assignments and tests had actually been written by another university student. It happened. Her first year in practice, Addy had argued a case against a junior college for expelling a student due to a low GPA when athletes with equally low classroom performance had been allowed to stay. She'd been able to prove false testing—papers being turned in by athletes that had actually been written by someone paid to write them on the athlete's behalf.

In lieu of an expensive civil lawsuit, the college had allowed Addy's client to remain enrolled and paid for a private tutor for her client, after which her client's performance had improved substantially. He'd graduated just below honors and entered a four-year degree program at a state college. The athletes who'd been involved in educational fraud had been expelled. She had no idea what had happened to them.

Addy's mind shot memories like bullets, reverberating back and forth, blocking her focus from the here and now.

From the third name on the spreadsheet of eleven. Right below Farley.

She'd seen it. She just didn't want to be in possession of the knowledge.

Didn't believe it. So she performed another search. This one for specific test score data. She rearranged the information by date, most recent first.

And the name rose to the top.

Mark Heber.

MARK WORKED HARD. He got home in time to finish the paper he had due by the end of the week for a freshman English class. Had a cup of hot chocolate with his grandmother while she sipped on chamomile tea. And he waited until he could slip outside his back door and sit in the dark with his beautiful neighbor.

She was already outside when he arrived, which surprised him. He'd been listening for her glass door to slide open. And he knew the second he sat down that something was not right.

The bottle of wine they'd opened the night before but hadn't finished, sat chilled on the table beside two empty wineglasses. Sensing that the wine was there for a purpose—that he was going to need it for some reason not yet known to him—he poured two glasses, leaving only a little bit at the bottom of the bottle.

It wasn't much if he found himself in sudden need of liquid tranquilizing.

She hadn't said a word yet.

So he started in. "You free Thursday evening?" Until he knew they had a problem, there wasn't one.

"Yes."

Nodding, he settled lower in his seat, his untouched glass of wine on the table beside him.

"I invited Jon to drop Abe off at my place," he said, watching her face for clues. She looked the same, albeit more formal than he was used to in her blue cotton pants, silk blouse and leather sandals. "I told him Nonnie and I would watch Abe for a while so he could have some time to himself."

"I'll bet he was thrilled."

Mark shrugged. Jon and "thrilled" didn't exactly go together. "He agreed readily enough. You want to join us?"

"Sure."

Okay, then. She'd agreed to a date with him. Of sorts.

How bad could things be?

The stricken look in her eyes as she peered up at him told him things were bad, and fear sliced through him.

"You're leaving."

"Yes."

"How soon?"

"By the weekend, I hope."

"You're dropping out of school midsemester?"

"I think so. I'm…still waiting to… I haven't had confirmation on that yet."

"What kind of confirmation do you need to drop out of school?"

"I need to know the consequences before I make my final decision."

Mark listened to her words, but what he heard her say was that there was still a chance she'd be staying.

"Have you given notice on the duplex?" He dealt with facts.

"My rent is prepaid through the end of the year."

"Can you sublet it? It's prohibited in my contract."

"I don't know."

She looked at him, but her eyes seemed almost vacant. He felt like he was seeing a stranger.

"You aren't drinking your wine."

Picking up her glass, she sipped and said, "You aren't drinking yours, either."

"I want to know what's going on."

To her credit, she didn't immediately assure him that everything was fine. She didn't say anything, which wasn't like her.

"Is it the nightmares? Did you have a bad night last night?"

Or had something else happened to her? A crime that merited calling the sheriff? Dear God, had she been raped?

Shaking her head, she smiled. Sort of. Her entire expression looked…broken. "I haven't had a nightmare in over a week. I'm out here tonight because I have to speak with you about something."

"Addy, whatever is wrong, we can deal with it." Did he sound as lovesick as he felt?

How did a guy who didn't believe in love feel lovesick?

"I know we haven't known each other long, but I think you'll agree that we've got something between us."

He held her gaze, and she nodded.

Feeling like he'd won a battle in a war he hadn't yet been drafted for, he marched onward, as any good soldier would do. "I'm not the type of guy who shies away from trouble," he told her. "If nothing else, I'm your friend. I'll do whatever I can to help you in any way I can. I just need to know what's bothering you."

"Would you please quit being so damned nice?" It was her voice, in a tone he'd never heard.

Her eyes glistened and Mark didn't want to hear any more.

CHAPTER TWENTY-SEVEN

Addy could deal with her own pain. She'd survived being nearly burned alive by her father. Survived listening to Ely's screams—and then the silence as her brother died. Survived losing her mother. And knowing that her father had set them all on fire.

She had no idea how to deal with knowing she'd caused someone else pain—someone she loved. If nothing else, this moment was teaching her something very clear about herself. She was nothing like her father.

"At least tell me this…" Mark's gaze was shadowed, but his concern was obvious as he turned toward her.

"What?"

"Did something happen to you today? Were you… molested in any way?"

"No! Of course not. I'd have told you…"

She stopped when she realized she'd pretty much admitted that she was withholding information from him.

Mark stood.

"Where are you going?"

Leaving his nearly full glass of wine on the table, he motioned toward his side of the duplex they'd shared for such a short time. In some ways that time seemed like forever.

A forever that she wanted more than anything else in life.

"I've got homework to do."

"Please, stay."

Watching her, his hands in his pockets, Mark didn't move—either to leave, or to sit.

"Please," she said again. She owed him this. Now. Before a new day dawned and he heard about it from someone else.

He sat. And her heart was more his than ever. His and shattering at the same time.

"I'm sorry for..." Everything. So, so sorry. "My mood," she finished lamely. She wasn't ready. How did one prepare to obliterate someone's faith in them?

She had no plan. As hard as she'd tried to figure out the best way to do this, the right way to handle the quagmire her life had become, she'd come up empty. It was the case of her life and she had no winning argument.

It didn't matter how she attempted to explain herself, hearing the words in her mind, they just sounded like excuses.

He sat a mere foot away from her. She could smell his musky cologne and wondered if he'd put it on just for her.

"You said you have something to tell me."

Yes. And she still didn't have the words. The way. She didn't know how to minimize his pain. How to make things right.

A PHONE RANG in the distance.

"That's my cell," Addy said, setting down her glass as she jumped up. "I have to get it."

At ten o'clock at night? The call lasted less than five minutes. One look at Addy's face as she came back outside and he knew that something had gone wrong.

Really wrong.

WILL HAD RECEIVED another threat. She'd called Greg Richards once and hung up, letting him know that Susan Farley had not met Montford's entrance standards. She hadn't expected to hear back from him.

Hadn't even known it was him when she'd heard her prepaid cell phone ring. She'd never had a call on the thing.

She hadn't recognized the number on the caller display when she'd run inside to get the phone.

But she'd answered because only Will and the sheriff knew the number.

Greg had purchased a prepaid cell, as well. Just in case.

The latest letter had arrived at Will's home. In his personal mail. There was no return address. It had a Phoenix postmark and was typed on the same generic letterhead. It, too, stated that Will should be liquefying his assets as he'd soon be ordered to pay a large sum of money.

Who the orders would be coming from was unclear. Ordered by an extortionist? Or by the courts?

The new letter had arrived on the same day Addy had met with Greg and turned over the list of names she'd compiled. As though the person behind it knew she was closing in. To hear that there'd been another letter had been upsetting enough. But that hadn't been the worst of Greg Richards's news. He'd read to her the dates of all three letters, asking her to check them against the spreadsheets she'd compiled that afternoon—just in case anything popped.

Something had.

The date of the first letter coincided with the week Mark Heber had accepted Montford's offer of admission.

She hadn't shared the news with Greg Richards. Not tonight. Tomorrow was soon enough. And she hadn't told the sheriff about the ten other people who'd been granted entrance into the university without qualifying to be there. He knew about Susan. That was all.

"I won't be leaving this weekend," she said, picking up her glass of wine as she took her seat next to Mark.

But he might be. Oh, not that weekend. But before

the semester was out. Unless Addy could figure out a way to stop that from happening.

"You got a call about school this late at night?"

Another mistake. "I… Can we talk about this tomorrow?"

"Yes." She tried to look away from the intensity in his gaze but didn't have the strength. Or the will.

He'd once told her that emotions messing with thought was the cause behind poor choices. He'd said it one time when they'd been talking about Ella. Until now, Addy's emotions had been so firmly under wrap that they'd never had the opportunity to interfere with her thought processes.

Will wanted her to stay in Shelter Valley. Greg agreed that, for now, it was in the best interests of the case to have Addy there.

And unbeknownst to both of them, Mark Heber's scholarship had just become a major red flag lawsuit in her investigation.

"I… There's so much I need to say, but right now I'm not at liberty to do that and…"

So much for being trusted with an undercover assignment.

Or maybe it was just that this was Mark.

And she wanted him to know.

MARK DIDN'T WANT to go to bed alone. Not with the sight and smell and sound of the woman next door so firmly ingrained in him that he couldn't walk away.

She was involved in something she wasn't at liberty to talk about. And she'd suddenly decided not to even finish out the semester. That didn't sound anything but bad.

He was losing her so quickly. Not that he'd ever expected permanence. They'd made that clear from the beginning. He'd just thought he'd have more time. ...

"I want to make love with you tonight." He put it right out there.

She didn't gasp or run away. She didn't even slosh her wine over the side of her glass. She sipped slowly, watching him over the rim, and then said, "We were going to wait until we were both in a position to do it right."

She hadn't said no.

"That was before."

"There'd be so much more potential for us to get hurt."

"I don't know about you, Addy, but my body's hurting so much now I can't possibly see how waiting any longer is going to do anything but hurt more."

His mouth was dry and his penis was hard. "Making love will create a bond between us, a deeper bond. Maybe it's what we need to hold us together through whatever lies ahead," he said.

Her eyes filled up. "Your timing is... You say the most incredible things."

"I could just be trying to justify it because I'm horny as hell." Reaching for her hand, he held it lightly. "If I'm wrong, please say so, but I'm worried that tonight might be our only chance at the 'future someday' that we talked about. If we let this chance go, we might never find each other again."

"And you think that if we make love, we will?"

"I don't know, but it makes sense to me that we'd have a better chance at it."

"You might hate me at some point in the near future."

There was no chance of that.

"I seriously doubt it. But even if I did, then at least we'd have made a great memory."

She didn't say a word. She didn't have to. The tears in her eyes and the smile on her face told him all he really needed to know.

ADDY DIDN'T HAVE a chance to think about the situation. She leaned in to kiss him without giving it any forethought. His lips had been there and they'd needed her lips on them.

And then only sensation existed. His mouth, larger than hers, covering hers, tenderly coaxing her lips apart. His tongue, touching her lips softly, inviting and waiting. Her tongue met his and she became someone new. Someone stronger. Bolder.

Someone who wasn't ashamed to spread her legs and straddle his knee, to open herself up to whatever he had in mind for her.

She was moist and needy and reaching for him. Her nipples tingled, awaiting his touch, his mouth. She pictured him naked, above her, below her, and was shocked at the images she conjured up.

"Let's go inside." Her fingers were reaching for the bottom of his T-shirt, sliding underneath, absorbing the heat of his skin. "I want this off," she added, excited by the unfamiliar raspiness in her tone. Expecting to be set on her feet, to stumble inside, Addy felt a rush as Mark stood, lifting her against him in one easy move, and carried her, still kissing her, to her back door. He slid that open somehow and the next thing she knew they were heading down the hall toward her room.

"Take this off," she groaned, pulling at the hem of his shirt. The carpet caressed the bottoms of her feet as he set her down and she wiggled her toes, feeling the threads between them. She grasped at the thick pile with her toes. Holding on. And gasped at the first sight of Mark Heber's chest.

He was not anything like the two guys she'd been with before. His chest was huge. Firm and hard and covered with thick black hair. His nipples were hard, prominent, urging her to lick them, suck on them.

She was ready to explode and he hadn't even unbuckled his pants.

LYING WITH A WOMAN was not a new experience for Mark. Lying with one, on top of one, underneath one—he was good with all of that. Had been having relations since before he'd quit high school.

But there was no bed like Addy's. No body like Addy's.

He couldn't touch her enough…couldn't kiss her

enough. He was ready to have his big moment and she was still fully dressed. He hadn't been this turned on his first time out.

Or any time after that.

And as he slowed himself physically, lifting her shirt with hands that trembled, he knew that no matter what secrets she held, they wouldn't be enough to make him hate her.

He loved her.

It was that simple. And that complicated.

That life-changing.

Adele Kennedy had turned a man who didn't believe into a believer.

AS MUCH AS HE wanted to, Mark couldn't spend the night in Addy's bed. Tucking her in, he kissed her one last time as he gathered his clothes and quietly left her room. He had to be home to hear Nonnie get out of bed if he was going to beat her to the bacon.

Dropping his clothes in a pile on her dining chair, he stepped into his jeans, pulling them up over a penis already getting hard as he relived some particularly memorable moments from the hours that had just changed his life yet again. He pulled his T-shirt over his head, letting it fall over the fly of his pants rather than tucking it in, and dropped the cell phone that kept him connected to Nonnie at all times in the back pocket that, in his teens, would have held a pack of cigarettes.

He'd been young and foolish once.

He'd paid a heavy price.

And he'd come out a man he could live with.

A man who was willing to pay whatever price he and Addy would have to pay to get to that future they'd talked about.

He'd been right. Making love with her had strengthened their bond. Making love had glued him to her for as long as she wanted him there.

He was halfway to the sliding glass door when he turned back. He couldn't just go without letting her know that the night had been about far more for him than just sex. He couldn't leave without communicating to her that she could count on him. No matter what. He'd leave her a note.

Her table was laden with folders and papers, pens and pencils. And her opened laptop computer.

He couldn't find a blank piece of paper so he reached for the legal pad next to the computer, intending to rip a page from the back.

He'd have done so easily, without reading a word of what she'd written, if his eye hadn't caught something he recognized as belonging to him.

Looking back, he saw that he hadn't been mistaken. It was right there. In handwritten script—*Mark Heber*. His name.

CHAPTER TWENTY-EIGHT

A SOUND FROM the kitchen woke her. Sitting straight up in bed, Addy listened. And realized she was naked. She didn't sleep naked.

Was someone in her house?

Shifting to pull the covers up over her breasts, her nipples came in contact with the sheet and felt…sore.

In an instant she remembered everything. The little bit of wine she'd had to drink could not be blamed for the wanton behavior she'd exhibited the night before.

Only love could have so transformed her.

Another shuffle from the other room had her tingling all over again. Mark was still there. Getting something to drink? Using the bathroom? She wanted him to come back to bed. Quickly.

Glancing at the clock, she calculated that they'd have another three hours together before either of them would need to leave.

Three hours before life caught up with them. She didn't want to waste a minute of that time being alone.

Out of bed before she'd completed the thought, Addy pulled on the light cotton robe she kept hanging on the hook on the back of her bedroom door and hurried down the hall toward the light at the end of it, belting her robe as she walked.

He'd turned on a light? Or had they left it on when they'd gone to bed?

Whatever she'd been expecting to see when she reached the kitchen fled from Addy's mind as she saw what was waiting for her.

Mark stood, staring at her, a sheaf of papers in his hand.

And, too late, she remembered that she'd been working before she'd gone outside the night before. She'd pulled more papers out to refer to during the phone call from Greg Richards.

"You're researching me." His tone was not fully accusatory. There was question there, as well, and Addy scrambled for words.

How much did he know? How much time did she have?

What did she have to say to keep him believing in her?

"This looks like some kind of background check." Not something she'd have thought of, but it could appear that way, she supposed.

"You've got my GED scores here. They're circled in red."

When one was being accused, the best defense was silence until the accuser spilled everything he knew and the conclusions he'd drawn.

"I had to get home in case Nonnie woke up and needed me. I was going to leave you a note."

She believed him.

And was in no position to lay blame in any case. She'd known, going in, that she was the bad guy here. She couldn't blame Mark for anything. No matter what happened from here on out.

He held up the paper he'd pulled from the stack. "This is a spreadsheet of Montford students who didn't meet entrance criteria," he said. The list of eleven.

Addy nodded. She knew she'd have to answer to this. She just hadn't realized it would be this soon.

She'd thought she'd be the one initiating the conversation.

And she'd expected to be dressed.

He was.

"Why are you doing this?"

"I did a lot of research. I was asked to look through a lot of tedious records and see if I could find anything that flagged itself as a potential lawsuit against the university." Was he going to hate her?

"I am a potential lawsuit?"

"I'm not at liberty to say."

She could have explained about the proven external economic value inherent in a Montford education. And how any deviation from equally applied principles for all applicants put the university at risk of lawsuit.

He was staring at her. "Is my education at risk?"

"It could be."

"Because you found me on this list?"

"I compiled the list." He was going to know eventually.

"Who else knows I'm on this list?"

"No one." Her "yet" was implied.

"What about the other names here?" His questions were getting harder to answer. "Does anyone know about them?"

"Only the one name I was originally looking at."

"Which one?"

"I'm not at liberty to say."

He was frowning. Studying her.

"But it's not me."

"No."

"Does our…association…have anything to do with this?" He held up the papers, his drawl more pronounced than it had ever been.

She'd looked up his file because of their association. But his name on that list of eleven—that would have shown up regardless if she'd known who he was or not.

"No."

"You didn't move in here to spy on me?"

Folding her arms over her chest, Adrianna forced herself to withstand his inquisition without getting defensive. She had it coming. "Absolutely not."

"Did you have sex with me to get more information out of me?"

"No."

His shoulders dropped. So did his chin. He continued to watch her—his gaze narrowed and piercing.

"For what it's worth, I was trying to tell you last night, on the patio."

"And then the phone rang. It had to do with this, didn't it?"

"Yes."

"What happens next?"

"I have a decision to make."

A raised eyebrow was the only response she got, and she knew her time to speak up or miss out on the chance forever was at hand.

"I have to decide whether I do what is ethically correct and turn over this list of names to the authorities that asked for them, or whether I throw it in the trash and pretend I never saw it."

"If you throw it away—this whole thing goes away?"

"Where your education is concerned, you mean?"

One nod—a very succinct up and down motion of the head she'd cradled between her breasts such a short time ago—was all she got.

"There's a chance that it will, yes."

"A chance?"

"They're looking at cases that could make the university vulnerable to lawsuits," she reminded him. "Someone else could feasibly find this same information. If they knew to look for it." She would be honest with Mark in terms of her own duplicity, but she absolutely could not reveal any information involving Will or any other students.

"If you turn in that list, what happens next?"

"I don't know."

"But you could make a pretty good guess."

He was a bright man. "Yes."

"And?"

"My guess is you'll lose the scholarship." She quickly added, "But you won't have to pay back the money already spent."

He nodded again, the tightening of his jaw the only evidence of the emotions that had to be roiling through him.

Addy took a deep breath, praying for the strength to get through this while she slowly unraveled inside.

He couldn't see that. Couldn't know what this was doing to her. She wasn't going to play the vulnerable-woman card. He didn't deserve that garbage.

"What are you going to do?" he finally asked.

"What would you have me do?" If he asked her to throw the list in the trash, would she?

Mark was silent for so long she figured he wasn't going to answer her. When he finally spoke, it was only to ask, "Who are you working for?"

"I can't disclose that information."

"Why not? Is someone forcing you to do this against your will? Are you in some kind of trouble?"

Addy's eyes filled with tears. Even now he was coming to her rescue. For the first time in her life she wished she was in trouble.

"No."

"Is someone blackmailing you?"

"No."

"That cop that was behind you yesterday—he has something to do with this, doesn't he?"

"I can't say."

"Are you part of an investigation?"

"As a suspect, you mean?"

His gaze narrowed again and, too late, she realized she'd just given him a clue. "Yeah, that's what I mean."

"No."

"So you're involved in an investigation, but not as a suspect."

Her silence told him what he wanted to know. But if she'd denied the allegation, he'd have known she was lying.

And that's why it had been wrong to sleep with him. She'd handed him the keys to her heart—to the ability to read through her subterfuge.

"Who are you?"

She didn't answer. She tried, but no words formed.

"What are you?"

"What does that mean?"

"Are you a cop?"

"No."

"What, then?"

"I'm a lawyer."

Mark's jaw dropped. He swung around toward

the door. Swung back. Stared at her as though she'd sprung up from the sewer, turned and left.

And Addy learned something new.

It took only one second for a heart to break.

CHAPTER TWENTY-NINE

MARK MADE BACON. And eggs and toast, too.

He sat at the kitchen table and forked food into his mouth, chewed and swallowed, all the while pretending that he didn't see his grandmother's knowing stare.

He couldn't answer to her. Not this morning.

Sometimes a man just needed space for himself.

It was something he couldn't help.

"You slept with her!"

"That's none of your damned business."

"Uh-oh. What happened?"

Mark jabbed at the last piece of fried egg on his plate, turned his fork prong down and shoved the egg into his mouth.

"You didn't hurt her, did you? She's different than the girls in Bierly. Some girls are just raised more fragile. Don't you worry none about it...."

Taking his plate to the sink, Mark ran water over the egg yolk and left the dish and his silverware to soak.

SHE HAD TO TURN over the list. No matter how much Addy loved Mark, the fact remained that his scholarship posed the most risk as being the cause of the threats against Will. The timing was right. The letters had started arriving almost to the day that Mark had accepted entrance into the university. It was too much of a coincidence for her to ignore.

Will was counting on her.

She'd not only given him her word, she'd taken payment for her professional services. While technically it could be argued that because there was no formally signed fee agreement, she was not beholden to professional ethics in this case, the argument would be weak at best. And wrong.

Wiping tears from her face, Addy sat at her kitchen table, dressed and ready to leave for campus as soon as she reapplied the makeup she'd cried off, and knew what she had to do.

But first, she picked up the prepaid cell phone given to her by Sheriff Richards and dialed. Mark's phone.

He still might not pick up if he saw the unidentified number on his caller display and suspected that it was her. She wouldn't blame him. But figured she had a better chance of getting him if he didn't recognize the number.

"Hello."

"It's Addy."

"I figured." And he'd still answered. She took that as a good sign.

"I'm getting ready to head out to campus to drop off yesterday's assignment. Nonnie calls me from the porch anytime she sees me out there." She was babbling. Stalling. And continued, anyway. "Do you want me to answer her?"

"If you want to."

"You don't mind if I'm in your house?"

"Do I have reason to mistrust your intentions with my grandmother?"

Oh, God. His answering hadn't been a good sign at all. It had just been a Mark thing to do.

"No," she said softly. "You don't. My affection for Nonnie has been sincere from the beginning."

As has my affection for you, she added silently, hoping he'd ask and give her the chance to say the words aloud.

"Feel free to go in, then."

Tears sprang to her eyes again and she swiped at them impatiently. "I just…I want you to know…I have to turn over the list, Mark."

"I figured as much."

"If I could find a way to let it go I would, but—"

"I get it," he interrupted. And added, "I'd like to know how much time I have. I'll need to make plans. To prepare my grandmother for travel."

"Just hang tight, will you? I'm hoping it won't come to that. And if it does, I'll make sure that you have all the time you need. At least until the end of the semester."

"I won't need long. We've got our home in Bierly to go back to."

She wanted to die. Right then and there. "Nonnie still didn't tell you?"

"Tell me what?"

"She sold the house in Bierly, Mark."

Silence was the only reply she received. Until she heard a tone signifying the call had been lost.

HE WANTED TO HIT something. Hard.

Stamping through the desert where he'd driven to cool off that second Thursday morning in October, Mark tried to find himself in the cacophony of violent thoughts and raging emotions that had taken possession of the man he'd once been.

It was almost comical the way things had stacked up against him. How was a guy supposed to fight things that were so completely out of his control? How was he supposed to fix them?

He'd thought about calling Nonnie, to reassure himself that Addy had been wrong when she'd told him that Nonnie sold the home she'd been born in. But he was afraid of what he might say to his grandmother if he found out the woman—the lawyer— he'd slept with had been right. So he'd pulled into an establishment offering free wireless service, gone online on his tablet and searched out recent closings in Bierly instead.

When he saw his home address right there, in black and white, he was beyond surprised.

The good news was, the savvy old lady had gotten a decent price for the place. She'd have safeguarded the sum, too. There was no doubt in his mind about that. Her money would sustain her until he could get back on at the plant, find a home in Bierly for them to rent.

It was when he pulled out his cell to call his former boss to ask for his old job back that he caught himself. He had a job. One he actually liked. With good benefits. Right there in Shelter Valley.

A town that he also liked.

The duplex was on loan to him only for as long as he was a student at the university—a condition of the scholarship—but there were other places to rent in town.

And someday, when he saved up the money, he'd find a school in Phoenix that would accept him and he'd get his safety engineering degree, too.

If he stayed, he wouldn't risk Nonnie's life with another long drive.

This was how a guy fixed things. He took what he'd learned and continued moving forward, one step at a time.

By the time he'd almost reached his truck, he'd convinced himself that life was good. And then he had a flashback: Addy, naked and open to him. He pushed the image away. Started walking faster—to the point where he was working up a sweat.

He remembered her soft skin. Her laughter. The vulnerable look in her eyes when he'd walked out on her that morning.

He almost made it out of the desert. Almost, but

not quite. When his truck was only feet away, when he knew he was going to have to drive back to town and face a life without Addy, Mark fell to his knees and wept.

And then, in control once more, he went home.

"SHE CAME BY."

He didn't want to talk about it.

"I asked her if you slept with her."

"I told you, you're overstepping your boundaries. I suggest you shut your trap."

"She said it was the most incredible night of her life. Those were her words. Most incredible."

What did the old lady want from him? His blood and guts on the table in front of her?

"She told me, Markie-boy."

"What? What did she tell you?" He hollered the words. Looking up from the homework due in an hour, which he now had no reason to complete, Mark glanced behind him at the frail woman in the wheelchair facing a computer with a gambling hand opened on it. His eyes dropped. "I'm sorry."

"I can't remember the last time you raised your voice at me."

He could. It had been the night she'd hauled his ass out of that bar and back to Bierly. The night the sixteen-year-old boy had become a real man.

Silence filled the room and Mark told himself he was thankful for it. He spent the next ten minutes reading the same six words on the same page, trying to find any meaning in them at all.

"She told me she's a lawyer."

He didn't want to know.

He read the line several more times.

"It doesn't change what we know about her, boy. It's her heart that matters, you know that."

"She lied."

"I imagine she did it for good cause."

"She's going to lose me my scholarship."

"I don't think so. But if it happens, it happens. You'll survive."

He wanted to argue. But couldn't. Because she was right. The problem was, he wasn't satisfied with just surviving anymore.

"She loves you, Mark."

It didn't matter. Love passed. And all that was left was the disappointment. And the moving on.

"I think she'd marry you if you asked her to."

Pushing away from the table, Mark yanked open the refrigerator door, grabbed the carton of milk and drank out of the container. Nonnie's frown be damned. He was what he was. An uneducated country boy from the hills of West Virginia.

"You love her, too."

"Don't you ever shut up?" He didn't raise his voice. Couldn't even raise enough muster to sound angry. He was what he was. Tired.

"You need me to ask her?"

"You sold the house."

"She told you."

He chuckled, failing to keep the bitterness inside of him. "Funny how she can tell me your secrets but manage to keep her own so well hidden."

"I sold the house over a month ago and told her the day I did it."

And the fact that Addy had withheld such an important piece of information from him was supposed to make him feel better? Endear her to him?

"I asked her not to tell you and she abided by my wishes. Until today. She told me you knew."

Didn't surprise him.

"She fits us, Markie-boy."

"She does not fit me." Mark sat back in his chair. He had to leave for his one class that day, and then go on to work. "Course she fits you. You're just steamed 'cause she lied to you. And I don't blame you. But don't be so cussedly holy that you lose the best thing that ever came your way."

Pushing out of his chair, he paced into the living room and back again. Twice and then a third time. "She's a damned lawyer, Nonnie! She's got more education than I'll ever have. Even if I don't lose the scholarship."

"There's more than one kind of learning, Markie-boy. She's got one, you got another. You fit. Just like I said. Seems to me, you two need each other."

It seemed to Mark that Ella had been right. Schooling changed people. Those with it moved on, leaving those without it feeling as though they'd never be good enough.

He couldn't spend the rest of his years feeling that way.

Not after a lifetime of it.

He wasn't the town drunk's dropout son anymore. And he couldn't be any woman's backwoods kept man.

Most of all he wasn't going to be the poor fool who was lied to. No matter what Nonnie wanted.

ADDY WAS ON CAMPUS midmorning on Thursday, dropping off Wednesday's assignment, when her cell phone vibrated in her bag.

Greg Richards was calling.

She called him back as soon as she was out of earshot.

"It might be over soon, Addy!" The man sounded almost jubilant.

"What?"

"One of the names on the list of female athletes you turned over yesterday—one of the women who was turned down for a scholarship that same year that Susan was granted her scholarship—lives in Phoenix. I went to the closest post office to her home address this morning, just on a hunch, and the postage stamp identically matched the stamp they use, down to a little bit of missing ink in the left corner of the ring due to a chipped rubber stamp! We know who sent the letters."

"Have you talked to her?"

"Not yet. I'm still in Phoenix, waiting for local backup, but with any luck, this will soon be over. I'll keep you posted."

CHAPTER THIRTY

ADDY'S CAR WAS in the driveway when Mark pulled in after class late Thursday morning. He ignored it.

Did he need to call and tell Addy not to come over that night for Abe's visit? Or would she just know not to show up? She was a lawyer. She'd be up on all of the social norms.

The car was still there half an hour later when he kissed his grandmother on the cheek and headed out the front door on his way to work. He saw it in his peripheral vision. He wasn't looking. It didn't matter.

"Mark?"

He stopped. If he'd looked, he'd have seen her sitting on the step just outside her front door. "Yeah?"

"They found what they were looking for," she said. He wasn't sure what that had to do with him.

"I don't know what effect that will have on anything where you're concerned, but they know that your education is not directly connected to what they were looking for."

He was sure that made sense to someone.

Shaking his head, he stared at her, raising one eyebrow. It was the best he could do without releasing the flood of disturbing emotions rumbling inside of him.

Why the heck he didn't just head to his truck he didn't know.

"I…also want you to know…now that my job here is more or less done…my name isn't Adele Kennedy."

She swallowed. He couldn't care less.

"It's Adrianna Keller. Adele lied to you, Mark. Adrianna never did."

Now she was splitting hairs. Or telling him something. Either way, he didn't care.

He had to get going or be late to work. "Thanks for letting me know," he said, and continued down the steps and out to his truck without looking back.

THERE WAS NOTHING for her to do but pack up and go. As eager as she'd been earlier in the week to get out of town and never look back, Addy was having a hard time getting her clothes into suitcases. She had to do the laundry first.

She couldn't pack up her kitchen stuff until she was sure she wouldn't need to cook another meal.

Until she connected with Will, she couldn't know about the exact timing. She was still on his payroll. Depending on how everything played out, he might still need a lawyer.

The sheets on her bed would need to be washed and packed. She wasn't ready to strip them off the mattress yet. They were one of the few physical reminders she had of Mark.

Addy took a bath instead. A long hot bath.

At two o'clock, Greg called back.

"She's in custody" were the first words out of the man's mouth. "Along with her brother. I'm still here, helping with the interrogation, making sure they have everything they need for an airtight case."

"What does her brother have to do with this?"

"He was the mastermind behind the plan. He figured that she deserved a hundred thousand dollars, at least, for having been denied the same opportunities Susan had been granted at Montford.

"I told her about the spreadsheet you came up with. As soon as she heard that, academically, she was worse off than Susan was, she backed down. And, incidentally, all of the other rejected applicants also had lower test scores than Susan."

Which didn't completely let Will off the hook. There were still ten students—eleven including Mark—who'd received the benefits of a Montford education without meeting the entrance qualifications.

"Once we got her downtown and she heard that she was being charged with blackmail and extortion, she changed her story, insisting then that she never intended to follow through on the demands for money."

"Threatening even without intent to extort money is a crime."

"Which is what I told her."

"Does Will know?"

"I called him just before I called you. If you hadn't caught that situation with Randi and Susan, we likely wouldn't have been able to stop this girl before she filed a suit," he said.

"I thought you just said she wasn't going to follow through on the monetary demands."

"She's not now. She was going to, no matter what she claimed after she realized she could do prison time. I saw a check from her brother made out to the courts in the amount of a filing fee on the desk in her living room."

"She'd hired an attorney?"

"I have no proof of that."

"Even if she'd filed and won, the school's insurance would have covered Will's losses since he was working in an official capacity," she said. "I'm very relieved to know that this really was just a disgruntled student believing she had a legitimate case. With the letters coming in such an underhanded fashion, I was having visions of someone with a personal vendetta against Will doing whatever it took to bring him down. I've seen some crazy, vindictive and vicious things in the seven years I've been in practice, and sometimes you pay a heavy price even when you're in the right."

"Well, I know that Will's eyes have been opened wide. You can believe that all policies and practices at Montford are going to get a thorough review and be strictly enforced from here on out."

She had to talk to Will about the liabilities involved with the eleven under-qualified students who'd been granted admission to the university. He couldn't take back those educations. Or the benefits they'd gained. And Montford could never withstand the hit if they attempted to compensate every similarly situated student who'd applied and been turned away. The most he could do was hope those eleven never came to light.

Which they would only if one of the students who was allowed entrance was not allowed to complete his education as the other ten had been allowed to do.

It was a matter of reasonable expectation....

"He asked me to have you call him," the sheriff was saying and then, telling her he'd be in touch, hung up.

She tried Will immediately. He wasn't in.

ADDY WASN'T A passive sort. She wasn't used to hanging around, waiting, surrendering control of the things that mattered most to her. She went into town, to the quaint women's clothing store, and bought herself a pair of sexy black leggings and a gauzy blouse that hung just below her thighs. A pair of insanely high wedges were next.

She might be practical. Conservative. But that didn't mean she had to feel undesirable. It didn't mean she couldn't be sexy when she needed to. She asked the saleslady to put her old clothes in the bag and wore her new outfit home.

If she'd crossed paths with anyone she used to know while she was in town, she hadn't realized it. Hadn't recognized them.

And that was how she needed it to be.

She wasn't hanging around Shelter Valley for any

reason having to do with her past. She was procrastinating because she'd given her heart away and couldn't pack up the rest of her things and leave without it.

Nonnie had told her Mark was off at five—in time to babysit. And when he arrived home, she'd be waiting for him. Either he was going to forgive her, or give her heart back.

And then she'd move home.

Will called while she was still downtown. She sat in her parked car and talked to him. While he was immeasurably relieved the threats had been dealt with, he was also concerned about the other areas of liability Addy had uncovered through her research. He asked her to continue to represent him as they sorted through everything. She'd have to take the Arizona bar exam, but she wasn't opposed to doing so.

She agreed to represent him on two conditions. Her first being that she be able to work from Colorado and travel to Shelter Valley only when absolutely necessary. The second condition had to do with Mark Heber.

What Will told her about him shocked her.

MARK HAD JUST finished working on a machine on the line, helping out the technician whose job it was to keep the machines in working repair, when he was paged to the front offices.

Four o'clock in the afternoon and he was getting paged? Pushing through the door from the factory to the office complex, Mark saw the police officer standing there before the other man saw him.

He wasn't just a police officer, he noted as he got closer. He was the sheriff. Mark's faculties nearly shut down.

Something had happened to Nonnie. He wasn't ready.

"Mark Heber?"

"Yeah, that's me."

A tanned hand reached out to him. "I'm Greg Richards."

The man's grip was strong, his shake friendly enough. "Good to meet you," Mark said automatically. His manners were Nonnie's doing. He'd made it his business to live a life that would honor her, not shame her.

"You, too," Richards said. "I'm here because your name came up in an investigation I was involved with. . . ."

This wasn't about Nonnie. Anything else was superfluous.

"I was made aware that you know about the fact that your Montford University education might be in question."

He nodded, not quite sure what was going on.

"Ordinarily I wouldn't have anything to do with such things, but because there was an investigation— and I believe it's best that the reasons for the investigation remain private—I am here to tell you that your education is not in jeopardy."

A brick fell from his shoulders. He hadn't even known it was there.

"Really?" He said the word like a cool guy who didn't give a damn when he felt anything but cool inside.

"You were administered an IQ test the day you met with your guidance counselor."

"An aptitude test," he clarified. "To assess my best course of study."

The sheriff shook his head. "Montford uses the exam sometimes to help with student placement when other test scores are unavailable, but it is a nationally accredited IQ exam."

So? Mark wasn't following any of this.

"IQ scores are kept confidential, and because they are not part of the official entrance qualifications, those scores are not included in any admittance files. However, they are on file in the guidance office."

Mark stood, without moving, summing up this man that Addy knew—even if just as a professional acquaintance.

"The particular IQ test you were administered is a legally accepted test that allows the university to override all other entrance qualifications, assuming the score is high enough."

Hot damn.

"You came out here to tell me I have a high IQ, Sheriff?"

"I'm here to tell you that the files you saw regarding your education have been destroyed and to inform you that any doubts placed on your right to be studying at the university or your right to the funds you've been awarded no longer exist."

"Addy sent you."

"I'm not at liberty to say how I came to know about your knowledge of the files. However, I will tell you that Ms. Keller did inform the university on your behalf that they would be putting themselves in jeopardy of a huge lawsuit if they denied your education after they'd let you enroll. However, the point was moot."

She'd turned on the people who'd hired her?

For him?

"It was important to her that you be told right away," the man said then, his gaze serious.

Mark got the message.

"Sheriff?" Greg Richards had started to walk away but turned back.

"The other names on that list…were they like me, legitimately allowed entrance due to criteria not noted in the admittance papers?"

"Yes."

"All eleven of them?"

"Yes."

So whatever lawsuit implications Addy had been hired to find were gone. Did that mean she was out of a job? Or that she'd be around longer while she kept looking?

She'd gone to the wall for him.

"One more thing."

"Sure." Richards stood casually, looking as if he'd stay there all day if Mark asked.

"Where would a guy go if he wanted to find out information on a fire that took place, probably in Colorado, at the Keller home a quarter of a century ago." He'd been thinking a lot about that fire. About Addy's aloneness.

The sheriff's easy expression tightened. "I'd leave that one alone."

"You know about it?" That shocked him. He'd had the impression he'd been the only one Addy had told about the tragedy.

The man appeared to consider his next words carefully and then said, "It happened here. Addy was born in Shelter Valley."

He could feel the truth shudder through him. And so much made sense. The recurrence of a nightmare she hadn't had for years. Her need to talk about something that had happened so long ago.

The breakdown on her back porch...

She'd been reliving the past because she'd come face-to-face with it.

Had she been out to her old neighborhood? Seen where the fire had taken place?

Had she borne that pain all alone?

Realizing that the sheriff of Shelter Valley had just gone out on a limb for him, understanding small-town protocol, Mark asked, "Is that why she was here... brought in to investigate whatever threats had been made? She knew someone involved?"

"Will Parsons."

"The university president, Will Parsons?"

"His family took her in after the fire. ..."

Mark came from a small close-knit town. And knew what he had to do. "I'd guess, since she's so well situated, there'd be a way to get hold of the case file on that fire."

Greg Richards frowned. "What are you getting at?"

"The memory of that night haunts her, Sheriff. I don't know what I can do to change that, but...I'd like to try." It was the right thing to do. Friends looked out for each other. A favor for a favor... "I was the fire investigator back in Bierly, where I come from. Fire forensics have only been around about ten years, but I'm pretty up on the newest studies. I was thinking maybe, if I could re-create the fire for her—figuratively—if I could take her to the site, live through it with her, she could see it through the eyes of an adult instead of a traumatized child. I'd been thinking I'd have to travel to Colorado to accomplish that, but if it's all right here..." He was talking faster than he was thinking. "Maybe, if we can help her there...she'd... consider staying..."

Because it was his only hope of keeping the love of his life.

After a long, piercing glance, the sheriff nodded, pulled a card from his top pocket and handed it to Mark. "Give me a call. I'll see what I can do. There are some times us guys have to stick together."

Richards grinned and Mark had a feeling he and the other man would get along just fine. He also knew that he would be the only one to help Addy through this. He'd figure out the truth of what happened, as best he could. He'd take Addy through the horror, and sit with her as long as it took her to lay the past to rest. No one else needed to know what her father had done. That secret would stay between the two of them.

Forever.

ADDY CLEANED UP her research. She checked in on Nonnie, who treated her as though nothing had changed, even complimenting her on her new outfit. When she returned home, she responded to email from her firm. There'd been a couple of requests for her services that looked interesting. She was ready for a new case.

She wrote back, requesting more information on both of them.

And she waited. She had to see Mark. In the morning she'd call Will. They were going to be in touch more regularly moving forward.

Maybe get to know each other as adults.

Someday, she'd like to meet the rest of the family again.

Not yet, though. She was too emotionally raw. Right now she just needed to be back home. To get her emotional footing back. She had what it took to make it on her own. She always had.

Maybe Mark would come see her in Colorado. Maybe he wouldn't.

Maybe, in time, she'd forget him.

She doubted it.

One step at a time.

By five, she was thinking about taking another bath. When her doorbell rang before she'd had a chance to run the water, she went to answer it, happy enough for the distraction.

She should have thought. At least long enough to look through the peephole.

Addy pulled open the door and was engulfed by a burst of noise that overwhelmed her.

"Welcome home, Adrianna!" The chorus of voices was loud enough to be heard on the next block. Male, female, young, old, there were at least twenty people on her stoop and spilling into the front yard, all of them smiling up at her as if she was a member of their family.

She didn't recognize a single one of them. Until one body separated from the crowd. And then a second, a third, a fourth and a fifth. Will Parsons. Randi. Becca—Addy knew her instantly. And the elder Mr. and Mrs. Parsons, as well.

Standing there, frozen to the spot, she had no idea what to do. Nothing to say. She hadn't been a member of a family for so long.

"Psst." The sound came from behind her. Nonnie was outside, on her porch. She must have been there all along—probably because she'd seen the crowd gathering and couldn't resist finding out what was going on.

Or maybe she'd been in on the whole thing from the beginning.

"Go hug 'em, girl! Go on." With one papery, blue-veined hand, Nonnie shooed Addy toward the five people at the bottom of her stairs. "They all know ya," Nonnie said. "But them five, they're family."

With tears threatening dangerously close, Addy stared at Nonnie, as though the older woman could save her from a step she didn't think she could take. How much did Nonnie know?

"Go on, girl," the woman said in the most firm tone of voice Addy had ever heard her use. "You got to do this if you're ever going to be able to love whole-heartedly again."

She could love wholeheartedly....

"Go!" Nonnie moved her chair forward and Addy stepped out of the way—straight into Becca's waiting arms. And Randi's. And Mr. and Mrs. Parsons's. She could hardly breathe. Weak and trembling, she couldn't stand. But she didn't need to. The people of Shelter Valley held her up, assuring her that they were never going to let her go.

CHAPTER THIRTY-ONE

MARK DIDN'T MAKE it to Adrianna's party Thursday evening. Nonnie had called, telling him about the gathering that she'd help coordinate. It didn't do any good, him telling her to mind her own business.

And if the meeting helped Adrianna, then he supposed Nonnie had been right to take part.

It wasn't that he was averse to meeting some of the town's most prominent citizens. He was sure he'd be meeting them soon enough—if Nonnie had her way. He just had something more pressing to do that night.

Rescheduling his time with Abe for that weekend, he started the evening by drinking a beer at the local bar with Sheriff Richards. The sheriff handed a satchel over to him under the condition that this confidential information be returned to him the next morning before anyone knew it was missing.

Mark didn't go out that night. Not after everyone had left Addy's house and Nonnie had settled in and the neighborhood had gone quiet. He sat in the chair in the living room and pored over investigative reports, timelines, descriptions of the scene of Addy's fire, of evidence retrieved from the scene, the processing of the evidence, charts depicting placement of the evidence, of the bodies, the coroner's reports. He read, and he lived through every single second of the night that Addy almost burned alive.

He choked up when he got to the part about the little girl who hadn't given up—who'd been found nearly unconscious, with third-degree burns down her back, but still screaming because she wanted her mother to be able to hear her. Addy's screams had led the firemen to her in time, providing them with her exact location so that the one-minute window they had to get to her was not wasted. Her screams had saved her life.

And it dawned on Mark, he'd seen Addy completely naked. He'd seen every private part of her. Kissed every intimate part of her body. But he'd never seen her back.

He knew now that hadn't been a coincidence. Addy had deliberately positioned herself so that he wouldn't ever see her back.

Obviously the plastic surgeons had done a good enough job that he hadn't felt any scars, but there'd be silvery lines visible—at the very least.

When he was finished reading, he drove to the big-box store that was open all night and then out to the cactus jelly plant to request permission to use a corner of their huge desert property to conduct some experiments.

On Friday morning, he rose before Nonnie did. Or rather, he got up out of the chair where he'd rested his head for an hour's nap, cooked up some bacon and left it in the warmer for his grandmother before stepping into the shower.

By 7:00 a.m., dressed in slacks and his nicest shirt, he presented himself at Addy's front door. He had to knock twice.

"Mark?" She'd clearly just come from the shower. She was dressed, in navy blue dress pants, a silk blouse and pumps, but her hair was pinned up and wet on the ends, and she wasn't wearing any makeup. "Is Nonnie okay?"

"The interfering old biddy is just fine," he said, not quite erasing the affection from his tone. He loved that old biddy.

"What's up, then?" She stood back in the shadows. "I was just getting ready…"

"May I come in?" He had a satchel on his shoulder. She could assume it was schoolwork.

Stepping back farther, she nodded toward the door. "Of course."

He set foot inside and Addy turned toward the hallway. "I'll just be a minute…"

Letting her go, Mark looked around for boxes or bins containing the belongings she'd be taking back to Colorado with her. The house looked just as lived in as it had the morning before—minus the mess on the kitchen table.

She was gone less than five minutes. "Sorry about that," she said, a forced smile on her face as she reentered the room. Her long blond hair was combed and pulled back in a bejeweled clip. Her makeup was impeccable. She looked ready to walk into a courtroom.

Or maybe she'd always looked that way and he just hadn't seen the lawyer in her.

"I've never actually associated with an attorney before."

"I've never associated with a man with a genius level IQ."

"I'm here to ask a favor."

"Okay. I'll do anything I can to help. You know that."

His hands in his pockets, he said, "Turn around and lift up your shirt."

"What?"

"You said you'd do what you can for me. It's a relatively small thing, I'm asking. Lift up your shirt. It's not like I haven't seen you naked before."

"I don't…"

Her gaze implored him and he wanted to give in to her. He thought about that little girl who'd just kept screaming and screaming through a raw, burned throat. Screaming when she couldn't even remember her own name. "Please," he said.

Slowly, Addy turned, raised her shirt and showed him skin that was unlike the pearly smoothness covering the rest of her body. Just as he'd suspected, her middle back was lined with silvery scars from that night long ago. Addy let him look as long as he needed to and by doing so, it showed Mark how much she trusted him. More importantly, Mark knew how much he loved her.

"Take a drive with me?"

ADDY SAT IN the passenger seat of Mark's truck because he asked her to. She was strong. A survivor. She could get through this and then she'd be on her way back to Colorado.

The reunion the night before had been lovely. A dream dating back long ago. For one evening, she'd been a member of the Parsons family, just like she'd once prayed she would be. She'd see them again. When they came to visit her in Colorado. And when she made occasional trips to Shelter Valley.

Would she see Mark, too?

She couldn't help but hope so.

The Parsonses were hoping she'd stay in Shelter Valley. But she couldn't. Will would help them understand.

"Where are we going?"

"I'm not at liberty to disclose that information." Mark threw her words from the other day back at her.

Staring straight ahead, Addy waited. Tried to stay tough. Surely the town had changed enough in twenty-five years to make it all unrecognizable. From the little bit she'd seen on her trip downtown, that was the case. Even the town square was different. Blessedly different. Not that she'd done more than glance at it.

Some of the stores had been the same, but she hadn't gone in them.

Still, she wasn't taking any chances. One never knew when a memory would hit, when recognition would strike.

She wanted no part of it.

The truck stopped in front of a building she didn't recognize. The Shelter Valley Sheriff's Office.

"Wait here."

Mark jumped down from the truck and went inside the building. He was gone a few minutes and returned without the satchel on his shoulder.

"Don't you have class today?" she asked him.

"Not until ten. And I've got perfect attendance, so I can miss if it comes to that. I know you went to bat for me. Thank you."

"You didn't need my help."

"I'm a genius," Mark said, grinning.

"I didn't need a test score to tell me that."

His smile faded. "I get that, you know," he said, watching the road, but glancing at her, too. Holding her gaze for a long few seconds. "I'm the one who needed the validation, which is ridiculous."

They were back on the road again. Going home, she hoped. But it didn't look like it. They seemed to be leaving town. And that was okay with her, too.

Mark didn't speak again until he pulled the truck to a stop. She figured that they really didn't have all that much to say to each other. She'd lied to him. She'd turned his questionable entrance qualifications over to the authorities when she could have thrown the evidence in the trash.

But his scholarship had been saved.

"Did you ask who filled out your scholarship application?"

Mark turned to her. "I thought you knew."

"There is no record of a scholarship for you in the database, which is all I had access to. Which means it was privately funded."

"What about Will Parsons? You could ask him."

She shook her head. "It didn't have anything to do with the investigation."

"I'm sure it was Nonnie."

And something occurred to her. "She always said she didn't fill out the application, but what if there wasn't one?"

Mark glanced at her again. And said, "There's no record of a scholarship."

"Right."

"Damn!" Mark slammed his hand on the steering wheel. "The old bat probably used her savings for the first semester fees and then sold her house and is using the money to fund the rest of the scholarship. She'd do that—set it up in the form of an all-expenses-paid scholarship that requires me to complete my education or pay it back."

"We don't know that."

"But that's what you're thinking, too, isn't it?"

"Yes."

It all made sense. And it answered the last question she had regarding Montford University.

"We're here," Mark said.

Addy glanced around. They were parked on the side of a road, a little ways out of town. There were some small homes around—all set on tiny lots at different angles. They were old. Mark hadn't parked in front of any of them.

He'd parked in front of an overgrown vacant lot.

Did he plan to buy the lot? To build a home on it? Was that why she was there? "Let's get out," he said, opening his door with a sideways glance in her direction. Because it seemed to matter to him, she opened her door. Climbed down from the truck. Walked a couple of feet out into the lot to stand beside him.

Nonnie had sold their home for a fairly large amount. Probably because of land. It had been in the family for long enough to be paid off. Even after the scholarship, they'd have money to invest. Maybe Mark had already bought the place.

She hoped not. It was barren. He could do so much better and in a less run-down neighborhood.

He was watching her.

"What?"

"Nothing." He looked around, surveying the land, and looked back at her. She had no idea what to say.

"What do you think of it?" he asked. It was like when someone showed up in a hideous dress and asked how they looked and you had to find something kind to say.

"I don't like it."

"You don't?"

She shook her head. "I'm sorry, Mark. I know I shouldn't say that, but I can't lie to you. I hope I never have to tell another lie in my life. It makes me sick. And I don't like this place. You and Nonnie shouldn't have to live here."

She wasn't being a snob. It wasn't about money. The neighborhood was filled with trash. Dirty. There was no attempt to make things nice. Nodding, his hands in his pockets, he kept staring at her.

"What?" she asked again, getting more tense by the second. He seemed to need something from her. She had no idea what it was.

"Nonnie says that you don't believe in love."

"Of course I do." She loved him. "I know it exists. I'm the one who told you that."

He shook his head. "You know it exists—you just don't believe that you'll ever find it. That it will last. You don't trust it."

Did he blame her? Her own father had murdered the woman he adored. She stared up at him openmouthed.

"I don't, do I?" she said.

He shrugged. "I don't know. That's just what Nonnie says."

"She's wrong."

"Okay."

But maybe she wasn't. She knew she loved Mark. He was there now. Being kind to her.

Which would indicate that she still had a chance with him. "Why are we here?"

"You don't recognize it, do you?"

Shaking her head, she looked around. "Not at all," she said. "I've never been here before. I—"

Mark's gaze was so intense it scared her. "Yes, you have."

How would he know?

She looked around. And then it hit her.

"No." Vigorously shaking her head, Addy backed up. One step. Then two. "No. Uh-uh. No." Stumbling, she backed into the street. Taking more backward steps. Away. She had to get away.

And she backed into something that didn't move. A rock-solid wall. Mark's arms came around her. "I have to go, Mark." She was leaning forward now, pulling away from him.

"Addy." His voice was firm, but gentle, too. Warm and soft. Like he'd said her name the night they'd slept together.

That night had been good.

So good.

Better than any night she could remember.

And then there was the other night she'd never forget.

"I want to relive the fire with you, Addy. So you can accept it for what it was and come out the other side. I'll sit with you in burning hell if that's as far as we get. I'll stay there with you if you can't get out. But you have to know this, Addy. He didn't do it."

What was he talking about? She had to go.

"Water," she choked.

A plastic bottle appeared in her vision. She stared at it. Mark loosened her grip on his arm, the arm that was holding her, and fastened her fingers, one at a time, around the cold, moist bottle of water.

With the bottle in her grasp, he unscrewed the lid, all the while holding her close with his other arm.

Shaking, she watched as the clear, cool, liquid splashed out on her hand.

"Your father didn't set the fire."

She was so thirsty.

"Greg Richards agrees, as does the fire marshal." Mark kept talking. She heard him.

"Twenty-five years ago, they didn't have scientific bases by which they determined causes of fires. They didn't have fire forensics labs like we do today. The conclusions were anecdotal, mostly based on logical guesswork."

She understood. But she couldn't look up. Didn't want to know, to remember any more than she already couldn't forget.

"Do you know what a flashover is?"

She shook her head.

"It's the time it takes from the moment a fire starts until the premises is engulfed in flames.

"The home your parents lived in, the materials it was made out of…" He could go into all of that later. Because he knew Addy well enough to know she'd want the answers. But she wasn't hearing him now.

So he went back to the important stuff. "We now have tests that prove that the flashover of the fire that night would have been less than five minutes."

The street was rough. She remembered it being smooth. She'd learned to ride her bike here. Her father had helped her. Over and over again, catching her every time she'd been about to fall. *Don't look down,* he'd said. *Look up. You won't fall if you look up.*

"The fire marshal back then had determined flashover to be twenty minutes," Mark said. "It was the only thing that made sense, the only thing that would have allowed your father to get from the origin of the fire, a common household chemical spill, to the spot next to your mother where his body was found. He didn't say anything specific about your father, only the flashover rate because it had to be in the report. I surmised how he reached that rate based on what you told me. I'm guessing he found your father's prints on the household chemical container and drew his conclusions from that."

Her father had wanted to be with her mother when she went. That's what Gran had told her. Or had it been a counselor? Someone had told her that.

"We also know that because of the saturation point of your father's lungs, based on medical evidence when he was found, there's no way he could have been at the origin of the fire. He'd have died instantly. And he didn't."

"H-h-h…" She tried to speak. Her throat was dry. "H-how?" Her throat stung so much it brought tears to her eyes. "How do you know this?" She finally forced the words out because she had to.

"I spent the night studying the police report," he told her. "And then running some experiments. I might be a freshman in the safety engineering program, but I've been working with fire since I was sixteen years old. I made certain, before I allowed anyone to put their safety in my hands, that I knew everything there was to know about the beast."

She believed him.

Because he was Mark.

She didn't trust love. She didn't trust men. But she trusted Mark.

"Daddy didn't kill us," she said, feeling like she was strangling, in the dark, alone.

"No, Adrianna, he didn't. The evidence suggests that he was trying to save your mother, not die with her."

She couldn't stand any longer. She was going to fall. Lightheaded, Addy expected to feel the hard ground beneath her body.

Instead, she was wrapped in a pair of strong arms that cradled her until she found the strength to stand again.

CHAPTER THIRTY-TWO

MUCH OF FRIDAY was a blur to Addy. She didn't start to feel human again until dinnertime when Mark suggested that they pick up Chinese.

"I'd rather make soup," she said, out of the blue. "Nonnie likes my potato soup. It was my mother's recipe. They found her recipe box in the fire. It was metal and the cards inside weren't damaged. Gran gave it to me when I was in high school."

They were in his truck, having spent much of the afternoon driving around Shelter Valley and then sitting out at the state park. She'd remembered so many things. Talked until her throat hurt.

And he'd talked, too. About trust. The lack of it. About a father who really did let him down.

And he'd called in to work to let them know he wouldn't be coming in that evening.

"We're close to the grocery store," he said now. "Do we need to stop for anything?"

"No." Shaking her head, she could clearly picture everything in her kitchen. In the entire duplex. She could clearly picture everything in her home in Colorado, too.

And where she'd stored the file of her most important papers, like her birth certificate.

She was back.

"I have everything I need."

"I don't." Mark looked over at her, but he drove right past the grocery store.

"What do you need? Maybe I have it?"

Was he going to sleep with her that night? She'd probably ask him to if he didn't offer. He didn't have to do anything, just lie there next to her.

"Oh, you have it," he said, and there was no mistaking the double edge in his tone.

"What is it?" What was hers was his. If he wanted it. Nothing she had was doing her any good alone.

"Your heart."

Was he kidding? "You've already got that. And here I thought they said you were a genius."

Pulling over to the side of the road, Mark kept his hands on the wheel as he looked at her.

"I don't just want you to love me, Addy, I want all of you. I want you to trust me enough to take a leap."

"Can I keep my fountain?"

"Of course."

"And your trust? Do I have that?" Without it, they didn't have a chance.

"Yes."

"You're sure?"

"I just have to get used to the lawyer thing," he said, his expression completely serious. "But I'm working on it."

"Okay."

"I want you to marry me."

She wanted that, too. Without a doubt, which surprised the heck out of her. "Soon."

He was on a four-year nonrefundable scholarship. He was asking her to live with him in Shelter Valley. And if she was going to give him her trust, this was the leap she had to make.

"Okay. On one condition."

"What's that?"

"You let me take the money I made on this last job—and it was a lot—and use it as a down payment on a nice house with everything handicap-accessible, including the bathrooms. All Nonnie wants is her independence and I want her to have it."

She was asking him to trust her. To accept that no matter where he was born, or how early he quit school, or what job he did, or how much education he had, he had nothing to prove to her. To accept that she loved him for who he was inside, not for what he could or could not provide.

Because as far as she was concerned, he already provided it all.

He provided everything that mattered most.

He hadn't answered her. Both hands were clenching the steering wheel so tightly she could see the whites of his knuckles.

"Mark?"

When he turned his head, she saw the struggle in those expressive blue eyes and her heart skipped a beat. But she couldn't take back her condition. They were who they were. Both of them. Either they were okay with that, or they weren't.

"I'm a genius."

She was going to lose him. He could help her get past her own fears and misperceptions, but he couldn't get past his own.

"I know," she said.

"I'd have to be an idiot to pass up the lifetime of heaven you're offering me."

Dared she hope?

"Nonnie didn't raise an idiot."

Seeing his struggle in the expressions chasing themselves across his face, she waited.

"I will not let my father's choices, or my mother's, rob me of my future," he told her, the words sounding more like a vow than any marriage ritual she could think of.

"Does this mean we can start looking at houses?"

"Can we have potato soup first?"

Addy figured they probably should.

* * * * *

LARGER-PRINT BOOKS!

HARLEQUIN *Presents*

PASSION GUARANTEED SEDUCTION

GET 2 FREE LARGER-PRINT NOVELS PLUS 2 FREE GIFTS!

YES! Please send me 2 FREE LARGER-PRINT Harlequin Presents® novels and my 2 FREE gifts (gifts are worth about $10). After receiving them, if I don't wish to receive any more books, I can return the shipping statement marked "cancel." If I don't cancel, I will receive 6 brand-new novels every month and be billed just $5.05 per book in the U.S. or $5.49 per book in Canada. That's a saving of at least 16% off the cover price! It's quite a bargain! Shipping and handling is just 50¢ per book in the U.S. and 75¢ per book in Canada.* I understand that accepting the 2 free books and gifts places me under no obligation to buy anything. I can always return a shipment and cancel at any time. Even if I never buy another book, the two free books and gifts are mine to keep forever.

176/376 HDN F43N

Name _____ (PLEASE PRINT) _____

Address _____ Apt. # _____

City _____ State/Prov. _____ Zip/Postal Code _____

Signature (if under 18, a parent or guardian must sign)

Mail to the **Harlequin® Reader Service:**
IN U.S.A.: P.O. Box 1867, Buffalo, NY 14240-1867
IN CANADA: P.O. Box 609, Fort Erie, Ontario L2A 5X3

**Are you a subscriber to Harlequin Presents books
and want to receive the larger-print edition?
Call 1-800-873-8635 today or visit us at www.ReaderService.com.**

* Terms and prices subject to change without notice. Prices do not include applicable taxes. Sales tax applicable in N.Y. Canadian residents will be charged applicable taxes. Offer not valid in Quebec. This offer is limited to one order per household. Not valid for current subscribers to Harlequin Presents Larger-Print books. All orders subject to credit approval. Credit or debit balances in a customer's account(s) may be offset by any other outstanding balance owed by or to the customer. Please allow 4 to 6 weeks for delivery. Offer available while quantities last.

Your Privacy—The Harlequin® Reader Service is committed to protecting your privacy. Our Privacy Policy is available online at www.ReaderService.com or upon request from the Harlequin Reader Service.

We make a portion of our mailing list available to reputable third parties that offer products we believe may interest you. If you prefer that we not exchange your name with third parties, or if you wish to clarify or modify your communication preferences, please visit us at www.ReaderService.com/consumerchoice or write to us at Harlequin Reader Service Preference Service, P.O. Box 9062, Buffalo, NY 14269. Include your complete name and address.

LARGER-PRINT BOOKS!

GET 2 FREE LARGER-PRINT NOVELS PLUS
2 FREE GIFTS!

✦HARLEQUIN®

Romance

From the Heart, For the Heart

YES! Please send me 2 FREE LARGER-PRINT Harlequin® Romance novels and my 2 FREE gifts (gifts are worth about $10). After receiving them, if I don't wish to receive any more books, I can return the shipping statement marked "cancel." If I don't cancel, I will receive 4 brand-new novels every month and be billed just $4.84 per book in the U.S. or $5.24 per book in Canada. That's a savings of at least 19% off the cover price! It's quite a bargain! Shipping and handling is just 50¢ per book in the U.S. and 75¢ per book in Canada.* I understand that accepting the 2 free books and gifts places me under no obligation to buy anything. I can always return a shipment and cancel at any time. Even if I never buy another book, the two free books and gifts are mine to keep forever.

119/319 HDN F43Y

Name	(PLEASE PRINT)	

Address		Apt. #

City	State/Prov.	Zip/Postal Code

Signature (if under 18, a parent or guardian must sign)

Mail to the **Harlequin® Reader Service:**
IN U.S.A.: P.O. Box 1867, Buffalo, NY 14240-1867
IN CANADA: P.O. Box 609, Fort Erie, Ontario L2A 5X3

Want to try two free books from another line?
Call 1-800-873-8635 or visit www.ReaderService.com.

* Terms and prices subject to change without notice. Prices do not include applicable taxes. Sales tax applicable in N.Y. Canadian residents will be charged applicable taxes. Offer not valid in Quebec. This offer is limited to one order per household. Not valid for current subscribers to Harlequin Romance Larger-Print books. All orders subject to credit approval. Credit or debit balances in a customer's account(s) may be offset by any other outstanding balance owed by or to the customer. Please allow 4 to 6 weeks for delivery. Offer available while quantities last.

Your Privacy—The Harlequin® Reader Service is committed to protecting your privacy. Our Privacy Policy is available online at www.ReaderService.com or upon request from the Harlequin Reader Service.

We make a portion of our mailing list available to reputable third parties that offer products we believe may interest you. If you prefer that we not exchange your name with third parties, or if you wish to clarify or modify your communication preferences, please visit us at www.ReaderService.com/consumerschoice or write to us at Harlequin Reader Service Preference Service, P.O. Box 9062, Buffalo, NY 14269. Include your complete name and address.

HRLP13R

ReaderService.com

Manage your account online!

- Review your order history
- Manage your payments
- Update your address

*We've designed
the Harlequin® Reader Service
website just for you.*

Enjoy all the features!

- Reader excerpts from any series
- Respond to mailings and special monthly offers
- Discover new series available to you
- Browse the Bonus Bucks catalog
- Share your feedback

Visit us at:
ReaderService.com